C000102161

TALES OF THE MACABRE

NEWTON WEBB

STEEL CROWN PRODUCTIONS

Copyright © 2023 by Newton Webb

All rights reserved.

No portion of this book may be reproduced in any form without written permission from the publisher or author, except as permitted by U.S. or U.K. copyright law.

CONTENTS

TALES OF THE MACABRE

Welcome to the debut collected works of Newton Webb. Tales of the Macabre is intended for mature audiences. This book includes the following tales of creeping horror:

1747 – The Grimsdyke Ghouls In the 16th century, a family kicked out of their homes in Grimsdyke found a new and murderous way to survive.

1864 – Smoke in the Sewers In 18th century London, a group of street urchins strive to escape their master. But in doing so they unleash a greater horror.

1958 – The Black Fog When the black fog rolls in, death follows. In 1950's Grimsdyke, two lovers encounter a horror unlike any other.

1961 – A Rose By Any Other Name A bank robber hiding from the law, Dennis commits a heinous crime. Soon, he'll learn to regret his actions.

2008 – Rock Bottom Aussie backpackers come face to face with primal adversaries in the cold peaks of Nepal.

2012 – The Platinum Service When you have great wealth, you can buy your way out of most things. But sometimes, actions bring unexpected consequences.

2013 – Festival of the Damned Four teenagers are hired to perform at a country fair, but they soon realise that they were each chosen for a very specific reason.

2013 – The Sinful Child Held captive in her father's basement, Amelia struggles to escape. But reality isn't always what it appears to be and soon she will learn an earth shattering secret.

2018 – Terror from the Trash Climate change is a very real threat to the world, but scientists find new perils as something long thought to be dead, awakens.

2020 – The Tattoo A hitchhiker and a lorry driver exchange tales on the road. Soon, they realise that neither of them is who they claim to be.

2020 – The Tokoloshe In South Africa there exists a demonic entity that can make wishes come true, but the consequences cannot always be predicted.

2022 – The Heir Apparent Keen to support his parents' failing farm, Keith asks his wealthy cousins for a position in the family firm. As he becomes more and more entrenched in the business, he discovers that limitless ambition can be murderous.

2022 – The Wrong Crowd Tim just wanted to apologise to his girlfriend, but he soon finds himself in peril when he realises that he has accidentally joined a very exclusive and very deadly club.

2024 – The Black Box Waking up from a coma after a severe accident, Jack finds that it is always better to read the small print when offering your body to medical science.

2348 – The Illusive Passenger In the distant future, a freighter captain picks up a most unusual cargo.

2518 – The Ghouls of Bangalore In outer space, greed and narcism still plague the human race. An engineer whose life is at its nadir learns a terrifying secret.

Newton's Macabre Tales span continents, with stories from the 17th century to the distant future, from Nepal, through Europe and South Africa. Some stories contain elements of humour, love, and passion, but all are imbued with soul shattering terror.

As you travel through time and space, you'll witness horrific consequences, mind bending paranormal activities and good people who took a wrong turn.

Each story is unique and offers a different perspective. So cradle your drink, and get comfy, because you are about to pierce the veil and witness the true nature of horror!

CHAPTER ONE

THE GRIMSDYKE GHOULS

JESSICA'S JOURNAL

N ote: The following extract is from an 18th-century diary purchased from an antique shop in Grimsdyke.

3rd October, 1747

Father lost his job today. We had to flee Grimsdyke. I don't know what happened. Nobody would tell me. Now they want to arrest him. Mother is furious. We have no coin and precious little food. Mother filled a cooking pot with utensils and I took my journal, writing roll and of course, my Bible.

4th October, 1747

We live in the caves now. Mother is dreadfully cross with Father. It's cold and wet by the sea. We can't have the fire outside in case it is seen, and the caves get too smoky if the fire is lit for long. I am so hungry. We have boiled some seaweed and some crabs, but Father can only forage after dark. I help him when I can as he doesn't see as well as I do at night.

11th October, 1747

I was out last night, foraging as usual, when a fisherman found me as he walked home across the beach. He was awfully kind, but Father was scared he might have told others where we were, so he hit him with a rock. When I started to cry, I was slapped. We have to be quiet. I helped Father carry the body back to the cave. Mother and Father are arguing now about what to do with him. They don't have the tools to bury him. I am reading the Bible now by the light of the fire. It is my only solace. I am so hungry.

Mother has come to an agreement. She is... It is nauseating to even write it. She is butchering the corpse. Heaven help us. It smells so good on the fire. I hate myself for even feeling temptation. Satan stalks us, I am sure and is pleased as we tumble ever closer to his embrace. I will not join him.

12th October, 1747

Mother and Father have stopped arguing now and have become inseparable. They bonded over their ghoulish feast last night and have come to terms with their new life. The bones wouldn't burn in the fire, so the blackened skull sits atop the pile and judges us. I judge us. The remaining flesh sits in the pools of seawater to pickle. The caves reek. I welcome the smoke now.

My parents are laughing now, more in love than ever. Father is talking about where he can find more flesh. What have we come to? I will not join them.

14th October, 1747

The hunger has left me weak in body and spirit. My teeth are loose, and my body is gaunt. Father had brought back the carcass of a smuggler, along with three barrels of rum. Finally, I couldn't hold back anymore. God help me, I gnawed on a freshly roasted piece of flesh. It was the most beautiful thing I'd ever tasted.

Then I remembered what it was and violently vomited it up. Mother and Father were filled with rage. They beat me for wasting food. They beat me for acting as though I was better than them. But I am better than them because I can still resist the Devil's temptation.

I know now what I must do for the sake of our immortal souls.

They are asleep. I apologised profusely. God forgive my deceit. I congratulated them on their cleverness. They celebrated their good fortune with the rum and I refilled their cups again and again. They made me wait outside in the rain while they engaged in carnal congress.

I spent the time wisely, gathering all the driftwood I could find, both dry and wet. When I returned, my parents were sound asleep and snoring. Father still had his trousers down. I waited to be sure then bound their hands and feet. I banked up the fire with wet wood until the cave was thick with smoke. Taking a brand to the pile of dry timber I'd left by the entrance, I blocked the cave with another fire. It was hot and fiery, a precursor to our inevitable fate. I hope that I can explain my actions to them when I see them again in Hell.

They woke from the coughing, but their cries were already weak. I put the last of the wood on the fire and sat sobbing outside until they fell silent. Lord have mercy on our souls.

15th October, 1747

Jeremiah found me on the road, weak from hunger and exhaustion. He is a sweet-hearted man, a widowed carpenter. I praise the Lord for sending him to me. He confessed to me whilst he nursed me to health that he cannot read, write or do sums. I have promised to repay his kindness by minding his home for him and managing his books.

He may not be fair of face, but he is noble of spirit.

And he looks delicious.

CHAPTER TWO

SMOKE IN THE SEWERS

1864, LONDON

The urchins, Tregor's Foxes, pressed themselves into every corner, every nook and cranny of the dank, brick basement. Metal hooks hung from the ceiling on long iron chains. The foetid smell of damp iron and old blood filled the room.

Mick wanted to look away, but he couldn't. Tregor always knew when they did that and punished them too. Mick sat next to his friend Evan, a Welsh lad who had been abandoned in the city as a toddler and raised by the Foxes. The two of them nestled together, enduring in solidarity.

A ring of light illuminated Tregor as he sat on a battered mahogany chair, his long tattered coat hanging from his heaving shoulders. With lips pursed, Tregor was breathing heavily through steepled fingers. His eyes, framed by thick, bushy eyebrows, focused with the intensity of a hawk.

"One more time," he growled, his voice low and gravelly.

Tim whimpered. He knelt on the cold flagstones, prostrating himself before his master. "I was carrying the package, so I was. Then I saw it. I saw it, Sir! It were red smoke but alive. I would be paste, Sir, actual paste, but the Shadow saved me... she..." he trailed off and trembled as Tregor's eye started twitching.

"Where is the parcel now?" Tregor asked quietly, his voice barely above a whisper.

Mick felt sick. He knew how this performance ended, how it *always* ended.

Tim closed his eyes. He knew too. Tears fell freely. "I lost it. I did."

"Lost it," Tregor roared. "You were carrying a parcel of opium? Then you saw some smoke that came alive and spirits that haunted you? Then you lost it?"

Tregor was on his feet with an explosive movement, his hand round Tim's scrawny neck as he hoisted him up high. His chair shot back into the serried ranks of terrified urchins. "You smoked it!" Tim couldn't speak even if he wanted to. His face reddened as he managed a last desperate squawk. Tregor dumped Tim down onto a metal hook. There was a sickening squelch, followed by high pitched screaming as Tim dangled, his shoulder impaled on the chain. Arterial blood sprayed red. Mick could feel it on his face. He ground his teeth as he tried to remain impassive. Every instinct cried out for him to wipe away his dying friend's gore.

"Nobody leaves this room while he lives." Tregor's one eye swung malevolently round the room. It met Mick's and paused.

He knows.

Mick shook, forcing himself to hold Tregor's gaze. He bit his lip as he trembled and prayed. He could taste blood before the baleful look moved on to the next urchin.

Tim was still screaming as Mick made his fateful decision.

Life with Tregor was death. Today, tomorrow, or in a week, he didn't know. But he knew. He *knew*. He had to get Maud out of here. They had to flee and soon.

He took one last look at Tim as the boy fell silent, his body slowly swaying on the hook as the movement stilled. Just another dead Fox in London.

A thunderous roar woke Mick. He was too tired to react as Tregor's boot crunched into his thigh.

"Up, up," Tregor bellowed. "You fat, lazy, miserable excuse for Foxes."

Mick's body ached from the cold floor. He pushed himself to his feet as the other children stirred round him. Maud was already up. She had to get up earlier than the rest of them to prepare the gruel. The watery meal got thinner every day, much like the Foxes.

They gathered together, cupping the bowls of gruel in their hands, as Tregor sat on his wooden chair. Mick's eyes kept wandering to the hook where Tim had died last night. The blood on the floor, walls and ceiling had dried. It was indistinguishable from the other stains now.

An enormous pile of boxes waited next to Tregor's chair and as the Foxes approached, he doled out the smuggled goods, each of them nailed shut, with oriental lettering inscribed on the top. Tregor instructed his Foxes as to where they should deliver their cargo. Tregor's deep-set eyes were hollow pits, pits that seemed to see everything, know everything. Mick didn't need to look down. He knew what was underneath him. The dark patina they were forced to stand on served to remind them of the consequences of failure.

Tregor gave Mick a box destined for Cheapside. He bowed obsequiously and backed away, avoiding eye contact. Mick waited for Maud to join him as Tregor gave her a box for Fleet Street. The two of them walked solemnly through the basement kingdom of Tregor's Night Foxes until they reached the grating. Unlike the rest of the building, this construction was new. The sewers, so recently built to cleanse London of the Big Stink, had instead become a conduit for all kinds of filth and villainy.

They clambered down round the other Foxes, who all flitted off on their nefarious errands. Brother and sister waited until the two of them were alone.

"Maud," Mick whispered, then repeated when she remained silent. "Maud, we ain't going back."

She spun round, wild-eyed. "You mustn't say that, brother. You mustn't!"

"Maud, if we go back, we'll die. Maybe today, maybe tomorrow, maybe in a month. But before too long we'll be proper dead." Mick took her hand. "I've made plans."

"What have you done, Mick?" Her brother led her down one side of the sewer. There was a maintenance cubby, nothing more than a platform with a grate above it, but it was reasonably dry.

Maud pulled back. "We'll be late. Please, Michael, I am begging you. Don't you be doing this. It's madness."

Mick pulled her harder, then worked free a loosened brick. A tiny bag, a silver crucifix and two silver candlesticks nestled alongside a box marked with Chinese letters, the twin to the ones they carried that made her recoil.

"Oh Mick, what did you do?" Maud gasped.

"Nothing. I turned up to make my delivery and the mark was dead, wasn't he? He was lying in his bed next to his bleeding pipe. I had to climb in through a window," Mick said.

"Tregor will—"

"Never know. We'll take this box, the money and leg it to the countryside, somewhere where Tregor will never find us." Mick held her tight, imploring her. "Please, Maud, don't choose death. Choose life."

But Maud no longer looked at him. She was looking behind him, her face wracked with terror.

Mick froze. A cold sweat ran down his back as he turned, expecting to see Tregor.

A girl, dressed in rags with long matted hair, faced them. Her face appeared pale and drained of blood. Her body was unnaturally white and brittle, looking like that of a corpse.

The stories they had whispered at bedtime, the rumours of sightings in the sewer, the urban legends they had pretended not to be scared by.

They were true.

It wasn't Tregor. It was the Shadow.

"Run," the Shadow squeaked.

Mick looked at her, dumbstruck. "What?"

"The smoke's coming. You gotta run." The Shadow pointed urgently down the sewer, before disappearing. The darkness swallowed up her pale form, leaving the urchins alone once more.

Mick looked at Maud. The unexpected combination of events overwhelmed their thought processes.

Mick ran to the cubby hole entrance and stared out, but she was gone.

"The red smoke that Tim saw," Maud muttered.

"I thought he was smoking the product like the grown-ups do." Mick wandered back to the sewer. It was then that he saw it. A ribbon of red smoke languidly coiling through the air. It seemed to turn as if sensing Mick.

Then it hurled towards him like an arrow. He spun and ran. "Open the bleeding grate, Maud. Run!"

But Maud didn't. She stood stock-still, trembling.

Mick pulled her to follow him to the ladder, but the smoke caught up with them, billowing round Maud. She screamed before choking, gagging on the sulphuric cloud as it prized her jaws open, streaming through her every orifice. Her body tensed, her arms thrust out as she spasmed in pain. Within moments, as Mick watched in horror, the cloud was absorbed, in its entirety, into his sister's body.

There was silence.

Mick caught his sister as she collapsed.

"Maud," Mick whimpered, eyes wide with concern. "You... okay?"

Maud stood up on her own feet, turning to him as though nothing had happened. Her eyes narrowed. "Three boxes of opium and some niknaks, Brother-Mine? You expected us to run away with that?" She eyed the stash with disdain. "Who would we even sell it to?"

"What happened?" Mick asked, climbing back down the ladder.

"I grew up. Now hide your stash and then let us go." Maud watched, tapping her feet patiently.

Mick looked at her. "You're different. It's the smoke. It's done something to you."

"Sometimes smoke is just smoke, Brother-Mine. How many types of smoke are there in this city, do you reckon? We are underneath heavy industry in a methane ridden sewer." Maud reached for her throat. "It was unpleasant, toxic even, but it has dissipated now. The pain gave me clarity. Now, hurry up, Brother-Mine. We are going."

"Stop calling me that!" Mick said angrily, cramming his stash back in the hole.

"What?" Maud handed him her box and he reluctantly put it in along with his own.

"Brother-Mine. You call me Mick, or if you're angry, Michael." He once more covered up the cubby hole and concealed it from view.

"Of course, 'Michael,' if that makes you happier." Maud smiled, a sinister expression crossing her face.

"What're we going to do now?" he asked. Part of him was furious that Maud was upturning his plans for them both. Part of him was relieved.

"*We* are going to do nothing." Her eyes narrowed. "But *I* am going to kill Tregor."

She turned and marched back down to the sewers.

"Maud!" Mick followed her as she headed towards the headquarters of the Night Foxes. She ignored him until he grabbed her shoulder, at which point she violently shrugged him off. "Maud, this is mental. It's suicide. It's a bleeding death sentence if we return with no boxes and no payment." He trotted behind her. "Remember Tim."

At that, Maud paused. She looked coldly over her shoulder. "I remember Tim. He was an abject lesson in what could happen if Tregor remains alive."

"What're you going to do?" Mick asked, his voice tinged with panic. "He does shits that're bigger than you."

"I told you, I'm going to kill him."

Mick was out of breath from the punishing pace Maud was keeping up. She, however, seemed unaffected. From the corner of his eye, he turned and, for the briefest of moments, he saw the pale sight of the Shadow watching them.

He cursed under his breath.

Maud had reached the ladder leading to the Night Foxes' basement. Mick made one last grab at her. She turned, shoving him with such a tremendous force that he skidded along the gantry on his back. He watched, surprised, as she clambered up the ladder. "Maud!" he shouted one last time. With fear gripping his heart, he glanced over his shoulder only to realise that the Shadow was watching them both. Her light blue eyes were wide with worry. Her ghostly face watched them intently.

Mick shook his head at the ghoulish spectre. He had no time for it. With a grim sense of resignation, he quickly scaled the ladder after Maud. If his sister was going to die, she would die alongside family.

The den was empty. The Foxes were all out on errands, except for Tregor's pet boy, Herb, who was hiding in the corner, dressed in his usual crudely patched and sewn finery, trying to stay out of sight of their master.

Mick entered to see Maud marching towards Tregor. Tregor roared, standing up to his full height, his fur coat splaying out behind him. "What are you doing, back so—"

Before he could finish, Maud dropped into a sprint and hurtled towards him. Her hands flicked out, her nails growing longer and sharper, like a falcon's talons. From her throat burst a hellish scream, a sound of animalistic fury.

Mick was stunned into inaction. He forced himself to lumber after her, fear causing his limbs to react slowly.

Tregor's eyes widened in shock. He threw his rum bottle at Maud. She smashed it to one side then leapt into the air, raking her claws across his face. A giant arm struck her, sending her tiny form flying.

She twisted in mid-air, kicking off from the wall to land on all fours on the floor.

Mick balled his fist and lashed out, punching Tregor's chest. It felt as though he had hit solid oak. Mick looked up just in time to see Tregor cuff him. He spiralled until he landed on the ground hard enough to force the wind out of him. Mick's eye narrowly missed one of the room's many dangling hooks. Blood filled his mouth and he spat it on the floor. His head was spinning. As he turned and tried to stand, his legs betrayed him, and his vision blurred.

He heard Maud hiss at Tregor before running at him again. Blood matted the arm of Tregor's fur coat. Fury made his features stretch, his veins bulge and his eyes narrow. Tregor howled with rage. He spat a string of savage curses, spittle projecting from his cracked lips. He lashed out with his boot.

Maud rolled to one side, ducking round one of the hanging hooks, dodging a brutal kick. Her hand flicked out and blood splattered from the back of Tregor's calves. He collapsed onto the floor. Cursing, he rolled onto his back and pulled a pistol from his jacket. The silver barrel gleamed in the dull light of the room.

BANG!

The first shot tore into Maud's shoulder, throwing her backwards. Tregor rose unsteadily to his feet, breathing heavily.

Mick let out a long, mournful moan. He crawled towards his sister's body on all fours.

The second shot took her in the eye. Her body collapsed onto the floor, twitching.

"You thought to kill me? *Me*!" Tregor fired a third round into her skull. "Tregor? I *am* fear made flesh. I *am* power incarnate." He fired a fourth round. "I *am* the monster in the night." He fired a fifth. "I *am* the devil that rules the underworld." The pistol clicked. All rounds were spent.

Tears filled Mick's eyes as he reached Maud, gently stroking the pulped remains of her face. He waited for Tregor to pick him up and place him on a hook as he had done with so many others before them.

Instead, he recoiled as Maud brushed Mick's hand to one side, sitting up. The bullets squeezed out of her body as her wounds knitted together. She looked Tregor in the eye with a venomous gaze and said, "I *am* Maud and I find *you* lacking."

"No," Tregor gasped, fear lighting up his eyes for the first time in many years. He threw the pistol to one side and pulled a cleaver from his belt with one hand, and a long knife with the other. Staggering on his injured leg, he queried, "What are you?"

"I told you. I am Maud, the new queen of the Night Foxes." As Maud threw herself forwards, Tregor lashed out with his cleaver. She jerked back, her hands moving with impossible speed to slash his wrist as it passed her. The cleaver clattered to the floor, falling from his limp grip.

He stumbled back.

Pressing forwards, she sidestepped a clumsy lunge from Tregor's knife. Sliding in closer, she lacerated the femoral artery in his thigh with her blade-like fingernails.

He stepped back to avoid a strike at his throat, but his legs gave out and he collapsed back onto the floor. His top hat rolled to the other side of the room, coming to a stop at Herb's feet.

Herb recoiled in terror, the back of his hand pressed against his mouth as he sobbed.

Tregor clutched at his thigh to stem the tide of blood as his red arterial flow joined the black stains left by Tim only the day before. As the red pool spread across the floor, Maud placed her hand on his heart and a roaring sound filled the chamber. Tregor's eyes glowed red as light erupted from them. The scent of roast pork filled the room. Tregor's corpse collapsed to the ground. Acrid, red smoke was rising out of the sockets where once his evil eyes had been. It coiled before Maud's jaw opened wide and she inhaled it into her body.

Mick vomited on the floor. He looked up to see Maud walk over to a hook and lower it.

Drawing back Tregor's head, she rammed the vicious hook through his back. Pulling on the chains, she raised him up. It made a grisly trophy for their regime change.

In the corner of the room, Herb was still shaking. With trepidation, he crawled towards the exit.

Maud took a step towards him and seeing her, Herb collapsed, curling up into a ball and whimpering.

"Maud... Herb's our mate," Mick said, as he slowly stood up. His body too was shaking after his adrenaline rush.

Maud levelled her gaze at her brother before finally nodding. "Of course." Turning to Herb, she said, "Get up. You will serve me as you served Tregor."

Herb was uncharacteristically silent as he nodded, his vast mop of curls unusually limp and lifeless, falling round his dumbstruck face as he kneeled in submission.

"How did you—?" Mick started.

"Not now. The important thing is that we find sustenance. Tregor's life was almost spent before I found him. He won't sustain my body for long." Maud looked back at the grate. "Herb, cook my brother something. In fact, prepare a full meal for everyone on their return. Not the thin scrapings Tregor used to give them. I want my Night-Foxes to be healthy."

Mick looked closely at Maud, trying to recognise any signs of the old Maud.

"Who are you?" he asked.

"Strength, power incarnate. That is all you need to know." She smiled at him. The warmth of her expression never quite reached her eyes, though. "Fear not, Brother-Mine. First, we must consolidate our power in the sewers, then we'll forge a new empire above ground." Maud walked towards the grate. "I have business to attend to. Stay with Herb and keep an eye on my new palace, meagre as it is."

Mick didn't know what to say. His day had gone from one terror to another. He sat back against the wall and tried to make sense of it all, feeling hollow. He slumped down, watching as the corpse of Tregor slowly rotated on its chain, regarding him through eyeless sockets.

Herb scampered to his feet and scuttled over to Mick. He pulled at Mick's sleeve. "Come on, mate, let's get into the kitchen. I can't bear it here any longer."

The two of them shuffled into the back room. The tiny stove was still burning from the morning's breakfast. Herb cursed as he touched the hot iron door, forgetting to first wrap his hand in a towel. He threw more coal into it, locked the door behind them, before collapsing onto a rickety wooden chair. Mick joined him. "What the fuck just happened, Mick?"

"Maud... I don't understand. It is like she is a completely different person."

Herb reached into one of the crates, pulling out a bottle of rum. "Tregor isn't going to care anymore, is he?" He poured a couple of large splashes into two tin mugs and handed one, his hands shaking, to Mick. He managed a weak smile. "That is a silver lining, at least."

The scent of rum churned Mick's stomach. "I can't. My stomach is ruined."

"Sip it, mate. It'll sort you out." Herb downed his mug, then refilled it. "What the hell just happened?" he asked again.

Mick took a sip, then another. Herb was right. It helped. "One thing after another. It's been a bastard of a day. I don't know how else to explain it."

"Well, have some more rum. That'll help." Herb sploshed a bit more of the dark fluid into his mug.

Mick took a deep breath. "Well, it turns out that Tim wasn't lying. We saw the Shadow. I thought she was going to kill us, but she was warning us about the red smoke, which also existed." He drank deep from his rum, his eyes damp. "It's in Maud now. I guess that is why she isn't worried about bullets and can roast people like chestnuts."

"That makes no sense. Which is about as much sense as watching our little Maud do... that." Herb pointed at the entrance leading into Tregor's chamber. Maud's chamber now.

"I think the Shadow has been following us since the red smoke." Mick scrunched up his eyes as he tried to make sense of it all. He failed dismally, exhaling loudly, his frustration obvious. "I don't understand any of it," he whispered. "Tregor's gone and we *should* feel safe. It's my sister, for God's sake. But—" Mick trailed off.

They sat quietly for a moment. On the stove, a large pan of water steamed. Herb reached over and threw in some bones. "This used to be Maud's job. Don't suppose she'll take it back and let me be queen, will she?"

Mick didn't respond to the weak quip.

"Are you sure she even is Maud?" Herb asked. "I don't recognise her."

This time Mick responded. His eyes, deadened by trauma, looked into Herb's. "That's my sister. I won't hear any different. The smoke has strengthened her, that's all."

"What was she going to do to me? Now, she has smoked Tregor?" Herb busied himself chopping vegetables. Mick heard the quaver in his voice all the same. "I can't see her wanting me as a pet. I wouldn't even know how to service her."

"Herb, she isn't going to hurt you. No more than she would've hurt Tim. She is your mate, our mate." Mick looked down at the floor. "This is a good thing. This is good for us." Even repeating it still didn't dispel the doubt in his mind. Everything about Maud was different. Her mannerisms and her stance. He barely recognised her from the shy, submissive sister he had grown up with.

Suddenly, what Herb had said finally clicked in Mick's mind. "And oi! If I find you've been servicing my sister, I'll wallop you right in the specials!"

Several hours later, Maud returned to take her place on Tregor's chair. Her skin seemed wan and stretched. Her eyes were dull and lifeless.

"Are you alright, pet?" Mick asked, concerned. He brought her a bowl of stew, but she waved it away.

"Thank you, Mick, even a body as young as mine burns out fast. Stew won't help me anymore. I need souls. Tregor's black, shrivelled excuse for one could not provide much sustenance." Maud smiled at him. "You will look after me, won't you, Mick?"

Mick put down the stew and held her head to his chest. "Of course, Maud, I promised, didn't I? We're family." For a moment, he could see the old Maud in her expression. "Maud, we gotta get rid of Tregor's body. It will scare the bejesus out of the others."

Maud contemplated his words for a while, then shook her head. "It should scare them, brother. The more they fear, the more they will obey."

And with that, the familial bond between the two siblings was gone again. Mick watched his sister sadly, wondering what thoughts were brewing behind her eyes.

The Foxes filtered into the chamber as the evening gradually traversed its inexorable journey towards night. The hulking corpse of Tregor hung in place, a stark testament to the new order. One by one, they sank to one knee, pledged fealty to Maud, and then retreated to the other side of the room. Bowls of thick stew, which would ordinarily be the height of luxury, proved cold comfort in the gruesome charnel house. Mick and Herb filtered through the urchins, telling them of the duel between Maud and Tregor, seeing the looks of disbelief.

Maud looked out over the scared children. "This is hard for you," she said. "You're scared. I can see it in your eyes. But I promise you, if you prove your loyalty to me, I will keep you safe. I will protect you from those who would destroy us."

She saw the urchins listening intently, their faces drawn and pale.

"From this seed, an army will grow," Maud thundered. "From the sewers, a new order will rise. I know you. I know all of your stories, how you've suffered. That ends now." She looked out over the frightened faces. "Together, we will teach the rest of the gangs that the Night Foxes are to be feared and respected."

Evan wouldn't make eye contact with Maud, he whispered to Mick, "This is too much, mate." Mick couldn't disagree with him.

It was night when the last Fox came in, hesitantly joining the group in the shadow of Tregor's body.

Maud banged her fist on the chair. "I welcome you all to a new era of the Night Foxes. The beast has been slain. Now, the wealth of the poppy trade shall belong to all of us, not just to Tregor."

A muted applause sounded.

"How did *you* kill Tregor?" Jack asked. He was the tallest of the Foxes, nineteen and already growing into an imposing figure.

Maud regarded him with an icy gaze. "I fought and slew him with my bare hands. If anyone feels they would make a better leader, they are welcome to try the same with me." She cocked her head to one side. "Would you like to claim the chair, Jack?" Jack was a head taller than Mick, two heads taller than Maud. Not that it would make a difference. Mick knew that the moment the words left Jack's mouth, Maud wouldn't let them go unpunished. Behind her, reluctantly, Mick moved to take his place at her side. Maud's eyes flicked round to where he stood and he felt a tremor of fear, not for his life, but for Jack's.

As Jack moved towards Mick's sister, Mick watched sadly. Another Fox was going to die. "Don't do it, Jack," he warned.

"Or what Mick? You think I'm scared of a lanky streak of piss like you?" If anything, Jack seemed emboldened by Mick's threat. Mick shook his head.

Maud stood up as Jack approached Mick. "Do not challenge Mick, challenge me. Take the chair if you can."

"Oh, piss off Maud." Jack absentmindedly made to backhand Maud out of the way as he continued towards Mick. She caught his wrist, snapping it in one movement.

Jack screamed with pain, his eyes wide with surprise.

He fell to one knee. Stepping closer, Maud placed her hand on his chest. His eyes smoked as he fell to the ground, dead.

As he died, Maud's eyes brightened. Her skin took on a rosy hue and she returned to her chair, reinvigorated. "Anyone else think they would make a better leader for the Night Foxes?"

They greeted her with silence, the occasional muttering of disbelief their only response. Maud pointed at two of the Foxes. "Dispose of the bodies." She released the chain, holding Tregor up. The demonstration was complete. She no longer required her trophy.

Mick had a restless night. Maud's talons outstretched, his sister's face loomed over him, haunting his dreams. It was almost a relief when Maud banged her chair, waking the Foxes. "Herb will make breakfast. Mick will collect today's boxes. Then everyone will wash. I will not have my legion, meagre as it is, soiled with dirt and decimated by disease."

Fear of Maud outweighed the Foxes' disgust of washing and they obeyed. After each Fox had washed, Herb handed them a thick bowl of warm gruel and a tin mug of water.

Mick went through into the dark recesses at the back of the main room with Tregor's key. He pulled out the boxes and stacked them next to Maud. She opened up Tregor's book, looked at its pages, and then handed it to Herb. "Assign the Foxes their deliveries." She waited patiently in her chair while Herb read out the assignments.

Mick took his assignment, bowing to Maud and taking his box from her. "Are you sure you don't want me to stay?" he whispered.

"Why would I want that, Brother-Mine?" she answered with a patronising smile.

"I..." Mick bit his lip. "You might need me."

Maud gave him an amused look. "I think you need my protection more than I need yours. Be gone, you have your task."

And that was it.

Mick took his box and walked towards the grate. He could feel his sister's eyes boring into the back of his skull.

The foetid stench of the sewers was a welcome reprieve. But Mick was sharply aware of a confused mixture of warring emotions that were battling within his brain. He knew he should be grateful to his sister and thankful for the red smoke that was empowering her, but instead he felt a profound awareness of a huge personal loss. Already he missed the close filial relationship they had always shared.

As he splashed through the damp tunnels, he felt an itch on his spine. Several times he turned and thought he caught a glimpse of someone, or something, following him. A flash of white, or a flicker of movement, was always on the edge of his vision.

He clutched at the box and increased his pace. He stopped to catch his breath, always watching behind him.

Rats swam through the thick waters and water dripped from the ceiling, but the Shadow didn't emerge. Somehow, though, he remained certain that she was still haunting him. He could feel her eyes on his back.

She hadn't harmed Tim, nor did she appear to want to hurt him. If anything, she had tried to warn them both. Could the Shadow be some sort of otherworldly nemesis to the red smoke? Was that possible?

Mick continued on his journey towards The Strand. The Shadow had indeed tried to warn them about the smoke, but Mick wondered if it was still something they should fear. Maud had torn through Tregor and saved them from his brutal reign. Part of him worried that she was no longer his sister, and the other part felt envy that the smoke had chosen his little sister, Maud, rather than him.

He increased his pace. The more he dwelled on Maud, the more uneasy he felt.

Opening up the grate, he climbed out into the busy London streets beside the river. Street sellers hawked their wares while others proffered less respectable delights from the shadows. Puddles of industrial oil and the scent of discarded night soil assailed his senses. Mick slid through the crowd.

He arrived at his next address. It read Jonathan Hargrave on the package. He knocked at the door, keeping a wary eye out for his competitors. He heard the clack of shoes on the floorboards before the door creaked open and a severe-looking face wearing tiny circular spectacles was looking down at him. His eyes narrowed with distaste before he held out a small brown pouch. It was heavy with coins that jangled against one another. Mick accepted it, thanking the man and tucking it into his vest before patting the outside of the fabric to be sure it had not slipped out of his grasp.

"You will inform your master that I will require double the quantities for the next shipment. My work has reached a sensitive point," Jonathan said, obviously eager to end the conversation and return to whatever he was up to.

"Right you are, guv'nor," Mick confirmed, flicking through the bag's contents before passing the package to his customer.

As Mick filtered through the backstreets on his return journey, he became aware of three children standing outside a bakery, watching him. He only recognised one of them, but they were all clearly members of the Silent Ones. "How's it going, lads?" Mick tried amiably.

The largest of them, a swarthy kid with lank, greasy hair, pulled out a knife and tapped it against his thigh.

Eyes widening, Mick backed away. His heart was thumping. "What ya doing, boys? The Foxes have an agreement with your master. We stay below ground except for deliveries and you control the surface."

The knife stopped tapping.

As one, the three children pounced. There would be no negotiation with the Silent Ones. Their tongues had been removed during their initiation to prevent them from sharing the gang's secrets.

Mick turned to sprint for the grate. It was a good four hundred metres. The surrounding civilians cursed and shouted as he raced through the jostling crowds, bumping from body to body. He could hear behind him the sounds of pursuit and increased his pace. Every second he imagined a knife plunging into him.

He was close now. If he'd had the energy, he would have spent it praying for more speed. As it was, he focused on the grate as his feet pounded over the cobbles. Ducking round a stall and vaulting a stack of barrels, he made it to the sewer entrance. With a last effort, he lifted the grate and jumped. Mick felt a hand grip his shirt for the briefest moment before his body-weight tore it out of his attacker's grip. As he plummeted down the shaft, Mick grasped at the ladder. The iron structure, covered in rust, cut cruelly into his hands before he could slam his feet onto the rungs halfway down. Old and rusted they might be, but at least they managed to hold his weight. His knees crunched painfully against the metal.

Breathing heavily, Mick looked up. The three faces loomed above him, eyes silently regarding him from the sewer grate. Mick took a moment to catch his breath before shouting out, "It doesn't have to be like this! You don't attack us. We don't attack you."

But of course, they couldn't respond even if they wanted to. One minute Mick was withering in the malevolent gaze of the mute urchins, the next moment, all three were gone.

Clambering down the rest of the ladder, he turned to limp home, his trousers sticking to his bleeding knees.

The foxes' den was quiet as Mick entered. Herb slowly stood, stirring a pot full of stew. He blinked at the state of Mick. "What happened to you? You look... well, you look like shit."

"The Silent Ones just tried to murder me in the bleeding street. They must know that Tregor is dead," Mick said. "It's been one hell of a day." He slumped down against the wall. "Where's Maud?"

"She's gone. She did the same thing yesterday. Just upped and went out for most of the day," Herb said.

Mick regarded Herb curiously. "How long is she away each day?"

Herb shrugged. "I'm not her keeper, mate. I stay quiet and keep out of sight as much as possible."

"You know you are still her best mate, right?" Mick whispered. "She has always cared for you."

Herb was silent for a long time before he said, "And I love Maud. If that's still her."

"You can't say that." Mick shook his head.

"I know I can't." Herb looked round, his face unusually pale. "That's the problem. It's the first time I've been unable to speak my mind in front of her. I don't know how she will react."

Mick accepted a large bowl of thick potato stew from Herb. Herb had added cabbage, onions, and lamb bones to give it flavour. He waited for it to cool as the steam wafted up. He barely noticed the taste. His thoughts were dark as he pondered his sister.

It was several hours before she returned. Only one of the other Foxes joined Mick and Herb as they waited for her.

Maud looked round the den imperiously. "Where is everyone?"

Mick shrugged. Herb remained silent. It was Evan who finally spoke. "They've run."

"Explain," Maud thundered, her voice thick with rage.

"The other gangs know that Tregor's dead. I don't know who ratted us out first. But someone must have spoken. The truce has been broken. It's carnage out there. It isn't a good time to be a Fox." Evan held out his hands. "The other gangs have either been attacking us or forcing us to join them. I had to run from the Dockers or I'd have got a boat hook between my shoulder blades."

"So much for my sewer legions," Maud snarled. "I don't have the power to deal with this now. I can't leave the sewers yet." She pounded her palm with her fist. "I need more life force." She slowly stopped, raising her gaze to Evan, a wintry smile stretching across her face as she stepped in close. "With your help, I can leave this sewer and hunt down the other gang leaders."

Evan nodded. Mick's eyes widened as he anticipated what was going to happen next. *She wouldn't. Not Evan.*

"Come here," Maud demanded.

"Maud please..." Mick begged.

Evan got up and walked over, ignoring Mick. When Evan was close enough, he smiled hopefully at Maud.

"You will be remembered," Maud said, reaching out to stroke Evan's cheek. Her other hand flew out and touched his chest. His eyes smoked as his body fell to the floor.

"Hell's teeth, Maud, what have you done?" Mick cried out, looking down at the corpse of his best friend.

"It was a strategic decision, Brother-Mine. Needed for the long term good." Maud regarded Mick closely. "I needed the power. Soon, I'll be able to leave the sewers and feed on those above."

"Who is next, then?" Mick said with disgust. "Me? Are you going to kill your brother? Or will it be Herb?"

A squeal sounded from behind them. "Don't drag me into it! I'm far too pretty to be killed." Herb looked at the smoking corpse of Evan. "Evan…" He sank down next to him.

Maud tapped her feet impatiently. "Eat well and get some sleep, brother. We are short-handed and don't have time for your weakness. Our delivery commitments outstretch our capacity. We will have to prioritise if we are to maintain control of the Night Foxes' business and hold the sewers." She looked at Evan's corpse. "We'll find the others soon. They will pay for stealing from me."

Mick didn't sleep. He sat scrunched up against the wall and closed his eyes, pretending. After an hour, Maud rose and left the den. He waited until she had left, stretching his aching muscles before clambering down into the sewers.

He followed her trail for about a dozen feet before a small voice startled him.

"Please don't."

Mick jumped. He spun round to see the Shadow watching him from a narrow side tunnel.

She approached slowly, cautiously. "Your name is Mick, isn't it?"

"How do you know that?" he asked, watching her warily. The spectre didn't seem all that threatening after the events of the last few days.

The Shadow walked closer. "I listen to everyone, but nobody ever sees me, or if they do, they run away." She bowed her head shyly. "I'm so sorry about your sister. She seemed nice. But you mustn't follow her. You mustn't."

"What do you know about my sister?" Mick said. His voice was louder than he intended. It echoed down the tunnels and sent the Shadow scuttling back into the tunnel.

Her face slowly returned, peeking round the corner. "Not here. You are too loud. Follow me."

Mick followed the Shadow. She led him through the stinking underground maze until they reached a section of what Mick had thought to be a wall. Instead, it transpired to be a door. The Shadow pulled at the handle and it swung open. The stench of dead fish hit him as he stepped inside a colossal basement full of huge vats of brine. Mick shivered in the unexpected cold. He could smell the salty, damp air. The walls and floors glistened with a white, powdery crust of salt. The floor crunched as he walked across it. It looked like a winter wonderland.

A small terrier came running up and barked at him.

Realisation dawned as he looked at the Shadow.

"You aren't a ghost," he said. Stepping closer to the filthy girl, he stroked her cheek with a finger. Her skin was warm and rough to his touch, not cold and smooth like marble or glass, nor ethereal like a ghost or shade. His finger left a trail, exposing her pale pink skin underneath as the white powder rubbed off onto his skin. "It's salt," he said in complete amazement.

"I don't think I am really a ghost, but sometimes I feel like I am not actually real either," she said shyly. "The workers at the cannery look straight past me without seeing. The children in the sewers run away from me."

Mick sat down. "Who are you?"

"My name is Tess. I live down here. My job is to look after Egg." She pointed at the terrier, who, recognising his name, yapped happily. Suddenly, a look of concentration flashed across her face and a flash of silver flew from her hand.

Mick turned to see a dead rat impaled on a small knife.

Egg ran and picked up the rat, bringing it to her. She took out the knife and dropped the rat in a bucket which already contained many of its fallen brethren. Finding a box, she sat down on it. "I used to feed Egg and he would kill the rats, but he is older now, and isn't as fast, so now I kill the rats and he picks them up." She scratched his ear and ruffled his fur.

"How long have you worked here?" Mick asked.

"All my life, I think." She screwed her eyes in concentration. "I don't remember not working here."

"You tried to warn us about the smoke," Mick said.

Tess nodded. "It has been in the sewer for a week now, ever since they tried to expand the sewers down south."

"What is it?"

"I don't know," Tess said, hanging her head. "It started off by entering the workmen. It would make them fight each other. When it ran out of people to fight, the body would drop dead and the smoke would look for a new body. It couldn't move far at first, but it seems able to travel further with each day."

Mick bit his lip. "It's in my sister now. How long has she got? Can we save her?"

"I'm so sorry." Tess looked down at the floor. "It only lasted an hour or so in the workmen. I don't know how it's lasted so long in your sister."

"Why didn't it enter your body?" Mick asked, regarding the scruffy rat catcher suspiciously.

"I don't know," Tess admitted. "I don't think it can see me. Nobody seems to see me."

Mick shook his head. "It has to be more than that. The Foxes thought you were a ghost, but we still saw you. The red smoke chased us. It chased Tim." He looked at his finger, the salt still staining it from where it had touched her face. "I don't think it likes salt."

"Or the smell of eels."

Mick snorted, scrunching up his nose. "Nobody likes the smell of eels."

"Oh," Tess said, curling her arms closely round her body as she looked down at the floor in shame..

"No offence," Mick said quickly.

"None taken." Tess smiled at him, forgiving him immediately.

Mick stood up and started to pace. "Maud disappeared for several hours yesterday."

Tess nodded. "She went back to where the smoke came from. I don't think the smoke can survive being far from its home."

"Will you help us get it out of my sister?"

Tess sat silently for a while and then nodded. "I don't know how to, but I will. If you promise me, I won't be alone anymore."

"If we get the smoke out of Maud, then I promise you that you can become a Night Fox. You can live with us and we'll be one big family." The salt crunched under Mick's feet as he paced round the cannery. "As for how. I think I have an idea. Come and find me first thing tomorrow morning."

Tess smiled shyly, her face lighting up even as the salt on her cheeks cracked

"I'll see you soon," Mick said. He stepped out into the sewer and raced back to the den.

On his return, Mick crept into the kitchen. Herb was fast asleep in one corner, seated on a stool. He had curled up, his head cradled on his knees. Mick stole past him to go through the cupboards. Finding what he was looking for, he slipped it into his pocket.

A few hours later, Maud returned. Mick continued to feign sleep until she announced loudly that it was time for the deliveries.

He looked at the creature his sister had become. "We won't be doing that today, Maud."

It regarded him curiously, "Won't we? Are you giving the orders now, Brother-Mine?" It shook its head dismissively. "You will take two deliveries today. You need to move fast."

"You ain't all-powerful, not yet at least." Mick straightened his shoulders and reached into his pocket. "Get out of my sister and we'll say no more of it."

Herb had woken up. He peeked out, his eyes wide with fear. Cautiously, he backed away to watch from the sanctuary of the kitchen.

The creature that had been Maud looked derisively at Mick's hand in his pocket and snorted dismissively. Its lips stretched open wide in mock surprise, then faded back into a smirk. Its gaze flickered back to the retreating chef and it smiled malevolently. "Herb has the right idea. You bent the knee to me before, Brother. Why choose to betray me now?"

"Because you ain't my sister. You've just stolen her body, wearing it like a jacket." Mick stepped forward. He tried to will more anger into his voice to mask the quavering fear that sapped the strength from his legs.

It chuckled. "No, I am not your sister. She is here, watching all I do. Right now, she is screaming at you not to be an idiot." The thing advanced on Mick, holding out its hand. Long talons emerged from her fingers.

Mick instinctively took a step back.

"But to be honest, this is all good timing," the creature declared. An unnaturally large smile was spreading across its face as its teeth sharpened into needlelike points. "Your life force will be enough for me to finally break free into the city above." It sniffed loudly before giggling again. "All those souls, just waiting to be harvested. When I'm strong enough, I'll bring my clan through the rift, too. It's been a very long time since we were last in Britain."

"Who are you?" Mick demanded.

"You can call me Mabli. Know that I have achieved where all my illustrious kin have failed. I have found a way back. They will hail me as their champion." Mabli narrowed its eyes. A twisted sort of smile spread across its face. It began to circle Mick with a confident, predatory gait. Mick stepped to one side, making sure that he always kept himself between his enemy and his escape route. "The Fomorians ruled these lands thousands of years ago. Back then, your kind called us gods. Now, I return to find that you worship a carpenter. Pathetic."

Mick gritted his teeth. "Mabli?"

Mabli cocked an eyebrow. "Yes?"

"Fuck off home." Mick pulled his hand out of his pocket and hurled a thick cloud of salt into the apparition's face. Mabli howled with pain and fury as its flesh smoked and burnt. Mick was already running. He lifted the grate and half climbed, half fell down to the sewers below. Landing on the gantry, he ran towards the cannery as fast as possible. Behind him, he heard Mabli. It roared in a horrific perversion of his sister's voice. He knew it couldn't be far behind him. It was faster. He prayed the salt had slowed it down enough.

His legs burned, but he forced himself forward. His lungs felt tight, sweat stung his eyes, and his chest was close to bursting. The wet gantries underneath glistened like black ice. Mick couldn't stop. He could hear the slapping sound of Mabli's naked feet pounding the sewer path. He expected to feel its talons raking across his back at any moment.

He saw Tess at the junction halfway to the cannery. Her eyes focused behind him, her hands flickered and two flashes of metal flew past him to thud into his pursuer.

"Where are you?" He heard Mabli cry out in frustration. "What manner of fae dares to interfere with the Fomorians?"

Mick stumbled. His legs were working like pistons. He could no longer concentrate on his running. His sole aim was to make it down the path and to keep breathing. At last Mick glimpsed the entrance to the cannery and almost passed out as relief flooded his system. The door was wide open, a parting gift from Tess.

Egg waited, yapping encouragingly and wagging his tail, as Mick slumped through the doorway and collapsed onto the salt lined crystalline floor. He rolled onto his back in the shadow of the huge pickling vats. They surrounded him, the last resting place of thousands of eels.

Egg licked his face as Mick lay on his back, shuddering breaths filling his lungs with precious air. The scent of decaying fish had never been so welcome. His throat tasted of copper and everything hurt as his body protested at the relentless, hammering abuse it had endured.

He blinked. When his eyes opened again he saw an enraged Mabli in the entranceway. A hideous parody of the Maud he remembered. It was no longer a pretty, happy face. The face had changed. It was gaunt, with great hollows beneath its cheeks. The creature's mouth gleamed with razor sharp fangs. Its eyes were like black glass. Lank ropes of hair hung down round its face, matted and unkempt.

Egg barked at the intruder, bravely blocking the entrance, tail down and growling. Mabli cast a look of disdain at the small dog, causing him to yelp and hide behind a vat.

A grin spread across Mabli's face, exposing its cracked and bleeding lips as the creature returned its attention to Mick. "Salt? You think you can stop me with poison?" Mabli stepped into the cannery. Its feet smoked where it trod on the salt lined floor. "You are so very wrong if you think this cave can protect you from the likes of me."

"No," Mick panted. He scrabbled on all fours to the iron stairs leading to the upper gantry. His lungs were burning, his muscles trembling. He staggered onto it and breathed deeply with shuddering sighs, the bitter taste of blood in his mouth.

Mabli followed him. "Yes. I've slaughtered legions in my time. I won't be stopped by a child," it said in a mocking tone. "Goodbye, *brother*, you've proved yourself to be quite the thorn in my side."

Reaching the upper gantry, Mick struggled to stand on unsteady feet. His limbs were on the verge of collapse.

"Ah, your last stand." It sneered at him. "Didn't think this through, did you? Pathetic."

"You have to fight this, Maud. Don't let it do this," Mick pleaded.

Mabli laughed. "Did you honestly expect that to work?"

Its hand blurred out towards Mick's heart. Mick stepped back, clutching at its wrist. His other hand grabbed Mabli's blouse and then he toppled backwards, dragging the creature with him.

The two of them fell into the vat of congealed fish. Thick, putrid liquid surrounded Mick's body. The long, slimy forms of dead eels wrapped themselves round him as he plunged down towards the bottom of the vat. He flailed with groping hands. Already exhausted, he fought to return to the surface for air. The viscous jelly sucked at his limbs, drawing him ever downward.

With an explosion of breath, he broke the surface, but almost immediately sank again. His limbs screamed with protest as he forced them to propel his body upward once more. As he kicked and pushed himself through the water, a sea of dead eel eyes bore witness to his struggle. All round him, he could see the huge fist sized bubbles as the red smoke popped and dispersed into the air.

Mick looked round for Mabli, for Maud, but it was still underwater. He ducked under, reaching through the coiling flesh, but he could feel nothing. Taking another deep breath, he dived through the tubular corpses, his desperation mounting. Suddenly, he felt something. His fingers pushed frantically until—*yes, cloth*! He grabbed at it and pulled his sister's body up to the surface.

She was unconscious.

His other hand scrabbled frantically at the slippery sides of the vat. His panicked cries echoed through the dark when he realised that there was no way out of his watery prison. He screamed with frustration and pounded his fist against the unyielding metal. His deadened legs churned the waters, a jellied soup that bobbed and surged round him.

All of a sudden, a strong wiry hand grasped his wrist. With a final burst of effort from his legs, Mick managed to push himself upwards just as he felt his head was about to explode from the blood pounding in his ears. Guided by his saviour, his fingers found the lip of the vat and he was able to pull himself up at last, out of the stinking water.

Under the dim light of flickering oil lamps, he saw Tess lying on her front. He passed Maud's cold, wet body up to her. Tess gripped her as best she could until she had the small girl by the armpits and was able to lift her up slowly onto the gantry. Maud's face was as white as a sheet. Her eyes were closed. Tess rolled her on to her front and slapped her sharply on her back, between the shoulder-blades.

Egg ran up and licked Maud's face, yelping, his tail wagging as he tried to understand what was going on.

Mick watched helplessly as the two of them battled to save Maud's life. His final reserves of energy were spent.

Don't be dead after all this, Maud. You can't be dead!

Suddenly, Maud coughed violently. She vomited up salt water through the holes in the iron gantry.

Leaving her to expel all the fluid she could.Mick half crawled, half slid towards his sister. He rubbed her back as she continued to clear her lungs. He wiped her slimy, wet hair off her face. He cleaned the slimy jelly away from her face and her eyes.

"Maud," he ventured nervously.

"Mick?" she answered quietly, her voice raw from the vomiting. Tears erupted from the small girl as she wept freely, curling into a ball and rocking backwards and forwards. Egg redoubled his efforts to lick at the distraught girl's face, his tail wagging hopefully.

"It's okay now, Maud." Mick patted her shoulder. He reached down to pull her into his arms and hugged her. Both their bodies were freezing cold and coated in slime, but they didn't care. Mick looked round for the smoke but, to his relief, he could see nothing.

Tess was sitting with her legs crossed, watching them. "It's gone now," she reassured them.

Maud shivered with the released adrenaline and the cold. "The Shadow?" she said, looking at Tess.

"A girl and our friend. She saved our lives," Mick confirmed.

Tess stood up straight, ramrod straight, and waved overly enthusiastically.

Maud gave her a weak smile in response, before being subsumed by another coughing fit.

Mick led the girls into the Foxes' Den. Tess held Egg close to her chest. He looked round curiously, then sniffed the air, his eyes widening as he caught the scent of a savoury potato stew emerging from the kitchen.

Herb slowly poked his head out.

"It's safe now, Herb. Maud's okay now. The smoke has gone," Mick said wearily.

"Who is your friend?" Herb asked, still unsure and reluctant to leave his sanctuary.

"I'm Tess," she answered shyly, beaming at him.

Herb squinted at her. "She seems unnaturally happy. I don't trust her."

"Stop it, Herb."

Mick pointed at Tess with his thumb. "We couldn't have saved Maud without her. I said she could stay with us," he grinned. "She doesn't need to be alone anymore. Maybe we all need each other?"

Egg barked.

"Sorry Egg," Mick apologised. "This is Egg. He is a ratter."

Herb knelt down and held out his arms. Egg jumped down from Tess and scampered over to him with his little tail wagging. He leapt into Herb's embrace. "Oh, I like you, Egg!" Herb looked into Egg's eyes. "I wouldn't feel lonely if I lived with you." Egg barked and licked Herb's face.

"So, what now, Mick?" Maud asked.

Mick walked over to Tregor's chair and kicked it over. "This becomes firewood. We ain't having a ruler. We got some money in Tregor's stash and what's left of his opium. We will do what needs to be done and we *will* do it together."

He looked at their faces and for the first time in years, the tightness in his chest relaxed as his heart felt the beginnings of something that might well be hope.

Deep within the sewers, a crack showed through the brickwork. It exposed a fissure which led down through the rocks to an ancient Roman temple dedicated to the pagan god Jupiter. A circle of fluted columns stood round a large, ornately carved marble altar which had cracked in half. The long forgotten skeletons of ancient Roman legionaries lay round the stone pedestal, entombed in their armour.

A red glow dimly shone through the base of the sundered altar.

CHAPTER THREE

THE BLACK FOG

11TH OCTOBER, 1958, GRIMSDYKE

The town of Grimsdyke slumbered. An ancient fishing village, its population had aged and dwindled. The brick buildings remained as a hollow shell for a diminished community.

Ted lay on the bonnet of his father's car. Next to him, Sue was decanting cider into two tin mugs. She pulled a face as some splashed onto her blouse.

Pulling out a fresh cigarette, he lit it and took a long drag. The tip flared with more energy and enthusiasm than he could ever remember feeling. Numbly, he accepted the mug with a grunt of appreciation.

He hated this town.

"Look." Sue pointed at a roiling fog bank, dark in hue. It was sweeping in from the sea and had already enveloped the lighthouse. The blazing fury of the bulb, guardian of the seas, had been quenched, swallowed by the thick, black shroud.

Ted sat up, for once interested in something other than his dismal life. "Isn't the whole point of lighthouses that they can pierce fog?"

Sue offered her mug to Ted. "I want to go home. I don't want to get caught in that."

Drinking the last of his cider, Ted gazed over at the fog. "It's stopped coming in."

"Ted!"

"Fine. Get in the car. I'll drive you home."

Leaping off the bonnet, he tossed the butt onto the damp grass. Clambering into the car, he checked his hair, making some adjustments to his pompadour before pursing his lips with approval. The radio crackled with the tail end of "Louie Louie" as the ignition fired.

The road rumbled under their wheels as they crawled through the narrow streets. Ted parked outside Sue's house and they shared a lingering kiss before she ran to her door and began the slow process of creeping silently inside, back to her bed.

Lighting another cigarette, Ted drifted home, listening to music and dreaming of escape. It was early in the morning when he finally parked up. Taking a beer out of the fridge, Ted sat down on the floral patterned sofa his mother had been so proud of and took a long swig. Lurching forward, he turned on the television and adjusted the dial until the plum tones of the BBC wafted over him.

His barely touched beer lay bereft as the velvet darkness of sleep enveloped him in its dark veil.

He was woken by his dad crashing about in the kitchen. Jumping up, he saw him filling the kettle.

"Sit down Dad, I'll make you some tea and toast."

Taking the kettle off him, he ushered his dad to the sofa.

"Mum'll be back soon. She'll do it." His dad settled his gaunt frame, enveloped in an oversized, cream woollen jumper, onto the sofa.

"Yeah, course she will, but let's treat her, eh?"

Ted shook his head. His mum had been dead for the last year. Gathering up the cups and saucers from yesterday, he filled the sink with hot, soapy water. As the kettle began to whistle on the stove, he filled a teapot and swore softly. The toast was burnt. He scraped off the black and then covered it with a thick slather of butter.

"Did Mum get any biscuits?" His dad called from the sofa.

"No, *Mum* didn't get any biscuits, Dad." Ted looked at a photo on the wall of the three of them. Even after a year, he still thought of his mum every day. He looked down at the burnt toast and smiled. She had always burnt the toast.

Then anger flowed through him. *If you hadn't killed yourself, then I'd be out of here, free to escape this cursed town.* Instead, he was left looking after his shambling wreck of a father. Since she had been found dead on the beach, his dad hadn't been able to work. He barely ate, just drank tea in front of the TV and rotted.

Ted didn't have that privilege. Instead, he had a job. In Grimsdyke that was a privilege in itself. Munching on a slice of buttered toast, he carried over his dad's breakfast.

"There you go, Dad." Ted slapped it down without ceremony on the side table.

"You are a good kid, son." His dad looked up at him with watery eyes as he munched on the toast.

Ted didn't respond. Still in yesterday's clothes, he brushed his teeth, corrected his hair and left for the harbour.

His manager, Bill, nodded at him with approval as he took up his station. Ted kept himself to himself, but always arrived early and worked hard. Anything to get out of that coffin of a house.

The others complained about dwindling fish stocks and about foreign imports taking their jobs. Ted didn't. He just kept his head down. As the others were let go one by one, Ted survived, day by day repairing boats, fixing nets and scraping barnacles off hulls. He took a grim pride in his work. He couldn't bring back his mum or fix his dad, but he was good with the boats.

As Ted worked to recaulk, pitch and debarnacle the Ocean Ghost, he overheard Old Pete talking about the lighthouse. Downing his tools, he wandered over.

"Both dead, how?"

Old Pete took his time. Unused to this much attention, he was savouring it. He'd lost his job years back but kept coming back out of habit to sit and smoke his pipe, drinking the odd cup of tea that Bill allowed him for old time's sake.

"The Black Fog claimed them last night. It rolled over the lighthouse and swallowed their souls." Old Pete took a deep drag from his pipe.

Ted was unimpressed. "That is great, Pete, but what did the police say?"

Spitting a gob of saliva onto the harbour decking, Pete snarled. "The blue bottles? Buzzing round, knowing nothing. They don't listen to the old tales."

"No Pete, they don't. They look at the evidence instead. Now, what did they say?"

Pete wafted a gnarled hand at Ted as if he was a foul stench. "They said it were death by misadventure because they found an empty bottle of whisky with them. Natural causes, my arse! They want a coroner's report. Waste of time! It were the fog, I'm telling you."

"Sure it was Pete." Ted walked back to the Ocean Ghost.

Old Pete, less than impressed by his dismissal, bellowed after him. "It were the fog, I tell you. It used to claim fishermen, but there ain't enough of them for it anymore, so it's coming to the land." Standing up, he shouted across the harbour."Do you all hear me? It is coming to the land!"

Bill turned round, annoyed. "Shut your trap, you crazy old coot, or I'll kick you off my dock, you hear me?"

Grumbling and muttering, Old Pete returned to his seat, sucked angrily on his pipe and watched the sea. Ted could see him mumbling, but thankfully could no longer hear him.

As six o'clock came round, Bill counted out Ted's day wages into his hand. Nodding his thanks, he strode off. It was getting colder so Ted quickened his pace. Stopping by the harbourside shop, he went up to Sue, who sold him some smokes and a bottle of local cider. He remembered his dad's request that morning and picked up a packet of biscuits.

"Shall I wait for you?" He leaned over the counter and gazed into her eyes.

Unimpressed, she pursed her lips. "No, go home, bath, change your clothes and pick me up at eight when you don't reek."

"Do you want dinner from the chippy?"

Sue shrugged. "It isn't like we have any other options in this town." She bagged his purchases for him.

Taking the bag from her, he gave her his cheekiest grin and leant over to kiss her cheek.

"Get off with yer. I'm working, you scoundrel." She softened the blow with a wink, then sniffed. "And you stink."

Refreshed, clean and wearing a rusted-iron, red shirt, he applied some expensive pomade to his hair and checked the mirror. *Looking sharp.* He tilted his head to a few other angles to be sure and then slung his leather jacket over his shoulders.

Driving to the chip shop, he picked up three fish and chips.

He dropped off one of the newspaper-wrapped parcels of food to his grateful dad, leaving the other two in the passenger seat, filling the car with the scent of salt and vinegar. He swung by the harbour to pick up Sue. She was all ready and waiting for him in a powder blue blouse and waving happily.

They drove to their favourite viewpoint overlooking the sea. Climbing onto the car bonnet they sat munching on the salty chips and drinking cider. Sue was burbling on about the lighthouse. Ted tried to block her out. The deaths at the lighthouse reminded him of his own mother's death the previous year. He drank deep and reflected that they should have bought a second bottle.

"Ted!" His eyes snapped open in annoyance as she pointed. The black fog had returned and was rolling in again. It had enveloped the lighthouse and showed no sign of stopping.

"Get in." He jumped down from the bonnet. Sue followed anxiously.

By the time they had reached Sue's house, the fog had already enveloped the streets. Forced to park up, he walked Sue to the door and began the slow walk home.

His hand out, he could only see a metre in front of him. The town was silent. Everyone was inside, he guessed. It wasn't far to his house, but as street lamps and bins loomed out of the fog at him, he was forced to slow his pace. The fog tasted of salt. It was getting thicker.

When his front door appeared out of the mist, he chucked his cigarette butt onto the floor and breathed a grateful sigh.

He walked into the front room.

"Mum?"

From the sofa, his mum turned round from where her arm was round Dad.

"What are you—" Ted blinked. "Is Dad ok?" He moved to check his dad's pulse.

His mum laughed with the same musical tinkle he remembered so painfully. "He is alright. We've just had a celebratory drink, that's all."

Dad opened his eyes and smiled sleepily. "Hello, son. Your mother is back. Isn't it wonderful?"

Ted looked back at his mum. "They said you were dead. We saw the body." He stepped back."Dad, shouldn't you be in bed? You don't look well."

She kissed the top of Dad's head as he gently nodded off. "He is fine here, Ted. Come and join us. It's been a long day for all of us."

Ted backed away.

Gesturing again, she patted the sofa next to her. "I haven't seen you in a year. Sit down. I'll explain everything."

Overloaded, Ted made for the door.

"Ted. You get back here this instant. Don't be rude!" The screeching tone echoed after him. "Ted!"

He stumbled through the cold fog once more, nearly tripping over a bin. round him, he could hear rustling. It could be anything in this damned weather. One hand stroked the wall to guide him through the streets. He nearly tripped over a second bin, then his shoulder smashed into a lamppost, causing him to hiss with pain. Without hesitation, Ted pressed on.

His mind was locked up, unable to process what was going on at home. *I saw her dead. Dead.* Who was that at home if it wasn't Mum? *Could it have been someone else in the mortuary?*

His breath was short, the emotional and physical stress getting to him. *I need a drink.* Finally, he reached Sue's house. He banged on the door with his fist. Then, without waiting, he went to the living room window and gasped.

"What the—" Jack was sitting on the sofa next to a gently nodding Sue. Jack. Jack, her eight-year-old brother. The same one who disappeared four years ago. He hadn't aged a day.

This isn't right. Without thinking, Ted kicked in the front door. It took three attempts.

He raced into the living room. Sue's head was nodding dreamily. Her eyes slowly blinked open. "Jack came back. Isn't it wonderful?"

"Where are your parents?" His heart thundered as he waited for the response.

"Sleeping upstairs. Why?" Sue looked confused. "What's wrong with the front door?"

Instead of answering, Ted stormed upstairs. Jack was screaming at him to stop.

The bedrooms and bathroom were empty. Ted tore downstairs. Jack bellowed at him. "Stop, stop! Sue, stop him. He is jealous!" Sue couldn't do anything but cry. Her head flopped down on her chest. She looked exhausted.

Ignoring the little snot, he stormed into the kitchen to find the bodies of Sue's parents. They had both collapsed onto the floor where they were lying with their arms wrapped round each other. Strangely, both had looks of serene euphoria on their faces.

"I told you to get out."

He turned slowly to see the tiny form of Jack staring at him with malice. "You are ruining everything."

Ted started forwards, then stopped as Jack's body shifted and twitched, the face contorting grotesquely.

Ted stopped in his tracks. He stared with horror.

There was a savage rip as Jack's shirt tore and a coiled mass of scales writhed through the rent fabric. His face seemed to shimmer.

'Jack' launched forwards. The sinuous body slid across the floor, jaws snapping, vicious, serrated teeth flashing, and monstrous eyes rolling back in its skull in anticipation of the kill. A sibilant hiss escaped before—

BANG!

Ted smashed a ceramic kettle into the creature's head.

BANG!

As the creature fell, its long snake-like tongue lolled out while its tail continued to convulse. Ted didn't stop hitting it until its skull was shattered and the beast was very, very dead.

A long, loud scream came from the front room.

Sue was slumped against the wall, her face pale. The body of the giant eel-like creature slowly morphed back into the form of young Jack.

"I can explain—" Ted started, dropping the kettle and holding up his hands.

"I saw the fucking snake, Ted," Sue snapped.

Ted breathed a sigh of relief, then turned to rummage through the kitchen drawers until he found a cleaver.

"I have to go. Dad is with one of those things. It is pretending to be Mum."

"What are they?"

"Who gives a shit? I have to go, and fast."

Racing to the door, Ted was halted by Sue grabbing his arm.

"Not without me, you don't."

"My mother has returned as a giant eel. You are staying here!" Ted tried to shrug Sue off.

She clung on. "You want me to stay alone in the house with that thing? You can sod right off, Ted."

Supporting her, he relented and they both stumbled out into the fog. The rustling sound was back. Sue gripped his arm tighter. He shook her and pressed a finger against her lips. It wasn't rustling he had heard earlier. It was slithering.

Peering through the windows of the houses as they passed, in every one they saw happy families relaxing on their sofas, everyone watching television, and most of them dosing. Still, there was always one family member awake, one family member who turned to look at Sue and Ted with a blank expression on their face.

They arrived at Ted's front door to find his father asleep on the sofa. Ted threw open the door, a cheery smile across his face. "How about that hug, Mum?" She beamed at him and patted the sofa.

The cleaver clunked right between her eyes. An inhuman scream burst from her lips.

Her body didn't change.

They waited for a moment. Ted shrugged hopefully. "Well, I guess Jack turned human when dead—"

"—It wasn't Jack, Ted," Sue said. She raced upstairs for a blanket to place over his dad. She tossed a second one over to Ted, who wrapped the corpse of the creature in it. His mum's face was still looking up at him.

They stayed watching the front door until the mist receded and the sun started to come up. The morning air was cool as he loaded the beast's body into his car and drove it down to the wharf. Ted broke into a supply closet in search of a tarpaulin and chains for the disposal of the body.

Once it was securely wrapped, he loaded the cumbersome bundle into a boat and sailed it out into deeper water. When he felt he was far enough away from shore, he heaved the body over the side of the boat and into the sea, grunting with the effort.

Exhausted from his exertions and a sleepless night, he flopped back and throttled the motor to head towards home. Looking over his shoulder, his blood ran cold and he cursed. The fog was rapidly returning.

He heard a sound and turned to see his dad was in the boat with him.

CHAPTER FOUR

A ROSE BY ANY OTHER NAME

2ND JUNE, 1961, KENT

It was cold and damp, a typical February morning in Kent, as Sara sat looking under the polythene sheets in her rockery. No matter what she tried, she couldn't recreate the gardens she'd seen in Crete. Her particular patch in Kent's garden of England just didn't have the baking sun or the right soil for it. She dug out the deep taproots of the dandelions that were more than happy to take over her attempt to recreate Eden.

"Tea and toast," Dennis bellowed from the bedroom window. She jumped. The small trowel slipped and cut through the root instead of neatly excavating it. Her husband was awake and from the sounds of it, was feeling the effects of last night down the Red Lion.

"Coming right up," she called back to him. It would be time to get Rory ready for school soon, anyway. Leaving the weeds in her bucket, Sara headed inside to boil the kettle.

Rory was already sitting at the kitchen table, gripping the latest edition of the Eagle comic in his hands. She poured him a glass of milk, which he duly ignored, his attention dominated by Dan Dare's adventures on the planet Venus. Making a fresh pot of tea, she grilled two slices of toast for Dennis, then set about a new batch for Rory and herself. "Rory, get this up to your dad." She handed him the plate and a chipped mug of milky tea. Rory could smell lavender as she leant over him. His eyes gleamed as he dashed to obey. Her eyes dropped down to his comic and she smiled.

She filled the sink with hot, soapy water and gently dropped the dishes into it. Popping into the living room, she collected the glasses from last night. Dennis had kept her up entertaining his old partner in crime, Reggie. It didn't take a master detective to tell that they had hit the whisky after the pub. *No wonder Dennis is in a foul mood.*

A frown crossed her brow. On the side table was a sales brochure for a jewellery shop in Hatton Garden and an AA Map of London. A sick feeling churned in her stomach. Dennis had promised her that the last job would be his final one. Their house in Kent was meant to be a retirement bolt hole where they could live off the proceeds of his past jobs.

Not again.

Dennis had made it this far through luck and skill, but that wouldn't last forever. As far as she was concerned, this job was the last straw.

Waving Dennis off to the Red Lion, she returned to fill the sink with the dishes from lunch. Rubbing the hot suds over the greasy plates, she reflected on the latest time she had been happy. It had been in Crete, on their honeymoon, drinking wine in the tavernas by the sea and basking in the scent of the salty sea, the sweet honeysuckle and the roasting lamb, the sounds of merriment, laughter and the gently lapping waves. The white-washed buildings stood in stark contrast to the colourful people and their vibrant way of life.

On her return, she had immediately set about recreating the beauty of Crete in her garden with a trellis, wooden decking, and the pride of her garden, a large rockery. But like her marriage, it had never really taken off. Like her marriage, it became choked by weeds and failed to grow. It just wilted.

The doorbell rang. Startled, Sara dropped the plate she was drying. It shattered into tiny pieces as it hit the tiled floor. Pausing in indecision, she looked at the broken crockery, threw her hands up, and answered the door.

"Hi, hi, hi." Her friend Hazel beamed at her. No matter the situation, Hazel always put a positive spin on things. Leading her into the kitchen, Hazel gasped at the shattered crockery, the two of them immediately set to clearing it up.

Crisis over, they settled down with cups of tea. "What's got you all riled up then, pet?" Hazel blew on her mug, displacing a gout of steam.

"I think Dennis is planning another job." Sara confessed. She looked down. "He said the last one would be the final job. He promised me. How could I have been so stupid?"

"Oh, Sara." Reaching over, Hazel stroked Sara's hand. "I suspected Reggie might be up to something." Looking her in the eyes, she asked, "Are you going to do what we discussed?"

"Of course, I'm done expecting him to change. I've got a taxi coming in an hour to take us to the train station. I'm going to pack up Rory's things and take him with me to stay at his Aunt Jane's."

"You are making the right decision. This is no life for a child." Hazel sipped at her tea.

"What about you?" asked Sara.

Hazel pulled a face. "We don't have kids to worry about. If Reggie goes down it won't change much for me. It isn't like he spends much time at home, anyway. He's always out with your Dennis." She laughed. "Sometimes, I wonder if it's you or Reggie that is Dennis's real wife."

Sara got up. "Well, Hazel, thank you so much. You have always been my best friend, but I had better get Rory ready."

"Good luck, Sara and godspeed."

There was a honk from outside.

"Rory!" she called. A small pale face appeared and then came running down the stairs. His knobbly knees poked out above long socks. Chucking a scarf round his neck, Sara pulled a woollen cap over his head. He could smell her lavender perfume as she adjusted his jacket. "Come along." She planted his suitcase in his hand and then opened the door to see... Dennis.

Dennis looked smug as he peeled off a note and handed it to the taxi driver. The taxi slowly reversed and left. Fear gripped her heart. "Den nis," she said. Her voice sounded thin and reedy. Warily, she put down the suitcase and walked towards him. "I told you, we have a kid now. We agreed, no more jobs."

"Is that why I find you skulking out of here like a thief? You coward. You couldn't even face me, could you?" He stepped towards her. "Our family stays together. Forever. You know that Sara."

"Go inside Rory. Wait in your bedroom," Sara ordered. Her stern, matronly voice quavered. "It's all going to be fine. Just go inside."

"Well then, we have matters to discuss, don't we?" Dennis pointed at the garage. "Why don't we step into my office and have a wee dram, eh?"

"Dennis..." She took a step back.

His eyes hardened. "You can step in there now, dear or I will drag you in by your treasonous hair. Do you understand?"

She looked at the garage. "Promise me you'll look after Rory and I'll do whatever you want."

"Oh, he'll be fine. I already have someone to take care of him. Someone who won't try to separate him from his dad." Dennis pointed. "Come along. Chop, Chop." He grinned. The smile failed to reach his eyes, which resembled cold, dead lumps of coal. "I haven't got all day."

"Where is Mum?" Rory asked, as Hazel cooked dinner.

"With your Aunt Jane," she said, smiling. "She had a right barney with your father and needed some time to really think about what is important in her life. Don't you worry, she'll be back soon enough. She's been very stressed recently."

She would never leave me here.

He looked down at his pork chop with roast potatoes and carrots. His appetite faded. Cutting them up and forking them into his mouth, he fell silent.

"Tell you what, why don't we plant a rose in the garden to show just how much we love her?" Hazel mixed him a glass of squash. "She would love that."

Rory nodded. "A red rose."

"Of course, I'll pick one up tomorrow. We can plant it together." Hazel beamed at him. "We are going to be great friends, Rory."

I don't want to be your friend. I want my mum.

After dinner, he excused himself. His dad was still down the pub. He'd been there since he'd argued with Mum. His plate was on the side. The gravy had grown cold. White patches of pork fat were congealing on the surface.

He heard the front door slam and the heavy tread of drunken footsteps as his dad returned.

Rory lay in bed, eyes open. Sleep eluded him. He knew his mother was never returning. Rory could feel it in his blood. He was trapped with his father, the ogre, the bogeyman—the ever-present source of fear in his life.

He didn't sleep that night.

In the morning, Rory lumbered out of bed, red-eyed and swaying from exhaustion. Hazel was waiting for him. A large bowl of porridge sat congealing on the table. Next to it was a glass of milk. Numbly, he consumed both before leaving to walk to school.

When Hazel had put the beef joint into the oven, she picked up a bowl of batter. "Come on, Rory. I got you a little something for your mum." Leading him outside, they walked down to the end of the garden to where Hazel had left a small white rose and, next to it, a trowel.

"Thank you, Hazel." A large trench of disturbed soil attracted Rory's attention. "What is that?"

Hazel was beating the batter to get the fresh air into it. "Leave that well alone Rory, that is just manure to help the garden. Look how vibrant it is becoming."

Rory looked round. Sure enough, for the first time, their garden was blooming despite the season. His mum's plants were looking healthy, green and sturdy. Her centrepiece, a small olive tree, was flowering for the first time with small crimson blooms.

The bushes of star jasmine were thick and luxurious. The star-shaped blooms they were named after blossomed with velvety red petals.

Clumps of oregano, rosemary, and thyme were spreading across the bed. Bees were buzzing happily, harvesting the fresh nectar. A wondrous sense of calm settled over Rory. Having successfully beaten enough fresh air into the batter, Hazel had disappeared inside to make Yorkshire puddings.

Rory looked at the trench.

If it's manure, then it'll be good for the rose.

Rory took out the rose and dug a small hole for it in the disturbed soil. He planted the rose in the middle of it and tamped down the earth. As he admired the rose, one of its thorns pricked him. He winced and looked at his finger. Blood welled up and he sucked it to staunch the bleeding.

His father was back home from the Red Lion, early for once. Reggie was with him and they both tucked into the roast beef.

"This is magnificent, thank you, Hazel." Dennis raised his pint to her. She beamed in response. "I got a little something for you this morning while I was out." He held out a small box.

Hazel opened it and squealed with excitement. It was a silver pendant with a mounted sapphire. Handing it to him, she excitedly asked him to put it on for her.

"Of course." He pulled her hair clear and clasped it shut.

Hazel ran to find a mirror, leaving Dennis to smirk at Reggie. They clinked pints as Dennis forked another two Yorkshire puddings onto his plate.

After dinner was over, they retreated into the living room for private conversation while Rory was banished to his room to read his comics.

It was early in the morning. The sky was still dark when Rory first woke up and heard it. A whisper, almost a sigh.

"Rory."

It could almost be a gust of wind. Rory snuggled down into his duvet, pulled a pillow over his head, and remained awake until the sun rose.

When he returned from school, he heard a scraping, a whimpering, then a bang. Creeping through the house, he saw his father slamming into Hazel through a crack in the kitchen door. She was mounted on the table, moaning with pleasure.

He backed away. Ditching his bag, he ran outside.

He walked slowly towards the rockery. The plants had exploded in size. He marvelled at the rich, verdant foliage, then saw the rose, his rose. It was already a large bush sporting dozens of red blooms. Its roots had covered the trench with a thick mass. Not one of the blooms was white. He raised one of the flowers to his nose and the scent... the scent was lavender. He had a sudden vision of his mother, of her thick cream jumper, of her rubber boots, of her cradling a cup of tea. He looked at the trench.

"Rory."

He heard it again. This time he listened to the faint whisper.

"Rory."

Looking down at the trench, he shuddered. A tear rolled down his cheek. "Mum?"

"Rory."

He placed his hand under the rose bush and pressed it against the soil. "Mum," he whispered. A sudden sharp prick lanced into his hand. He jerked it back. Thorns were visible in the soil. His hand was bleeding.

"Rory, I'm sorry, I'm just so hungry."

Rory backed away from the rockery, creeping back inside the house. He hid in his bedroom until he was summoned to dinner.

Dennis was home early from the pub for once, he'd brought Reggie and they were tucking into the roast beef as Rory came down. Raising his pint, Dennis graciously toasted. "Compliments to the chef. You make a fine meal, Hazel."

Chuckling, Reggie clinked with him.

"Come here, Hazel." Dennis held out a small box. "This morning, I was having a good old look round and I found you a token, a small token, of my appreciation." Hazel squealed with glee and clacked over in high heels and apron.

Her eyes widening theatrically, she held up the box for everyone to admire.

Opening the box, she revealed a platinum bracelet.

Eyes widening, she clipped it round her dainty wrist.

Dennis smiled through a mouth full of Yorkshire pudding. He forked another onto his plate for good measure.

Rory had finished his meal and was sitting politely when his dad looked up at him. "Fetch the whisky and two glasses, son. The men need to talk."

Rory smiled and did as Dennis told him.

He waited in his bedroom, listening to the commotion downstairs. After about an hour, the front door slammed shut. Walking downstairs to the kitchen, he saw Hazel dancing round as she gathered up the dishes.

"You know Dad hid another present for you." Rory gathered up some plates and brought them over to Hazel as she put her rubber gloves on at the sink. "He was talking about it with Reggie, about where to hide it." Rory went back to grab the empty whisky glasses. "He buried it outside by the rose bush. Something about a ring."

Clasping her hands together and peeling off the yellow washing-up gloves, Hazel leapt about with excitement. "You have to show me where exactly."

"I don't know," Rory said dubiously. "I don't want to get into trouble."

Hazel gripped his hands, her eyes feverish with glee. "Rory! You can trust me. We are best friends."

"Okay, but you must act surprised when he shows it to you," Rory warned.

Hazel had already opened the back door. "Yes, yes."

Rory led her to the rose bush. "It's down there." He pointed.

Peering down, Hazel poked at the bush with her hand. "Oh, it's all thorny. Where is it, Rory?"

"It's just under the soil, by the roots," Rory said.

Placing her head under the leaves, she scrabbled under the bush on her knees. "Oh Rory, I can't find–Rory, I am stuck!"

Rory watched dispassionately as Hazel started to choke. Rose branches coiled round her throat. The thick scent of lavender wafted up from the rose bush as it shivered. Its thorns laced into her skin.

"Rory." The sound drifted to him in the breeze.

Rory smiled. "Compliments to the chef. Hazel makes a fine meal, Mum."

Rory was waiting at the kitchen table when the front door slammed open, indicating that Dennis had come home from the Red Lion. He was drunk and stumbling.

"What are you doing up?" he slurred at Rory.

Rory looked up, his face crestfallen. "It's Hazel. She is hurt."

"What?" Dennis started forwards, correcting his gait after almost tripping. "Where is she?"

Rory pointed at the back door. "She was in the garden, Dad, in her high heels and fell down. I didn't want to call the authorities because..."

"Never call the authorities," Dennis bellowed. "We don't want their kind sniffing round here thinking they are better than us."

Dennis stumbled outside. He could see the distant shape of Hazel through the dense foliage. "Hazel? Hazel." He looked down at her with horror. The roots bound her to the soil. Her limbs were tied with rose branches as thick thorns punctured her skin. She was a dried sack of skin. A large red rose blossomed out of her mouth.

A claw hammer smashed into the back of Dennis's skull. He spun furiously. "What the–"

"Our family stays together. Forever. You know that, Dad." Rory held the bloody claw hammer to one side as he stared down at his father.

Dennis growled and tried to lurch forwards before falling backwards into the beckoning branches of the rose bush.

The scent of lavender filled the air as Dennis was entombed by nature.

Rory sat on the train to Nottingham, reading the latest issue of The Eagle. He hummed a tune to himself. Beside him sat a cutting of a red rose bush in a plain terracotta pot. The delicate scent of lavender wafted across the carriage.

CHAPTER FIVE

ROCK BOTTOM

3RD MARCH, 2008, NEPAL

The Tuk Tuk bounced merrily over the rocky mountain track. Wilbur and Francis were happily singing along to Green Day's 'American Idiot' album. The wind was bitter, but they were seasoned travellers and dressed appropriately. The climate in Nepal was a far cry from Australia.

Francis passed Wilbur a bottle of the local rotgut, a drink called raksi that blew away the cold like a fist through cobwebs. Wilbur took a medicinal-grade swig, holding onto the steering wheel with his other hand.

Driving over a rogue stone, the Tuk Tuk jumped, raksi splashed all over Wilbur's face and into his huge, bushy beard. He gripped the steering wheel as the vehicle swerved on the road. They looked at each other, and both erupted into peals of laughter. The album flicked onto its title track, and they reached new levels of volume, if not ability.

Francis took the bottle off his friend. "Steady there, mate. I can already taste the beer at the hostel. Let's not fuck it up."

"I wonder if any other tourists will be there? This has been the loneliest walkabout I've ever had."

"That is what happens when a cheapskate books the tickets off-season." Francis pointed accusingly as he swigged from the bottle.

"Oh fuck off mate–" Wilbur started, before a loud whump sounded, heralding a cascade of rocks "–shit!" The Tuk Tuk swerved round them until, with a crack, followed by several smaller thuds, it tumbled off the track.

Gripping the steering wheel, he clung on for dear life as it began rolling and sliding down the ravine.

Bang. Smash. Pain. Silence.

Water was running over his leg and arm. Fuck. He was lying in a shallow stream at the bottom of the ravine. Francis was gone. He cried out an expletive as his leg informed him it was broken. Looking down, the bone was visible through the skin. He fought down panic by taking a deep breath.

Grunting with pain, he shifted his position. Why didn't these things have seat belts? Rolling over, he levered up the Tuk Tuk and slid out from under it. Vision blurred. He roared with pain, almost blacking out. Sliding across the wet rocks, he levered himself up against the cold stone.

"Fuck me dead. Are you alright, mate?" A voice floated down from the top of the ravine.

Relief flooded through Wilbur's system. Francis was alive! Wilbur bellowed back up at him. "I only went and broke my bloody leg, mate. I can see the cunting bone!"

"Nothing major then, you'll be alright. Pat on the back, stubby in your hand and a bit of physio, and you'll be bouncing like a joey." There was a brief pause. "I saved the Raksi."

Wilbur chuckled, "Oh good one, mate, pass it down, will you?"

"Get stuffed prick! I'm going on to the village. I'll grab some locals and I'll be back, pronto."

Leaning back against the rock face, Wilbur looked at his broken leg. Something would have to be done about that.

"Oi mate, can you keep an eye out down there? I lost my bloody hat!"

"I thought you'd fucked off? Sure, why not? I'll have a jog round, shall I?" Wilbur yelled back.

"Too right, well, see you in a couple of hours, then."

After waiting to see if anything else echoed from above, he assumed he was alone.

Somehow, he'd lost a trainer in the fall. He still had his other one, though. Gingerly, he pulled his leg up so that he could remove the trainer and pull out the shoe-lace. Small scrub trees grew wherever enough dirt could accumulate. He uprooted several of them, using the clasp knife he always kept in his pocket to cut off the side branches. Pulling off his canvas belt, he arranged the trunks on either side of the break, with the belt wrapped round the fracture. Tying the lace round the splint, he took a deep breath and muttered, "Oh, you cunt," then jerked the belt tight, screamed and blacked out.

He didn't know how long he'd been out, but when he came to, he saw a large dog sitting on its haunches on the other side of the ravine. It was watching him. "Oh, you furry bastard." He saw it had his missing shoe in its mouth.

"Big bugger, aren't you mate?" he warily noted the lack of a collar. "Reckon you ain't a dog after all, are you wolfie? Tell you what, how about you stay on your side, and I stay on mine, eh?"

The wolf cocked his head on one side and regarded him coolly, then laid down and resumed gnawing on the trainer. Wilbur leaned forwards and finished off his splint by tightening the lace. Wincing, he finished by tightening the belt. Now Wilbur had set the break, the pain was merely unbearable.

Rifling through his pockets, he found his phone was still working, albeit with a cracked screen and no signal. A sharpie pen, some tissues (used) and an empty protein bar wrapper. Nothing game-changing there. Sitting idly, he decided that he needed some company. Ferreting round him until he found a particularly attractive rock, he drew a face on it. Critically appraising his piece of art, he added hair and, with some deliberation, a moustache.

"Welcome to my ravine, Tess." He waited patiently. "Ah, not much of a talker then? That's a shame."

After a while, the wolf dropped off the chewed remnants of his shoe, sniffed the air and slowly started stalking towards him.

"No, mate, we discussed this. This is my side. That's your side over there, you dumb drongo." When subtle diplomacy failed, Wilbur resorted to roaring. "Fuck off, you furry prick!" and hurled a stone that smacked the wolf on the shoulder. He growled in response and started to leap forwards, only to receive a stone bowled right between his eyes. Yelping, he scampered back down the ravine.

"Off you go," Wilbur gathered up a pile of stones in case his hairy nemesis returned. Looking down at the heap, he moved Tess next to it. "You look after those now, girl."

Looking at the torn carcass of his shoe, he swore at length. Their luggage had scattered who knows where. Shame, he had duct tape in there. That would have sorted his leg out. Could do all sorts with duct tape, maybe even make some weapons in case the wolf returned for his other shoe. Sitting back, he gently sang "Basket Case".

As it got dark, he saw three pairs of eyes glowing a fiery white, padding down the ravine. Fear gripped him as he levered himself up, "Oh, you wanker, dialled up your uncles, eh? You bastard." He pulled off his jacket and wrapped the denim round his left arm, his clasp knife at the ready, in his right. "Come on then, you bunch of stinking wombats!" His voice sounded weak and reedy to his ears, so he added a few choice expletives until he had reached a suitably rage-filled bass tone.

For a while, everyone stood still, watching each other, eyes locked. Then the wolves leapt forwards in unison. The first one jumped. Wilbur raised his arm with its denim shield and as the wolf locked its teeth round it, he stabbed the animal furiously in the throat. Blood gushed over them both as the dying animal fell away. The other wolf tore into his leg as he stabbed down into the back of its neck. The final wolf barreled into his chest. Its fangs sought his throat as he fell backwards, the hot foetid breath washed over him as he tried to ward off the savage beast. In the brawl, he noticed the scab between the eyes.

So, his old friend had come back for the other shoe. Bastard. His clasp knife had disappeared in the fall and he reached round for anything else. White-hot pain lanced through him as the wolf trod on his broken leg in the scramble.

Tess.

His free hand suddenly felt her cool touch as Wilbur grasped her and smashed her into the side of the wolf's skull. Knocked to one side, it made one last furious attack, but Tess met him in midair and its skull crumbled. Just to be sure, Wilbur introduced him to Tess a few more times. Leaning back, breathing heavily and bleeding freely, he cradled Tess to his chest and passed out.

He woke to feel his legs being bandaged by a group of villagers. Francis loomed over him. Pointing at the wolf carcasses surrounding Wilbur, he asked, "Are those the bastards who shit in my hat?"

Wilbur nodded. "Ate my shoe too."

Francis shook his head in disgust. "No wonder you killed the hairy cunts," and passed him a bottle of raksi.

CHAPTER SIX

THE PLATINUM SERVICE

Friday, 2th March, 2012

'Initiation'. Oliver sat at his new desk, looking at the email invitation. The location was marked as being at 'The Datacentre' the time was half five in the evening. He texted his girlfriend to let her know he'd be late home.

It was his first day at Dragon Insurance and he wanted to make a good impression. What was limiting him so far was finding something to do. Frustrated, he leant over and spoke to the grey man next to him. "Roger?"

Bleary-eyed, Roger turned and looked at him with distaste. "What is it?"

"Is there any work I could pick up? I've read all the documentation, and I'm up to date with all the terms, including Lloyds Gross Gross."

Roger looked as though he'd swallowed something nasty. "It's Friday. Nobody works on a Friday. The Wolfpack hits it hard on Thursday. If you want to be one of the boys, you'll learn to respect that. Just keep your head down and stay quiet."

"Roger?" Oliver persisted.

"What?"

Oliver pointed at his screen. "Where is the Datacentre? We've a team meeting there tonight at five-thirty. I need to let the missus know when I'll be back."

"When you'll be back? *Never* give a time to your other half. Never. You are setting yourself up for failure. The Datacentre is the code name for a strip club." Roger slurped his coffee, then tapped on the keyboard just enough to stop the screensaver from appearing. Grease from his morning bacon sandwich caused the keys to gleam. "We go to Diamond Girls. Most of the boys have girlfriends there. It's harmless fun. As it's your initiation, we'll probably end up at a brothel."

Oliver blinked. "I'm sorry, I have a girlfriend. I can't go to a brothel. She isn't going to be happy about the strip club either."

"Are you simple? Why would you tell her? You absolute moron." Roger turned to face Oliver. "You have to go. It's mandatory team building. You won't last long here if you don't join the Wolfpack."

Five hundred and fifty pounds a day. A six-month contract. That is one hundred and thirty-two thousand a year if they extend.

"I'll be there," Oliver promised.

"Too right." Roger resumed staring into space as his hangover held his mind in impenetrable chains. "You'll know it is close to five-thirty when everyone turns off their location tracking and Dave hides his kippah in his desk drawer." He murmured, looking vacant. "That is when the wolf pack goes out on the hunt."

"Right." Oliver began the exhausting process of looking busy whilst simultaneously doing absolutely nothing. He had previously done some programming work in the public sector, so he had perfected the art. It just sucked.

Oliver had finished all the documentation and was reviewing the database line by line, drilling through it. It was painstaking and tedious. The code was a hodgepodge of different coding styles, which slowed him down. Everyone had their own naming standard and way of doing things which led to some unusual design choices.

It's five hundred and fifty pounds a day. Suck it up.

At five-thirty, the boys in perfect synchronicity locked their computers and began to circle Stevo's desk. Oliver, looking up at them, nervously stood and joined them.

"Are we ready, lads, for another night on the prowl?" Stevo smirked and leaned back in his chair. "First round is on the newbie."

Dave reached up, removed his kippah, sliding it into his jacket pocket. The other men disabled the location tracking on their phones so their wives would be none the wiser.

"Last chance Dickie." Stevo called over to one of the coders who was still at his desk. He looked up briefly and then shook his head.

Roger leaned in to whisper in Oliver's ear. "Dickie recently got in trouble with the missus. They only communicate via letters on the kitchen table. He shares them on the team Signal group."

"There is a team Signal group?" Oliver muttered.

"Yeah, prove yourself tonight and they'll add you." Roger pointed with his thumb at Dickie. "Anyway, he has to return home on time every night or she will leave him and take half his portfolio. He is worried sick that she'll leave him with the kids, so he only has lunchtime appointments now."

"Bloody hell." Oliver shook his head. "No wonder he needs therapy at lunch."

The conversation stopped. Everyone looked at Oliver.

"Therapy?" Stevo looked like he had swallowed something foul. "Fucking therapy? Like, tell me about your father?" The rest of the team cackled. "All I'd say to my therapist would be, 'My father was a fucking legend.' Jesus Oliver, you are so green."

"So—" Oliver tried.

"Hookers. Dickie orders his hookers at lunchtime to save his marriage. I mean, it's a beta move, but she has him over a barrel." Roger confided.

"Pub," Stevo ordered and with that, the pack descended upon the closest pub, The Bull, for the first drink.

Gathered round Stevo, they supped their bottles of lagers. Oliver had ordered a pint of ale.

"Rookie mistake." Roger pointed at the pint. "You gotta play the long game here. Bottles of lager slow down the drinking so you can last longer. You don't want to get to the Datacentre and find yourself unable to unload, do you?"

Oliver raised his pint. "I don't really drink lager. I'll just skip the next round."

"The hell you will, nobody skips a round. Next, you'll try to order a soft drink." Roger slurped out of his bottle of Becks. "Next pub is All Bar One. At this time of the day it is rammed full of east European fanny. We buy them a bottle of prosecco, chill out with them for a while and then—"

Stevo interrupted. "Then we hit the Datacentre!"

A chorus of cheers erupted from the wolf pack as they clinked their bottles together.

Oliver grinned nervously. His phone chirped in his pocket and he reached for it.

"Don't you dare." Stevo pointed his finger directly at Oliver's face. "No bitches when the wolf pack hunts."

Five hundred and fifty a day. Besides, it can't be that important.

All Bar One proved to be a bit of an anti-climax after another four bottles of truly abhorrent lager. They watched as Dave alternated between sending bottles of prosecco to tables of all girls and then calling them skanks when they refused to come over and join the wolf pack.

When Oliver suggested he got a round in, Stevo shook his head. "Nah, enough of these bitches. It's time to get the real thing."

A chorus of "Datacentre, Datacentre, Datacentre!" erupted.

Bundling into the back of a black cab, the motley crew headed off to Earls Court. As the cab bounced round alongside the river Thames, they cackled in the back.

"I've already selected mine. Jasmin. She has everything, a tiny waist, massive breasts, blonde hair. She is the real deal," Roger stated, holding up his phone. He showed her profile.

Stevo smirked. "Dealers choice as always, Mrs. Geurts knows her pussy. She always finds me the best one for the night. Don't worry about the wife seeing my search history, either."

"I think it is time," Dave said slowly, nodding. "Those whores at All Bar One pissed me right off. Only the Platinum Service will do."

A chorus of applause and high fives erupted.

"You madman!" Stevo shook his head in admiration. "Two and a half grand? No fanny is that good, mate, trust me. You can get top-notch action for three hundred maximum, including anal."

"What can I say? We don't compromise in the wolf pack." Dave smirked. "I'm due some top quality tail."

Oliver had been sitting quietly. "I thought we were just going to a strip club or something. I don't want to cheat on my girlfriend."

"What?" Disgust lingered in the cab as the temperature lowered. "I thought you wanted to be one of the wolf pack? We don't have beta males in our team."

"You need to think about what you just said and develop some fucking loyalty," Roger snapped. "We are all married, but we still bond together. It is what makes us an elite team."

The taxi lurched as it drove over some hidden bump.

As the group righted itself, Stevo sneered. "Sit this one out. We'll call this week 'probation'. Next Thursday, when we head to the data centre, we will do your initiation again and see if you can man up."

Oliver sat uncomfortably as the others muttered round him. He was ordered to the nearest pub to get a round of beers in and 'post spuff sambucas'.

When the lads all disappeared off, hooting and howling about how they were about to perform, Oliver sat quietly. He nursed a bottle of Becks and pulled out his phone. Five missed calls and a text message from his girlfriend.

"I wanted to tell you in person, but it's late and I'm going to bed. I went and got tested. I'm pregnant. We need to talk about this."

Fuck

He typed back a message saying he would be finished up at the pub in about an hour and would then head straight home, but Sarah didn't reply. He hoped it was because she was asleep.

About twenty-five minutes later, the boys started to filter in. Arms raised like football champions, they proclaimed their victory and, raising their shot, immediately downing it with aplomb. After relating tall tales about their conquests, they waited patiently for Dave to return.

They almost didn't notice his return. He slipped in quietly and sat down, pushing the shot away from himself.

Roger looked round at the others. "Dave? The shot is right there."

"I see it, Roger. I don't want it."

"You what?"

"I said I don't want it. I have just had the most amazing spiritual experience. It really put a lot of things into perspective for me and I don't want to ruin it with more alcohol." The others looked at him dumbfounded. "In fact, I am going to head home now. Thanks for a good night, lads."

"Thanks for a good night? What happened in there?" Stevo looked horrified.

"I'm not allowed to say, but it was worth every penny." Dave smiled at them. He practically gleamed with self-assurance.

He walked away from the table, leaving his beer and the shot, to the wolf pack's mute silence.

"What the fuck did they do to Dave?" Roger looked as though he was going to be sick.

Stevo straightened his shoulders. "Doesn't matter. He'll come to his senses. Once a member of the wolf pack, always a member of the wolf pack. New kid, you can do his shot. I'll have his beer."

Oliver, aged thirty-four and older than Dave, ignored the reference to being a kid and sculled the shot. The beer was foul anyway. The sambuca burned as it went down. He listened quietly as the boys all discussed the 'Dave Situation.'

After thirty minutes of disdain and theories about what the Platinum Service could be, Stevo raised his hand. "Right, I'm drinking myself sober. Dave's gone and ruined the night. Let's go."

The wolf pack emptied their drinks down their throats and lurched off in different directions to find their way home.

Oliver returned to find his girlfriend sound asleep. He lumbered round the bedroom, drunkenly removing his clothes in a manner he hoped was suitably stealthy, but nonetheless, she woke sleepily and looked up at him.

"Oliver, what time is it?"

"Go back to sleep, Sarah. We'll talk in the morning." Oliver walked over and stroked her hair. "I'm so happy for us."

Sarah smiled and slid back into sleep.

Sitting on the edge of their bed, Oliver was still drunk as he pondered his options.

If I just do six months at Dragon Insurance, we'll have enough money to move into a bigger flat. We could hit our ISA limit for once, build a nest egg.

He looked down at Sarah. She wouldn't understand if he told her he had to sleep with an escort for the job. Even he thought it sounded pathetic.

He lay down on the bed. It was all about the child now. He would send out his CV for new contracts with a similar day rate, but ultimately, he had to do what was best for them all in the long run.

Next morning Oliver woke up with a heavy hangover, groaning as he stretched out into the sheets. He could smell chipolatas frying downstairs and his stomach gurgled.

Sarah came up moments later. On a tray was black coffee. The acrid scent was ambrosia to him. Two plates of baked sausages and tomatoes on sourdough toast joined it and he eagerly sat up in bed to receive it.

"Can we talk?" Sarah asked as she joined him with her own plate.

Oliver took his first sip of coffee and leaned back with appreciation. "Absolutely. I was awake last night thinking about our baby. I am so excited for us."

"Awake? After the skinful you had?" Sarah pulled a wry smile.

"Well, not for long, but the pondering was intense and very... Well, it was very deep." Oliver slurped down another gulp of the black gold.

Sarah bit off half a sausage. Chewing on it, she looked round the tiny studio flat. "Can we even afford to have a child?"

"Absolutely." Oliver looked straight into her eyes. "One hundred percent. I don't really get on board with the particular brand of toxic masculinity at Dragon Insurance. But, for five hundred and fifty pounds a day, we can get a nice two-bedroom apartment and even start saving up a nest egg for our baby. If I get renewed, perhaps we could even think about buying a place."

Laughing, Sarah jabbed him in the ribs, causing him to almost spill his coffee over the white Egyptian cotton sheets. "Buy a place? Come on, let's keep things realistic. Nobody can afford to buy in today's market."

"Seriously, the amount I'm getting. Hell, I might even get more when we renew. All I have to do is keep my head down and rub along with the boys." Oliver beamed earnestly at her.

"That is all, huh? I'm glad you feel that way. It's a huge step." Sarah snuggled in closer to him.

Oliver put his arm round her. "It is a massive step, but one we'll take together. This is going to be good for us."

Collecting the empty crockery, Sarah watched as Oliver slumped back into bed. "Seriously, back to sleep after a coffee?"

"Five fifty a day. My liver wrote the cheque," Oliver mumbled as he pulled the pillows tighter to his face. "Five fifty."

Monday, 5th March, 2012

On Monday, Oliver strolled into the office to find the wolf pack clustered round Dave's desk. He was loading his stuff into his briefcase.

"What do you mean? You haven't turned into Jesus for Christ's sake." Stevo was pacing. "Look, don't make a rash decision. You are one of us."

"Many things clicked into place with me on Friday, mate. I woke up and over breakfast, I told my wife everything. We were honest with each other for the first time ever." Dave smiled. "It wasn't easy. We both cried—"

"—Oh, for fucks sake." Roger muttered.

"But we stopped arguing. It feels as though we are best friends again. All the drinking, all the women, was just me externalising that I was deeply unhappy with who I am. The Platinum Service just brought all of this home to me. Dickie, I really think—"

"—Fuck off, I'm fine, thank you, you prick," Dickie sneered at Dave. "I used to think you were alright. Now, I see you for who you really are. A self-righteous piece of shit. I. See. You!"

Oliver sat down at his computer and avoided the confrontation, logging in to bring up his emails. His ears followed the argument.

As he reached the door, Dave turned to the team. "Try the Platinum Service, guys. You don't have to live like this."

Stevo leaned back in his chair. "Go on then, fuck off."

Dave shrugged and left. Silence filled the office as everyone looked round at each other.

Oliver tapped away at his computer, loading up his programming software and working through the first of his assigned bugs.

Muttering next to him drew his attention.

"Never would have seen that coming. Dave was a legend. The Platinum Service made him into a beta bitch." Roger was distraught. "I won't use it. Got my usual whores. I never needed anything fancy. My life is perfect."

Oliver gave him a wan smile and returned awkwardly to his work. Someone had to do some coding. The others were all busy chatting and unleashing righteous indignation. Dave had been moved from the ranks of "Legend" to "Traitor". It was unnerving to see them turn so quickly on their own, particularly after Friday's continuous pledges of loyalty and brotherhood.

Stevo rallied the troops in the evening and led them down to the Bull, where the conversation veered between continued rage at Dave and just how happy everyone was with their idyllic life.

Oliver got home at nine. The boys had steered clear of the Data-centre, so he got back in time to reheat dinner and sit on the sofa with Sarah.

"Your breath is pure alcohol." Sarah wrinkled her nose as Oliver forked the contents of chicken curry into his mouth. "How much of this five-fifty a day is being spent on drinks?"

Oliver grinned. "It's tax deductible, business entertaining. It is expected when you are one of the boys."

"You know, you always said you were a computer programmer, not a professional drinker."

Puffing out his chest, Oliver looked down upon her. "When you are earning the big bucks, you have to do the grime to get paid for your time."

Sarah pulled a face but returned her attention to the TV. Oliver paid little attention to it. Finishing his curry, he leant back and declared that he would have a shower and then turn in for an early night.

Thursday, 8th March, 2012

On Thursday night, Oliver returned home much later. Thursday was the new Friday in the city and it was two o'clock in the morning before he stumbled back.. After the Bull and All Bar One, the wolf pack had descended on Diamond Delights, a strip club.

Sarah was woken by him slumping down next to her.

"For fucks sake, Olly, I have to be up at six for work." She rolled towards him. "You reek of perfume. Where did you go?"

"The boys wanted to go to a strip club," Oliver confessed.

Sarah's eyes flickered open and Oliver immediately regretted his honesty. "I've been making sandwiches for both of us to save money and you have frittered away our money on strippers? Your life isn't a non-stop bachelor party." She shook her head. "Olly, you used to be so proud of your job."

"Listen, it's five—" He never got to finish.

"—If you say five-fifty a day again, I swear I will scream. How much of that five-fifty are you actually keeping if you are down the pub every night and going on to strip clubs? Don't forget you have to pay tax too."

Oliver made the mistake of patting her shoulder. She flinched under his touch.

"Listen, I make more than enough for a bit of unwinding after work. This is where the real meetings happen. This is where we discuss what's happening in the office."

"Bollocks." Sarah rolled over.

Friday, 9th March, 2012

In the morning, Oliver woke to find that Sarah had already left for work. She hadn't made him sandwiches for lunch, not that it mattered. He had been binning the sandwiches when he went to the office, anyway. The boys would go out for a pint and a pub lunch or head to a proper sandwich joint. Oliver wasn't going to be scorned for having homemade sandwiches.

She won't need to be up at six every morning when we have a child. She can quit her job as a nurse. I'll be the breadwinner.

Getting out of bed, he made himself a coffee. Two spoons of sugar and two spoons of Nescafé. *We should get a coffee machine like the Americans have on TV.* He poured semi-skimmed milk absentmindedly over his Weetabix as he sat at the table in his underpants, reviewing his life.

He pondered on how he could fix his current dilemma. The way he saw it, Sarah had never understood money. She was a staunch saver and very protective of their money, but she didn't understand that you have to invest some cash if you want to make it into the big league. In his mind's eye, he had already sketched out what he needed for promotion. Better suits were a must. He was still wearing his M&S interview suit and Clark's shoes. He needed to see a tailor, buy three suits and also invest in a pair of Church's shoes.

It would be a good idea to buy Stevo an appointment. Get him on side.

Mentally, he was committed to hiring an escort to prove himself to the wolf pack this evening. His initiation was going to be flawless this time. Oliver was determined to show that he could be an apex predator like the rest of the boys.

The office was quiet when he arrived. Roger was the first one in, hunched over his keyboard, working off the hangover by munching on his bacon sandwich. His cheeks sagged as he sipped at a giant latte. The

Telegraph online news moved across his screen as he clicked through articles.

Oliver gave him a quick salute as he entered, getting a perfunctory nod from him in return as he started his PC and began the process of loading up. The first email was a calendar invite, 'Datacentre' at five-thirty. With a grin, he clicked 'Accept.' With Sarah kicking off at home, he needed a good night out.

A cluster of new bugs had been raised, and he skimmed through them for easy wins. Accepting the first, he was able to submit fixes for two of them even before Stevo marched in through the door at nine. Scanning the bugs, Oliver looked for something challenging to keep him going through till lunch-time. There was an obscure rounding bug that Roger had tried to fix twice and failed. Oliver accepted it with a hungry grin and began pouring through the code. Roger might be better at networking, but he didn't have Oliver's analytical mind. Oliver tracked through the code, making notes and sketching out the data flow on a ring-bound A4 pad.

Friday lunch was a pair of pints and a steak and ale pie at The Bull while they started talking through the pros and cons of various prospects for Oliver's first time at the Datacentre. It seemed like the world was at Oliver's fingertips.

When you earn this much money, you can have whatever you want.

He shook his head as he looked at the different girls on offer in the online catalogue.

Why did people bother desperately chatting up women in nightclubs? You can pick and choose here. Order champagne and women come to you.

His analytical mind, of which he was so proud, neglected to remind him of Dave's repeated failed attempts to lure girls over with champagne. The taste of ale and testosterone flowing through his system blanked out his higher functions as they all laughed at lewd jokes.

At 52, the oldest of the group, Roger, was imparting his wisdom. "The problem with women is that once they hit twenty-five, they are essentially ruined. So it is essential to have children early because when they hit thirty, you aren't going to want to go anywhere near them."

Nodding, Stevo raised his glass. "My wife is twenty-eight. We have an arrangement. She doesn't bother me. I don't bother her. As long as she keeps herself tidy and doesn't embarrass me in public, we are all good. She knows she is easily replaceable if she lets herself go." Stevo raised a finger in warning. "The alternative is to end up like Dickie, where the wife is in control, so you have to get your release in lunchtime appointments. That is no way to live a life."

Oliver didn't mention that Sarah was thirty-two and he found her immensely attractive. Nor did he say that he loved her. Weak comments like that wouldn't do anything to further his position within the group.

When he got back from lunch, he looked at the test scripts. He had nailed it. The tests were all green, the rounding error was solved. Satisfied, he looked round for new bugs to pick up.

He had solved another three bugs by the time that the wolf pack started to gather, circling Stevo's desk at five-thirty.

It was time for his initiation.

This time he knew what to expect and he was in the right headspace.

The boys drank their tiny bottles of Becks whilst making big statements about the problem with Britain today and the idiocy of woke culture. Without Dave, the girls at All Bar One went unhassled as instead, the wolf pack sat waiting for them to come to them. Sadly, as Stevo noted, the girls tonight were frigid and none took the first move.

They led Oliver to the Datacentre. He didn't know why he had such grandiose expectations. In his imagination, he had seen the Datacentre as a Victorian mansion, with Mrs. Geurts clapping her hands together and a series of elaborately dressed women dancing out in a line, waiting to be chosen.

The reality was far more practical. After advice from the considerably more experienced wolf pack, Oliver had reviewed the catalogue and decided to leave the decision to Mrs. Geurts.

The building was modern, resembling a hotel. Mrs. Geurts was a middle-aged woman dressed in a severe dark grey suit and sitting at a desk in the entrance lobby. A short cut black bob framed a stern face.

Stifling his disappointment, he was led to the woman by Stevo. "Mrs. Geurts, my friend Oliver needs someone experienced, blond, with good breasts, but slim. Not a Tonka truck."

Slipping a well practised, taut smile over her inscrutable face, Mrs Geurts pulled a key from a pegboard. "I believe Candy will fit the bill. She knows how to handle a gentleman new to the more professional arts." Handing over a card machine, she keyed in three hundred pounds.

Oliver hesitated. "It'll show on your statement as PG Holdings," she said, looking amused at the expression of relief on his face.

He took his key. The others picked up their keys and paid Mrs. Geurts. They ascended the stairs. The building was clean but everything looked cheap. The carpet was plain and thin, the walls painted an off white colour.

The boys filtered off until Oliver was left outside room thirty-one grasping his key. Buoyed up with overpriced lager, he took a deep breath and inserted the key. He wasn't cheating on Sarah. This was team building, that's all.

Opening the door, he found a small cell with a single bed. A bedside table held a selection of condoms, a box of tissues and a bottle of lubricant with a pump top. There was an IKEA chair at the foot of the bed.

Sitting on the bed was a beautiful blond girl. She checked her phone. "Standard service today, I see, no extras?" Patting the bed beside her, she looked up at Oliver. "Take off your clothes. You can hang them on the chair there."

"Right. Okay then." With nervous fingers he unbuttoned his shirt. Sliding out of his clothes, apart from an awkward moment hopping round with his trousers that refused to come off, he hung them on the chair whilst Candy tapped on her phone.

"All done?" She smiled and motioned again for him to join her. He moved down to the bed and went to kiss her. "No, no. No kissing, you naughty boy."

"Sorry," Oliver said, embarrassed. He sat there, unsure of how to proceed.

Reaching over to the table, Candy picked up a condom and opened up the wrapper. "Why don't you lean back while I pop this on, eh?"

Oliver gratefully obeyed. She slid the latex-free condom over his erect member whilst he lay there. Nervously, he twiddled his feet until the task was complete. She clambered on top of him and slid down onto his shaft. After that, the rest was more manageable.

Twenty minutes later, fully dressed, Oliver was in the local pub waiting for the boys to assemble. Stevo was first in, so had the circle of after spuff sambucas waiting. Stevo's was obviously empty, face down on the table. When Oliver picked up his shot, he was greeted with a roar of primal triumph. He had passed the test and was one of the wolf pack.

As the boys filtered in, all crowing their victories, they wanted all the details. Oliver glossed over the awkwardness, the clinical simplicity of the act. Instead, he went with an understated description of the event masquerading his discomfort as being gentlemanly. Regardless of his laconic recital, the boys lapped it up and cheered at the appropriate moments.

When he got home, Sarah was asleep or pretending to be. He showered, then climbed in next to her.

Saturday, 10th March, 2012

Oliver lay in bed with a hangover while Sarah slid out, made herself some breakfast and went out for a jog. He could tell that she was annoyed at him for coming home drunk last night and decided eventually to confront her about it over lunch.

"No," she said, her eyes as steel. "I don't care that you came home drunk on a Friday night. I am not the fun police. I care that you have come home drunk every night."

Oliver shrugged. "Look, team building is—"

"—So you say. Repeatedly. I'm surprised you haven't mentioned the five-fifty a day yet. You should tattoo it on your forehead."

"I don't think you understand just how much money that really is." Oliver pushed his fork at the desultory salad in front of him. Quinoa salad, and cheese and tomato quiche weren't going to cut it today. He was going to need to order a McDonalds from UberEats.

"I'm not an idiot. I understand how important it is to have money when raising a child. But at the moment, I have an absentee boyfriend and I absolutely will not allow my child to have an absentee father." Sarah stabbed her fork into her quiche, savagely spearing a segment.

Oliver leaned back. "Your child? Don't you mean "Our child"?"

"How can it be our child? You are never here," Sarah said coldly.

Oliver put down his fork. "I'm going out."

"Of course you are. Good to see that you choose avoidance as your primary coping mechanism. Very healthy." Sarah tore the quiche off the fork and glared daggers at Oliver.

Why the hell would I want to stay here with 'This'?

Muttering a half-hearted "Whatever," Oliver marched out of the front door into the drizzle. Slate grey clouds matched Sarah's mood as he left her behind.

The rest of the weekend passed slowly. It was like being trapped in the house with a velociraptor. A heartless abuser. Oliver began to rethink the whole parenthood angle. All he wanted was to return to the office. A lifetime with Sarah was not looking appealing at all.

Monday, 12th March, 2012

Oliver arrived at the office early, beating even Roger. He sat down at his desk, munching a bacon and egg sandwich. He grimly noted earlier that his previously lean torso was filling out after all the beers. Oliver eyed the bacon and egg sandwich critically. *This won't help.* It was needed though. After a weekend of the cold shoulder, he needed some warmth in his life.

Roger settled down next to him. "You're in early."

"Girlfriend is kicking off," Oliver grumbled. He started looking for bugs to squash. At least in the office, he felt valued.

"You need to nip that in the bud. She has to understand who is in charge," Roger advised. "If you don't, she'll only keep on whining. It's deeply ingrained in the female nature to try to supplant the patriarchy wherever they sense weakness."

Oliver nodded politely, though privately he suspected that Roger didn't know what he was talking about. "We were fine. She just doesn't like that I'm out all the time."

"Of course, she doesn't. Women want to keep an eye on their men so they can be in control. You need a clear delineation. The home is her territory. The office is yours." Roger pulled out his bacon sandwich, grease dribbled down his hands. "Does she have a job?"

"She is a nurse." Oliver admitted, after pausing to chew.

Roger had no such compunctions and spoke through his sandwich. "That is your problem then. She thinks she is your equal because she has a job. Even though I doubt it pays nearly as much."

Darkly, Oliver reflected that maybe when the child was born and Sarah became wholly dependent on his income, she might simmer down. Then he immediately regretted the thought. Oliver loved Sarah. He really did, and he didn't want a servant. He wanted a best friend.

Oliver thought of Dave and came to a solution. He pinged out a calendar invite. "Datacentre at five-thirty."

"Fuck me, Oliver." Roger grinned. "On a Monday? Yes! You are one of us now. An apex predator! Who are you going for? Anyone in mind."

Leaning back, Oliver smiled. "I do, in fact. I am going for the Platinum Service."

The boys clustered round Mrs. Geurts, receiving their keycards and heading to their allocated rooms. Oliver took a deep breath as he prepared to spend two and a half thousand pounds. Smiling nervously at Mrs. Geurts, he said tentatively, "I think I'm ready. I would like the platinum service, please."

Mrs. Geurt's face grew serious. "Of course. A few terms and conditions first. The Platinum Service is our premium product. It will bring you to new heights of pleasure and relaxation. However, we have a strict rule that each customer can only use it once, so we will need to take a copy of your ID for our records."

Oliver listened intently as she continued to lay out the terms and conditions. "Furthermore, we require a gentleman's agreement to *never* discuss what happens in that room with anyone else." Programming the card machine. Mrs. Geurts slid it across the desk.

"Ah, why do you need my ID? I don't want to give my ID to a place like... well, I am a private man." Oliver blathered.

"Unfortunately, the Platinum Service is a victim of its own success. Its sheer potency can grow addictive. We have the one time rule to protect our valued clients from themselves." Mrs. Geurts tapped the card machine.

Oliver hesitated. "It isn't drugs, is it?"

"We cannot discuss the Platinum Service in any way other than its cost. Which is two thousand, five hundred pounds. It is worth every penny, or we wouldn't have the one time rule."

Definitely drugs, then. Oh god, please don't let it be meth.

He thought of the baby. He thought of Sarah. *If this brings me clarity like Dave, it's worth it.* At less than five day's pay, it would be worth it.

He handed over his driver's licence and paid the money.

Mrs Geurts picked up the phone and dialled up an assistant to escort him upstairs to the top floor. Nervous energy competed with excitement at the prospect of this ultimate treat. The assistant, a long-haired brunette with a black lacy dress, gave him a coquettish smile. Her lip gloss gleamed in the soft downlights.

Taking him by the hand, she led him up the stairs. Oliver eyed her up and down.

Is she the Platinum Service? This could be all right.

At the top of the stairs was just one short corridor with two doors, one marked "Maintenance NO ENTRY". The other locked. The assistant pulled out the key with a flourish and unlocked the door. Opening it, she gestured. Oliver stepped through. The corridor continued a short way until he reached a pair of curtains. Behind him, he heard the door click shut and lock. Oliver sped up, his blood almost feverish as he felt himself growing engorged with excitement. Flicking the curtains to one side, he stormed through.

What the fuck?

The room was relatively spacious. In one corner was a leather armchair. A bottle of cucumber water stood next to a crystal glass. The sound of ocean waves was playing in the background. Oliver's eyes, however, were fixed on the room's centrepiece.

On the far wall was a hole, surrounded by padded faux leather, with two roll bars on either side for gaining purchase. Oliver had paid two and a half thousand pounds, almost five day's pay for a fucking glory hole.

After staring at it in mute disbelief, acceptance finally kicked in and he stormed back to find the door locked. He pounded on it and shouted, demanding to be let out and refunded.

When that failed, he walked up to the hole and peered through. Nothing but jet black darkness awaited him.

He shouted through it, asking to speak to Mrs. Geurts. Nothing. No movement, no sound.

He paced round the room, infuriated. He looked at the cucumber water. He looked at the hole. Shaking his head, he made a decision. Unzipping his flies, he approached the hole.

Here goes nothing.

The assistant came for him an hour later. He vaguely heard the click of the lock as he sat in a daze, sipping at the cucumber water. His entire body felt relaxed, as though he had just come out of a long massage.

Mutely, he watched her approach. He was deep in his own thoughts, but all good things must come to an end.

He stood up slowly. His legs felt like jelly, but grew in strength as he followed the assistant to the door.

"Did you have a good time?" she asked quietly, with a knowing smile.

"That was quite the experience. It wasn't at all what I expected," Oliver said. The world carried a residual sense of stillness to it. Sounds felt muted, colours felt brighter, more discordant.

He passed Mrs. Geurts and stepped outside into the chill of the evening air.

He could see the pub in the distance. The wolf pack was waiting for him. But he wanted to get back home to Sarah. He dropped them a text. "I'm knackered. I'm heading home, boys. See you Monday."

Hailing a taxi, he climbed in, avoiding the tube, and enjoying the quiet luxury of being driven straight back to his flat. Closing his eyes, he thought about what he really wanted out of life and how he could achieve it. The wolf pack had been a distraction, an attempt to fit in. It was unwarranted. Over half of the team's bugs were solved by him and by him alone. He was more important to them than they were to him.

The jewelled lights of London flitted by as the taxi rumbled along the roads. He looked out at the boats on the River Thames as a plan started to formulate in his mind. If he played this right, he could achieve every single one of his goals.

In the background, some kind of smooth jazz came through the radio. The cloying scent of three Christmas tree air fresheners permeated the car as he sat back, holding the support on the side. He hadn't spared any time for Sarah. Worse, he had neglected to consider that being a nurse, she worked equally hard and needed some time to unwind.

I've been a prick.

When the taxi stopped outside the house. He gave the driver his fee and a ten-pound note as a tip.

Opening the front door, he headed straight to the kitchen. Making up a pair of hot chocolates, he sprinkled some dark chocolate flakes over the top and carried them upstairs. Seeing Sarah lying in bed, the lights off, he placed down their mugs.

"Hey Sare, I know you are awake. I brought you hot chocolate. Do you mind if I apologise?" Oliver held out her mug.

Rolling over and rubbing the sleep out of her eyes, Sarah regarded him critically. Shuffling up to a seated position, she accepted the peace offering.

"I had a... therapeutic session today which put many things into perspective. I was able to take a step back and see things from your position for perhaps the first time since I took on this contract and I wanted to apologise for my behaviour." Oliver sat down on the bed next to her and took his mug. The thick, dark chocolate was still too hot to drink, so he blew on it gently.

"I found the culture and the money all a bit overwhelming. I hadn't experienced anything like that before and I felt I had joined a different way of life." He took a deep breath. Exhaling slowly, he reflected, "What I didn't realise was that the lifestyle didn't represent me, nor did I see how the toxic behaviour of others at the office was affecting my home life."

Sarah viewed him thoughtfully. "Change can be difficult, especially when you face change at work and at home simultaneously."

"I'll be back earlier on Monday. The hours are still long, but if they want me to be involved in meetings, they can do them in the office." Oliver leaned back against the headboard, his head cooled by the solid pine. "How about we order a pizza and watch something on Netflix? Spend a night in, just you and I?"

"Sounds good. It's been a long time," Sarah said. She snuggled in closer as they sipped their hot chocolates in silence.

When the empty mugs were placed on the bedside table, they kissed gently, hands wandered and they made love slowly, sensually.

As Oliver looked into Sarah's eyes, all he could think about was the padded hole in the wall. Every time he tried to focus on her, his attention wandered until his eyes closed. He visualised himself thrusting into that faux leather orifice. When they finished and rolled apart, sweaty and tired, she looked at him with a curious expression. He was worried she would confront him about it, but instead, she got up, went to the toilet and they faded into sleep.

Monday, 19th March, 2012

Oliver arrived early again on Monday. The weekend had been relaxing. They'd gone for a long walk in Richmond Park on Saturday, then for a roast dinner on Sunday for the first time in a month. They'd spent quality time together.

Loading up the bugs, he chose himself a couple of easy ones to start the day with. Stevo had sent a project over for him to take on. Rewriting the Bordereau reports for their new reinsurer, Oliver smiled. Proper work for once, not just crushing bugs.

Roger walked up behind him. "The Bordereau reports are mine. I always work on them."

"Sorry Roger, a rounding bug has cropped up in the Specialty reports. You can look at that instead. Stevo assigned the reports to me." Oliver typed on, growing aware of the ever-increasing silence from Roger. Finally, he turned, feeling eyes burning through the back of his skull to see Roger staring at him malevolently.

"I see you." Roger pointed his finger level with Oliver's face.

Oliver eyed him coolly. "I am not interested in arguing, Roger. I have no personal problems with you. Let's just focus on getting our work done."

"You are a snake." Roger took his seat next to him. Opening up his bacon sandwich. "Those are my reports. I've earned that project. I am loyal. You should have heard what everyone said when you ditched the team on Friday." He took a deep bite before mumbling through a mouth full of grease, bread and meat. "They don't trust you."

"They trust me to get my work done ahead of schedule, for it to be low in bugs and lead to an improvement in the surrounding codebase." Oliver shrugged. "Ultimately, that is more important than how long I stay down the pub or how many drinks I have."

Roger's lip curled. "That Platinum Service is toxic. It ruins everyone it touches. You had potential, kid."

"Uh-huh." Oliver focused on his screen. The existing code base for the Bordereau reports was a mess. He'd need to recode it all to bring it up to standard.

Monday night. Oliver was home before Sarah. He set up a few candles round the sofa and ordered their favourite pizza and a tub of ice cream from Papa Johns. He was flicking through the programs on Netflix, looking for a potential movie when Sarah walked in.

The warmth from the weekend had vanished. Sarah was brandishing her phone like a weapon. "What the hell is PG Holdings? Because it sure isn't tea bags at two and a half thousand pounds?"

Oliver's heart skipped a beat. "It is a one-time intensive therapy. It is what helped me so much on Friday. I really needed it. I think *we* really needed it."

"We?" Sarah walked over to the sofa. "Oliver, you keep telling me how rich we are and how I don't understand money, so perhaps you could explain simply why we have no money in our current account and we are in debt on our credit card."

"Think of it as an investment. I needed a realignment to set myself straight. I am not going down the pub anymore and it was one-time therapy. They actually don't let you have more than one session." Oliver looked at her serenely, gently patting the sofa next to him.

Looking down at the sofa, she raised an eyebrow. "I'm not a dog Olly."

"I know." He smiled at her.

"Listen, I know you are making changes, but we can't be in debt when the baby comes along. I only get so much maternity leave. Things are going to be tight." Sarah said, her eyes worried.

"Just keep an eye on your banking app. Watch the money flood in each week and those numbers rocket. I understand why you are concerned. But it was just some teething issues. It's to be expected."

Sarah sat down dubiously. "Well, are there any more teething issues for me to be aware of? Because I'm not feeling very secure right now."

"Everything is fine, Sarah. It's all going to be okay." Oliver stroked her hair. "I'm going to take care of us both."

They sat back on the sofa and watched Cruel Intentions. When the pizza and ice cream arrived, they ate contentedly and reached a quiet acceptance, if not quite yet an understanding.

Later that night, they made love again. Once again, Oliver's mind was filled with memories of the padded hole in the wall.

Saturday, 25th March, 2012

It was evening. The streets were getting busy as groups of marauding revellers searched for pubs and bars to start their night. Oliver had no such compunction. He was standing outside the 'Datacentre'.

The Platinum Service had loomed in his mind all week. The concept of a glory hole had always repulsed him, yet now the memory of its warm, mysterious touch obsessed him. Oliver wondered what the woman on the other side looked like. He visualised a young blonde. He could almost see a red cocktail dress.

He'd thought about it and nothing else at work. His work had degraded. More bugs were being raised against it. His speed was slowing down.

Oliver decided he needed one more session of the Platinum Service to get it out of his head. He would need a new credit card. Otherwise, Sarah would be worried. He would also need a new form of ID.

He picked up his phone and texted his brother, asking if they could go out to lunch at the weekend.

The next problem was Mrs. Geurts. She would recognise him. Looking at the opening hours of the Datacentre, he saw it was open seven days a week. He was willing to guess that she wasn't working every day. He decided to try at the weekend and see if they had someone else on the front desk.

That time was now.

In one hand, Oliver had a new credit card that Sarah wouldn't be able to check. In the other, he had his brother Ralph's driving licence. They looked similar, even though David was two years younger than him. It had taken lunch at Belgos to persuade him. Oliver had lied and told him it was for a prank in the office. After a few steins of Flemish beer, his brother had agreed and handed it over.

Looking through the door, his supposition that they would have a different Madame on duty at the weekend had been correct. A severe-looking blonde was sitting at the counter, her hair pulled back into a ponytail and her eyes framed by a pair of thin spectacles.

As he approached, she looked up. "Welcome. How can I be of assistance today?"

"I would like to try the Platinum Service, please."

Eyeing him, she judged him quietly and then curtly ran through the cost, secrecy policy and the stipulation that you could only use the service once.

Oliver nodded rapidly. He was fully erect already. His breathing was shallow in anticipation.

It took all of his willpower not to run to the room. Instead, he was meekly led there by an assistant called Jessica.

As the door clicked behind him, he wasted no time, unzipping his flies and pulling down his briefs. He grabbed the roll bars on each side of the hole and began rapidly thrusting. He could hear gagging sounds on the other side and grinned. An animalistic expression of primal lust distorted his face.

An hour later, he was found reclining on the chair by the assistant, who gently led him out of the room.

Sunday, 26th March, 2012

Oliver hadn't slept that night. Thoughts of the Platinum Service dominated his mind. He had tried everything, hot chocolate, showers, even sneaking to the bathroom to relieve himself. That hole just echoed in his visions. He wanted more of it. He needed it.

After a sleepless night, at six, Sarah got out of bed. He had listened to her sleeping most of the night next to him. "Right, I'm making us tea. Then you can tell me what kept you up all night."

Oliver lay in bed, exhausted. *How do I explain this?*

When Sarah returned twenty minutes later, she had bacon sandwiches with her. "Thought you might be hungry." She popped his mug of tea next to him and his breakfast. He looked at it forlornly. His appetite for food, for drink, was non-existent. All he wanted was to return to the Datacentre.

"Now, then, what's on your mind?" Sarah looked at him kindly.

"I... I've been having a lot of stress at work. I am working on these reports. It's tough." Oliver tried. He couldn't tell if Sarah believed him or not, but she nodded sympathetically.

Patting him on the shoulder, she asked him what she could do to help.

Oliver looked her in the eyes, then his vision dropped to her mouth and his body reacted. Reaching for her hand, he guided it into place. When she began to work his shaft, he slid his hand round the back of her head and pushed it slowly down.

"Oh, all right. Head pushing now, is it?" She grumbled, but acquiesced. As her head moved into position and the anticipation sent him into a whirl of excitement, she suddenly snapped her head back.

"What is this?" she asked. Pulling back the sheets, she reached back, got her phone and turned on its torch function.

"What is what?" Oliver looked down in a panic. Then he saw it, his eyes widening with alarm. A handful of black, soot-like spots were showing on his erect member. The surrounding veins looked dark and swollen.

Sarah took a photo.

"Don't do that. Delete it," Oliver said, horrified.

"I've never seen anything like this. It looks like a sexually transmitted infection, but it's like nothing I've ever seen before." She moved back to lie down next to him. "Have you been cheating on me?"

Oliver blinked. The question was cold, matter of fact and clinical. "No, I would never."

"If it wasn't for sudden onset and the veins, I'd say it was penile melanoma. When did you start to get these symptoms?" Sarah asked, immediately in work mode.

"I didn't. I don't know. You are the first person to spot them."

She reached up to his forehead. "Hmmm, I need to get my thermometer. It feels like a temperature. But it could be just because you've been under the duvet."

Oliver sat up. He felt shell shocked. All he could think was, the Platinum Service did this. He closed his eyes. Even though he knew the cause, he couldn't help but want to use it again.

Sarah disappeared and returned with her infrared thermometer. Shining it on his forehead, she nodded grimly. "Yep, you have a temperature. We need to book you in with the doctor when surgery opens at nine." She looked at him coolly. "You are sure this isn't an STI? It's very sudden. Do you promise me you haven't been cheating?"

Oliver looked her straight back into her eyes and lied. "I would never cheat on you."

Sarah returned with some aspirin for his fever. He gratefully swallowed them with a mouthful of tea. His sense of taste had gone, leaving the drink lifeless and drab. The Datacentre opened at three o'clock. e He would return and give them a piece of his mind.

"You should try to get some of that bacon sandwich down you." Sarah tried.

Oliver shook his head. He had no interest in food or drink. He knew what he wanted. He knew what he needed.

Oliver walked the streets. Sarah had managed to get him a doctor's appointment. They had prescribed him antibiotics and had taken a battery of blood tests. No definitive diagnosis. He felt worse. He was alternating between freezing cold and boiling hot. His jaw was aching and his throat felt dry even when he drank water.

He found himself sitting outside the Datacentre waiting for it to open. As he shivered, he saw Mrs. Geurts walking towards the front door.

"Mrs Geurts." He called towards her. She stopped and regarded him critically.

"Let me open up and then we can talk in about thirty minutes," she said professionally.

The door opened. Oliver stopped pacing and came in.

"May I help you, sir?" Mrs. Geurts had the same look on her face that she always did. Quiet, professional, calm.

"The Platinum Service gave me a disease! I want a refund." Oliver demanded.

Mrs Geurts looked concerned. She asked for his name. Checking her records, she tutted. "As I thought. You have a Platinum Service over a week ago." Looking up at him, she eyed him critically. "What are your symptoms and when did you first notice them?"

"Except for I didn't ., I last used the Platinum Service yesterday under the name of Ralph Kinley.

Mrs. Geurts froze. "You falsified your data." She shook her head. "The Platinum Service is only to be allowed once per customer. We were very clear. It is to be used in moderation only."

"What do you mean? That's just marketing." Oliver ranted. "How often do you clean that hole?"

Hissing, Mrs. Geurts motioned for the security guard to return to his post. "Never, *ever* reveal the secret of the Platinum Service."

"Yeah? Well, right now, I am considering tweeting not only what it is, but also the fact that I caught a *fucking* disease from your skanky hole." Oliver's voice sounded strained. His throat felt so dry.

"Mr Kinley, we rigorously test all of our performers and keep our facilities spotless. I can see that you are upset, though, so allow me to offer you a complimentary session of the Platinum Service. Tiffany can take you there right now."

Oliver gazed levelly at her.

This is an addiction.

Addiction is a social construct. You are just making use of two and a half thousand pounds worth of entertainment.

This is making me ill.

You are on medication now. You'll be better in no time. Besides, it's probably nothing to do with the Platinum Service. You aren't a doctor. How would you know?

"Okay," he rasped. Relief and disappointment in himself washed over him in equal measure. Tiffany took him by the hand and led him upstairs.

Monday, 27th March, 2012

When Sarah woke on Monday, she found Oliver shaking. He still wasn't eating. The darkened veins had turned black and were spreading up his torso. His jaw hung slack. He could barely speak. His head wobbled on his shoulders as the muscles weakened.

She immediately dialled for an ambulance, looking at him with concern. She helped him down the stairs and into the ambulance bed, wiping a bit of drool from his face with a tissue. Sarah sat in the back with him and held his hand.

Oliver was lifted into a chair and wheeled into A&E. He groaned and shivered. Adjusting the blanket, Sarah looked at him, worried. "I'm sorry, Olly, I have to get to work. I'll come back and see you straight afterwards."

He mumbled something, but it wasn't clear. Sarah patted his head, knowing that she was leaving him in safe hands while she went to begin her shift. The ambulance had taken him to St. George's Hospital, not to the hospital where she worked, the Chelsea and Westminster. Gathering her things, she clutched his hand, giving him one last worried look.

Oliver lay in bed until a need to go to the loo forced him to rise. He staggered to the bathroom and released a stream of urine into the toilet, clutching onto the roll bar.

Looking at his phone, he loaded up Uber and ordered a cab. Staggering to the front entrance, he collapsed into the taxi, spending his last strength. The taxi driver looked horrified as he drove him to his predetermined destination—the Datacentre.

When he arrived, his legs had completely given up. He tried to explain to the taxi driver that he needed help, but his voice wouldn't work. His jaw had lost all muscular control now and hung slack.

"Fucking junkies," the taxi driver swore at him. Then looking round, swore again before getting out and dragging Oliver to the pavement outside the Datacentre. "Someone else's problem now."

As the uber raced off, no doubt after leaving him a one-star review, the Datacentre doors opened. Mrs. Geurts directed the security guard to carry Oliver like a swaddling babe. "Don't you worry, sir, we'll take care of you."

Oliver was carried to the top floor. Even in his condition, he grew excited when he saw the entrance to the Platinum Service. However, they did not go through that door. Instead, Mrs Geurts led him to the door marked "Maintenance NO ENTRY". Unlocking it and holding it open for the security guard, she beckoned them on. Oliver's eyes widened in horror as he was carried round the bend in the long corridor.

He couldn't. His throat was ruined. He couldn't cry out or scream.

Behind the hole for the Platinum Service, a grey-haired man in a suit had his head strapped to the wall. An IV drip was attached to his wrists.

Mrs. Geurts undid the leather restraints and the man collapsed to the ground. Grunting with the effort, she dragged the body to one side as the security guard placed Oliver in the position the old man had previously occupied. He felt rough hands strap his head against the wall. An IV drip was attached to his wrist, a catheter was inserted into his penis.

Tears rolled down his face as he knelt there for however long. He didn't see what they had done with the previous occupant. After a while, he heard the sounds of someone walking in. "What is this shit?" He heard them complain as they paced the room behind the wall.

Minutes later, Oliver heard them unzip. He wanted to shout, to scream, but his throat was no longer capable of speech.

Moments later, his throat had other duties to perform as a thick, girthy member was forced into it. His eyes wept unabated as his first client received the Platinum Service.

Chapter Seven

FESTIVAL OF THE DAMNED

1st May, 2013, Huddersford, Kent

The coach pulled into Huddersford station. As it came to an abrupt stop and the brakes screeched, Faith stirred in Elsie's lap. Stroking her hair, Elsie smiled at the mousey little girl. "Wake up, sleepy head, we've arrived."

Elsie watched as Faith looked round her and out of the coach windows. She scrunched her eyes and rubbed the sleep out of them. The town was milling with people on their way to work. They could hear the dense chatter of a town small enough for people to recognise their neighbours but big enough to fill a depot with commuters.

"Come along, poppet." She gestured to the exit. Shouldering her backpack, she guided Faith up and out of her seat. The two of them joined the queue of people as they made their way down the cramped gangway.

A tall, burly boy in his late teens was waiting by the luggage bags. He leaned back against the coach and grinned when he saw Elsie. "Name's Blake. Now, tell me, what's a beautiful girl like you doing in a shithole like this?"

Elsie winced at the boy's clumsy chat-up line as she shuffled along with the other disembarking passengers towards the luggage hold. She looked up at him nervously and smiled. "Work, how about you?"

He looked up as they threw his bag out of the luggage area and leant down to grab it, slinging it over his shoulder. His muscular arms bulged under its weight. Elsie's much smaller bag appeared and she gripped it, pulling it clear with effort.

"I got a shitty gig dressing up like a bird for a country fair." He grinned. "They called it an acting job. I almost dismissed it because I've never done acting in my life. But a job's a job. What's your name and your—" he squinted at Faith "—sister's name?"

"Elsie, this is—"

"My name's Faith," her sister chipped in, stretching out her hand confidently. Blake shook it politely. "My sister's doing the same thing. She is dressing up as a rabbit. I am going to do it too, but I had to bring my own costume." Faith rummaged round in Elsie's backpack and found a pair of bunny ears to stick on her head.

"Hey, my battery charger's missing." A gangly looking teen was going through his bag. Panic gripped Elsie. She had only one real possession of value. Quickly opening up her bag, she rummaged round with a sense of encroaching dread.

Elsie stopped, biting her bottom lip to hold back the tears. It was gone. She had also been robbed.

"Are you okay?" Blake asked.

Faith came over and held her hand. Elsie shook her head. "Not really, it's gone. The only photo I have of my mother and me, before she... There isn't another copy. I should have sold the stupid silver frame and put it in something cheaper." Grief wracked her. *Idiot. You stupid idiot.* "It was all I had left of her."

Faith and Elsie had been to Brighton for a day out with their mother. They'd taken the photo on the pier. She'd never see her mother again.

"I'm sorry, girl." Blake went in for a hug. Elsie pushed him away, eyes wide with horror. "Whoa, sorry, I misjudged that situation."

Elsie gasped. "No, it is... I just don't like to be touched. I'm sorry, that is all. Thank you for your kindness."

The other victim had marched up to the coach driver and was busy haranguing him. Elsie looked at Blake. "I'm sorry again, please excuse me," she said, before joining him.

The driver, a haggard, middle-aged man with a balding pate, was shrugging. "Nothing I can do, mate. Call this number. It's lost property. They'll help you."

"Hey, are you guys going to this festival thing? I overheard you chatting." Elsie turned to see a short girl with her black hair cut into a bob, the tips dyed purple. "I mean, total drag, but it's easy money, right? I'm... 'The Fox', sometimes called Zoe." She mimicked a sexy growl.

"I'm Elsie, and I'm 'The Hare'." Elsie smiled wanly. The theft had torpedoed her appetite for social interaction.

"I'm Blake, and I'm 'The Pheasant'." Holding out his hand, Blake shook her hand with enthusiasm.

"Sorry, I must call this number. Come on, Faith."

Faith shook her head. "I'm staying with these two."

Elsie grabbed her arm. "The hell you are. You need to stick with me."

As she dragged Faith away with her, she saw Zoe looking at them with a bemused expression on her face.

"Why couldn't I stay with them?" Faith asked.

Elsie gave her a hug, then looked deep into her eyes. "It's just us now. We have to stick together. There is nobody else for us. Do you understand?"

"I know. I just wish things were like they were before." Faith's lip trembled. "I miss my room."

"We can't go back, Faith, you know that." Elsie stroked her hair. "Not anymore."

Faith nodded and Elsie called lost property. It took fifteen minutes of queueing to get to a human voice and another five to help the bored sounding operator fill out their form. They left her with absolutely no confidence that they would find it.

With a sunken feeling in her chest, she and Faith re-joined the other actors, who were waiting expectantly.

As she strode towards them, she loaded up the route on her phone. "It's a three-mile walk to the village from here." Elsie saw that it was all uphill and muttered a quiet curse.

Blake patted her on the shoulder. "I'll get us a taxi, no worries."

Elsie flinched. "We don't have any money."

"Ha." Blake reached down and grabbed her luggage. "Don't you worry, I get a bit of scratch from my gran. I can pay. It's only up the hill."

"Any room for a Fox in that taxi?" The newcomer slid her hand up Blake's muscular arm.

Blake winked. "Always room for a Fox, girlio."

"I'll pay half." Blake turned, annoyed to see another male pitching in. It was the gangly teen with the missing phone. "I'm playing the Badger. Name's Calvin, ain't it."

"Why are you the Badger? You're half my size. I'll tell you what mate, you let me be the Badger and I'll let you join our taxi." Blake pointed with Elsie's bag to a taxi rank on the other side of the coach station.

"Whatever, I don't mind. I'm just doing this for the money. I'll play any animal, really. I don't know if we get to–"

"–Perfect, then it's settled. *I'm* the Badger and *you* are the Pheasant."

Zoe followed him as Blake marched towards the taxis. "And a big, strong badger you are too."

Grimacing at the transparent flirtation, Elsie followed her luggage as Blake carried it for them.

"Come on, Elsie," Faith said, tugging her towards the waiting cars. Elsie surrendered to the inevitable and followed them as they assembled round a six-seater minivan.

The minivan drove them up a winding road to the top of the hill, where scattered houses gave way to a dense cluster of four-bed dwellings built in the last century. Miniature gardens, flawlessly manicured, were paired with well-maintained brick homes. Dogs watched from the gates and curtains twitched at the windows as the locals watched vigilantly.

"Look at the forest!" Calvin had his face pressed up against the window. They peered out. Sure enough, acres upon acres of fruit trees stretched into the distance down the hill from the village.

Faith watched, eyes wide. She had spent her life in Elephant and Castle. The countryside was new to her and this... this was a whole lot of nature.

"Well, I can't wait to get out of this hellhole and back to civilisation." Zoe pulled out a vanity mirror and adjusted her makeup.

Relaxing between Zoe and Elsie, Blake leaned back. "I don't mind it. Experiencing a bit of the outdoors could be fun."

"And I love that." Zoe leaned into him. He instinctively put his arm round her. Elsie's eyes rolled.

The taxi dropped them all off at the village pub where they were to meet their contact Geoff, who would brief them on their gig at the festival. As they walked into the pub, they saw the friendly, curious smiles of the local villagers with their tankards of cider. Wooden picnic tables were scattered across a grassy garden. Picking one as far away from the locals as possible, they all congregated. A group of kids chased each other round a giant bush on one side of the pub garden. Faith watched them enviously, but settled down next to Elsie.

Zoe shivered at the cold air and nestled into Blake for warmth.

"Well, that didn't take long," Calvin snarked.

Blake grinned amiably while Zoe narrowed her eyes at the remark.

"Look at you." A rotund man with tortoiseshell rimmed glasses and a vibrant waistcoat bounced towards them. "What a marvellous bunch of beautiful thespians we have here, brimming with vim and vigour." Circling the table, his twinkling eyes graced them with a welcoming smile. "Oh, I used to tread the boards myself in my youth in the village hall. How I remember the acrid scent of the greasepaint, the heat of the lights and the ghastly lack of pockets."

"Sorry, I'm Elsie. Who are you?" She suspected the answer, but it was always better to check.

"I'm sorry! Oh, gracious me. I'm Geoff." Geoff laughed. "What a buffoon! I apologise profoundly. You must have thought I was lampooning you like an absolute cad. I tell you what, how about I get you all some lovely freshly squeezed lemonade and brief you about your coming performance?"

Blake pointed to the locals nearby. "Actually, I think I'd rather have a cider. I'm nineteen, not nine."

Geoff preened, tucking his thumbs into his waistcoat. "But of course! Our cider is the best in Britain. Award-winning. That is why you are here! In its divine magnificence, the woods call for a festival in its honour and if successful, it rewards us all with fifty years of hearty harvests." Geoff took a moment to drink in the wisdom of his own words before seeming to remember them. "Of course, a pint for the young sir. Anyone else?"

A chorus of hands shot up, including Faith, who had her hand dragged down by Elsie. Geoff noticed her as if for the first time.

A frown crossed his face as he leaned in. "And who is this? A fifth actor? Most irregular."

"I need to keep an eye on her. She'll stay in the dressing rooms," Elsie said.

Pulling out a pair of bunny ears, Faith put them on. "I'm a bunny."

Geoff roared with laughter, "A leveret! Of course."

"No, I'm a bunny. I was most clear." Faith regarded the man with a disgruntled look. Elsie gently rested her hand on Faith's arm.

"Of course, a baby hare. I'm just sorry that we don't have a role for you on the stage. This festival"–he looked round, waving his arm expansively at the orchard–"is over a thousand years old. Every fifty years, we put on the festival to renew our vows to Cernunnos."

The teens looked at him blankly, except for Zoe, who was snuggling deep into Blake's chest.

"Care Snu Nose?" Faith attempted.

"Care-Nu-Nos! The Horned God, the lord of fertility. He was called Pan by the Greeks and Bacchus by the Romans. He ensures a plentiful harvest and healthy herds." Looking round with fake discretion, he whispered, "He is also the god of libations and other more adult pursuits." Geoff chuckled. "But you should wait a few years until you find out about those pleasures."

"Gross!" Elsie muttered.

"Now then, pints of cider for the men and halves for the ladies." Geoff turned to go.

"I'll have a whole pint, please," Elsie said.

"And me," Zoe chipped in.

Geoff gave a nervous chuckle. "Oh, of course, the modern generation. What a marvel. It is quite impossible to fathom."

As he walked away, Zoe looked up from where she had attached herself limpet-like to Blake. "So that just happened."

"Yep, we've officially been patronised." Elsie shrugged. "But we are getting paid."

"I don't like him. He's weird." Faith wriggled in her seat, her legs dangling down. "I wanted to be part of the festival."

Smiling at Faith, Zoe returned her attention to Blake.

Calvin pointed at the two of them. "So, that, this, bit fast innit."

"What do you mean?" Blake said, his heavy brow furrowed.

Calvin laughed bitterly. "What do I mean? You met five minutes ago and now you are what? Dating?"

"Is the little bird jealous?" Zoe gave a wicked smile, her eyes gleaming.

"She's just cold." Blake put his arm round Zoe and gave her a warm hug.

"Freezing." Zoe slid a hand up Blake's thigh, causing him to look embarrassed.

Elsie pulled her phone out of her pocket and was googling Cernunnos. "Oh my god, it turns out, Cernunnos is a thing. That is disgusting. They used to host orgies in his name. It's where the Christian harvest festival came from."

"Christian orgies?" Zoe gagged. "Sandal sex. I bet they all do it while wearing socks and cardigans. I hope they don't do that tonight. Imagine Geoff's fat, liver-spotted belly sashaying round."

"Child present," Elsie warned.

Faith giggled.

"How did the church go from orgies to sticking candles in oranges?" Zoe said.

"That is Christingle. Harvest Festival is the one where you take packets of instant noodles and tins of soup to church," Blake said. When the others looked at him, he shrugged, embarrassed. "I used to go with my gran to church on Sundays to make sure she got there okay?"

Geoff chose that moment to appear with a tray of cider tankards and crisps. "I have ordered some chips for you to fatten my budding thespians up for the festival."

He handed out four sheets of laminated cards. "These are your lines. I numbered them for the order you'll speak in. The high priest will say his lines, then..." Geoff paused expectantly.

Elsie raised her hand, "I say mine."

"Very good and so forth. Then we get a closing statement from the 'high priest', who will end it with..." Geoff braced himself, "Release the hounds." He waved theatrically and boomed. "That's my favourite part. Then you must run through the woods back to the pub wearing your masks the whole way. After a five-minute head start, you'll be chased by a chosen group of villagers wearing hound masks. If they touch you, you just fall to the ground with a shriek. They'll tie your hands with a hemp rope and lead you back to the festival where the high priest will give a reading."

"What happens if we make it back to the pub?" Elsie asked.

"Well, your rooms are here so you'll get a good night's sleep. But you'll also get a reward." Geoff winked, his jowls jiggling from the movement. "*Two hundred and fifty* pounds. I'll be waiting back here with four envelopes and I truly hope you all make it back. This is a wonderful opportunity to have a starring role in a once a century cultural event. I'm immensely jealous of you all."

Elsie smiled politely. "And our payment?"

"Oh, good lord, yes. Of course, of course. You'll be paid in full in the morning. You can order a taxi to the coach station using the pub landline. Now, do you have any bags to drop off? We have reserved rooms for you here."

They looked at their luggage and affirmed.

"Then follow me, my marvellous herd, and let's get you settled." Geoff took them upstairs and doled out the room keys, apologising that there was only one bed for Elsie and Faith.

Elsie, Faith and Calvin regrouped round the picnic table. Several plates of thick cut chips arrived, steaming.

"Shouldn't we wait..." Faith started.

"No," Elsie and Calvin said immediately in unison. "I think the other two are busy," Elsie said, blowing on a chip to cool it down.

Faith giggled.

"They weren't joking." Calvin had taken a long slurp of cider. "This is delicious!"

Picking up a tankard and taking a sip. Elsie's eyes widened. "This is delicious."

"Let me, let me!" Faith reached out.

"Absolutely not. You are far too young." Elsie took another sup. "And this is far too delicious to share."

"But Elsie!" pleaded Faith.

"No buts," Elsie said sternly.

"Where was that rule earlier?" Zoe said, stalking towards them, lips pursed and glowing from ear to ear.

Blake followed behind her, smiling amiably. "Alright, everyone?"

"That didn't take long," muttered Calvin. He looked at his cider sourly.

Settling down, Blake looked at the half-empty plates of chips. "Thanks for waiting."

"Well, we didn't know if you'd be joining us," Elsie said, looking round for a distraction. She lifted her tankard. "Have you tried the cider?"

Blake took a gulp. His eyes closed and he murmured with contentment. He took another sip before he could reopen them. "Fuck me, this is good."

Zoe smirked. "I bet I have tasted something better." Elsie chose to ignore her. When she realised nobody was paying her any attention, Zoe glowered, gulping down the cider with a sour expression.

"No wonder they keep winning best in Britain. This is great." Blake enthused. He had already finished his pint.

"Anyone want another?" Blake raised his empty tankard.

Looking at her half-full tankard, Elsie shrugged. "Yes, please."

"I'll get them," Calvin offered.

"It's alright, I already offered, mate." Blake grinned, starting to rise.

"No, I said I'll get them." Calvin spluttered. His face was red and angry. "I want to buy them."

"Jesus! Alright, mate. Whatever, I was just being nice." Blake sat back down, embarrassed. "I didn't mean to cause upset."

"It's fine." Calvin rose, leaving his barely touched cider on the table as he went to get a round.

Waiting until he was inside, Zoe looked at the others. "What a little psycho."

"What was all that about?" Elsie asked. Blake shrugged.

They sat awkwardly until Calvin returned and handed each of them a tankard of cider.

Taking another sip of her cider, Elsie rose. "This cider is going right through me. Did anyone notice where the toilets are?"

"Just head straight to the left. They are by the fireplace." Blake said.

Elsie walked inside. The pub was comfy. Stone walls were covered with old paintings and countryside knick-knacks, horseshoes, awards for their cider, mounted animal heads, and even an ornate crossbow above the bar. The warm sound of friendly banter echoed round the walls. As she walked past a subdued fire, the scent of cider, bleach and smoke filled her nostrils.

She found the toilet quickly enough, sitting down and closing her eyes. This is it. This is the day life begins anew for her and Faith.

Elsie emerged from the pub to hear loud swearing. Quickening her pace, she reached the exit and saw Calvin standing, pointing and yelling at Faith who, in contrast, was laughing at him.

"You stupid bitch," Calvin vented. Calvin's finger was pointing like the barrel of a gun. Blake had his palm against Calvin's chest, blocking him from Faith.

Elsie sped up. "What is going on?" Calvin turned round, shocked. "Why are you swearing at my sister? She is only fourteen. What did she do?"

"*She* drank your cider. I was defending you," Calvin protested.

"What the fuck is it to you? She is my sister. That was my cider. She is my responsibility." Elsie was close to the table now and showed no sign of slowing down. Anger coursed through her voice.

Calvin blathered something unintelligible that she assumed was his pathetic attempt at an apology.

"What's going on here?" A group of men from a neighbouring table had risen. "Everyone is trying to have a nice quiet pint here."

Blake imposed his bulk between Elsie and Calvin, gently separating them. "Come on, let's just sit down quietly and not get sacked...." He turned to the offended locals. "Sorry lads, it's all good."

Elsie turned round to where her sister was swaying. She quietly whispered to Faith. "And you. What were you thinking?"

"I just wanted to join in," Faith said quietly. "I thought it would be funny."

"Does it look like they are laughing? We're here to work. You've just caused a scene."

Elsie looked at Blake and Zoe, who were quietly looking at each other. "I'm sorry about this." The awkward atmosphere hung between them all like a fog.

"Don't worry about it, mate," Blake said. He gave her a slight smile before his gaze returned to his tankard.

Elsie bit her lip. "Faith, go upstairs to our room." Faith looked like she would protest for a moment before storming off upstairs. Her eyes looked tearful.

"Let me buy you another drink," Calvin offered.

"No, thank you. I've gone right off drinking. I'm going to chill out upstairs before the festival starts." Elsie looked at the empty cider and mentally cursed. That had been a lie. Elsie hadn't gone off drinking. If anything, she could murder another cider. Maybe she could grab another after she got paid tomorrow.

Blake cheerfully broke the ice by talking about his adventures in his hometown.

Getting up, Elsie gave Calvin a venomous look. The lovely spring day had been utterly ruined. First, she had been robbed, then Faith and Calvin had conspired to ruin the drinks. This would've been a wonderful opportunity for her sister and her to pretend that they lived an everyday life.

"I'm going to disappear upstairs," Elsie stood up. "I'm not really in the mood to drink, anyway."

Zoe leaned in and whispered in Blake's ear. He gave a shy smile. "I think we might go upstairs too," Blake said.

"You are all leaving me on my own? I just got a round in." Calvin looked round. "Zoe has barely touched hers."

Blake leant over and necked Zoe's cider, belching appreciatively. "Much appreciated, mate. I'll be down later. I'll buy you one before we leave."

They left Calvin looking into his cider. A bitter air surrounded him.

When they were halfway to the pub door, Zoe moved towards Elsie. "So, he is a psycho then. One in every team, I guess."

"He is an entitled prick," Elsie muttered. "Thanks for protecting Faith, Blake. I really appreciated it. She is a good kid, just an idiot sometimes."

"Aren't we all, mate? No worries." Blake paused awkwardly, disengaging from Zoe, the pub entrance being too narrow for them to enter entwined. Elsie patiently waited to let them handle the logistics.

"Do you want a pint to take upstairs, Elsie?" Blake asked. "I don't mind getting you one."

"Thank you, but I think I'm just going to go up and play with my phone." Elsie watched as Zoe oozed over Blake and left them to it. They seemed oblivious to the previous drama. She headed upstairs. Her eyes narrowed as she entered the shared bedroom with Faith. Curled up on the bed, she slurred, "I don't feel well."

"You absolute idiot. What were you thinking?" Elsie sat next to her. Out of habit, she checked her forehead. It seemed fine.

"I've had cider before. This feels different. I can't move my legs." Faith's voice was growing more slurred.

Elsie looked her up and down. "Show me." Faith moved her limbs. They twitched like a zombies. "Any nausea?"

"No, just very sleepy," Faith murmured in a barely legible tone.

Elsie brushed her hair out of her eyes. "You wait here, poppet."

Elsie calmly left the room. As soon as she closed the door, her eyes flared. Swearing, she stormed down the stairs. Blake and Zoe were just coming up.

"That prick drugged my cider. Faith is paralytic, zombified." Zoe's eyes opened wide.

Blake held up his hands. "Let's not jump to conclusions. She is only little. Maybe she just can't handle cider. It's quite strong."

"This isn't her first pint, Blake, much as it should have been. Besides, she is fourteen, not six." Elsie pushed past them.

"Elsie, wait." Zoe grabbed her shoulder. "Listen, he's going to get what's coming to him, but let's be smart about this, right?" Elsie turned to listen to Zoe. "We need a fourth person to do this shitty festival, or they just might call the whole thing off. I can't afford to lose the five hundred pounds, can you? Please, Elsie."

"If you think—" Fury blazed in Elsie's eyes.

"—We are going to confront him. But we aren't going to do anything stupid. We'll let him know that we know. Then after the festival we show him exactly how we treat sleaze balls that drug women," Zoe said. "Do you understand?"

"Fine. I'll keep it quiet, but I'm talking to him now." Elsie looked round at the rest of the pub's inhabitants. "Wouldn't want to upset the Last of the Summer Wine again, would we?"

"I'll come too," Blake said evenly.

The three of them walked outside to where Calvin was sitting alone at the picnic table. He was muttering into his pint. Elsie sat opposite him, her face stormy. Blake sat next to him. He gripped Calvin's shoulder with vice-like strength.

"Get off." Calvin jerked but couldn't dislodge the big man. "What the—"

"Don't make a scene, Calvin. The only reason that I'm not kicking the living shit out of you is that we've a job to do and we need the money. Do you understand?" Elsie's eyes were ice cold. They locked onto him as she repeated. "Do you... understand?"

Calvin slumped. "I haven't done—"

Zoe tossed a small baggie of tablets onto the table. "Well, well, just look at what he had in his pockets."

"They are medicine." Calvin muttered.

"In an unmarked baggy? Sure, go on then, take one," Elsie urged.

Calvin looked round. "I've already had my medicine today."

Elsie leaned forwards. "Stop lying. We know what you've done. Just admit it."

Calvin's face darkened. "It's so easy for chads like you." He thumbed at Blake. "You just got off the coach and immediately got laid. Women don't give a shit about the little guys. I didn't choose to be this height. What do you expect me to do?"

He looked at them all, then shook his head. "I found the answer to my problems just a week ago. I might not be big like Blake, but I'm smarter. I'm cleverer than he'll ever be."

Blake snorted.

Then Calvin told them a story about true love.

27th April, 2013, Truro, Cornwall

"Calvin, right?" Turning round, Calvin saw Emily. His eyes widened. "Do you remember me? I was in your year at school."

Pulling out his spliff, his face flushed. "Emily." He more than remembered her. He had loved her from the shadows, but never had the courage to ask her out. "What are you doing here?"

Looking down at her textbooks, she cocked an eyebrow. "The same as you, I'll wager. College."

"Oh yeah, I mean, yeah, that makes sense." *Stupid*. Calvin shuffled nervously on the spot.

"That cigarette smells interesting. Mind if I have a toke?" Emily smiled, her hair blowing in the Cornish sea breeze.

Calvin handed it over without thinking. "Sure, it's good stuff. My mate knows the supplier."

"I'm pretty new here. I don't suppose you fancy introducing me to the Student Union, do you?"

His heart thudded in his chest. *This is it. This is my one chance.* "Sure." *I can't screw this up. It has to be perfect.* "Let's meet up later, say, at four?"

"That sounds perfect. Four it is then." Emily winked at him.

Calvin ditched class. Emily was his priority. Texting his mate, he gave him a shopping list of drugs. Then, showering, Calvin wet shaved. After drying off, he put on his Ben Sherman polo shirt and his cleanest pair of jeans. Lynx Java deodorant and Hugo Boss aftershave added the finishing touch.

It was close to three. Calvin checked his phone and hurried out to meet his mate.

"You've quite the night planned." His mate smirked.

Ignoring the snarky remark, Calvin asked, "Have you got everything?"

"Ounce of weed, one Rohypnol, one Viagra. I have a gram of coke if you plan on going clubbing later? If you give me more time, I could get my hands on some MDMA."

Calvin shook his head. *Perfect.* He handed over the money and shuffled over to the Student Union Bar.

Inside, The Pixies were playing as they found a table. Calvin's eyes flashed with excitement as she settled down. She had never seemed more beautiful.

"Fancy a drink?" he asked nervously. He had gamed this out in his head a hundred times, but now it was happening for real.

"Thank you, I'll have a cider please," Emily replied as he had anticipated. *Yes, yes.*

He ordered a pint of Stella Artois for himself and a cider for Emily. Looking down at the drinks, Calvin had a moment of indecision. She seemed so relaxed and friendly in his company. *Could I win her over with my personality?*

The moment ended. Calvin's mind snapped shut, fuelled by a bitter cynicism. *Chads get the girls, those over six feet, with muscles, money and power.* He dropped the Rohypnol into her cider. *This is the only way you'll ever get to sleep with a girl as flawless as Emily.* Love? That was reserved for other people, certainly not for the likes of him.

Regretfully, he handed the cider over to her. Ruefully, Calvin wished there was another way.

"Is everything alright?" Emily asked.

He smiled back at her. "Yeah, it's all good." Pointing at the cider, he said, "It's Kopparberg, the good stuff."

She drank the cider.

He only made it halfway through his pint before she began to stumble with her words.

"Let's grab some fresh air, eh?" Calvin suggested. "A bit of a smokey smoke to chill out."

"I'm really sorry. I guess I must have been more tired than I thought." She nearly tripped. He caught her.

Leaning against the student union wall, they puffed on Calvin's spliff.

"I'm really sorry, Calvin, I'll make it up to you, but I think I need to get home," Emily slurred.

"It's okay, I'll get a cab. Make sure you get home alright." He had his arm round her, pulling her towards the taxi stand.

She texted him her home address. He swiped ignore on the notification screen. Lowering her into the taxi, he climbed in on the other side.

"If she is sick, it's a fifty quid fine," the driver warned.

Calvin pulled out fifty in notes and showed the driver he had the cash. Emily reached for her wallet but fell unconscious. Calvin gave the driver his address. Then he popped the Viagra. *Thirty minutes to kick in.* Viagra wasn't necessary. As he looked at his perfect angel, his body reacted immediately.

In the morning, he was lying in bed smoking a spliff. Emily's eyes widened as she woke in horror.

"I'm sorry. I didn't mean the night to end like this," she mumbled, shaking her head. "I just wanted a friend at college. This isn't what I'm like."

"It's okay, I understand," Calvin said honestly. *You'll end up with a doctor, a lawyer or a rugby player. Some men get all the luck, but at least I had one perfect night.*

She lumbered out of bed, nervously concealing her nakedness as she looked for her clothes.

He watched her, drinking in his last moments before the dream expired.

"I've got to go, but I will text you," she promised, hurriedly finding the exit to his flat.

No, you won't. Calvin took a final puff before stamping out the roll-up.

He might not have won the genetic lottery, but he was self-aware. He knew how the world worked. Calvin just had to be more intelligent, more cunning than the chads of this world. Emily was a classic Stacy, a girl who would normally be forever out of his reach. Sighing, Calvin smiled. Some chad was going to be a very lucky man.

Not last night, though. He had beaten the system at its own game. The underdog isn't necessarily a bad place to be. Nobody ever suspects the quiet loser.

The letterbox banged. Getting out of bed, Calvin wandered towards the door. He picked up a cardboard invitation. He had been asked to read a script at a shitty country fair.

A guaranteed five hundred quid?

He chuckled. The universe was finally turning his way. This was proving to be the best week of his life.

1st May, 2013, Huddersford, Kent

"You are sick." Elsie looked at Calvin. She felt ill seeing the worm's face. She rose and backed away from the table. "I'm going upstairs to look after Faith. I can't wait for this whole horror story of a festival to end."

Blake let go of Calvin, who glared at him. A mixture of shame and indignation was painted across Calvin's face as he sniffed.

"Come on, Zoe, let's get another cider. We've a few hours until the festival starts. Let's make the most of it."

Zoe, for once bereft of her customary salacious expression, solemnly rose. She looked at Calvin with disgust before grabbing her bag to join Elsie and Blake as they headed back to the pub.

Elsie was watching from the pub entrance. Calvin had been unmasked, another predator in a world of them. He might have escaped justice this time, but she was on to him, as were the others. She and Faith had been through enough. This was just yet another piece of evidence that nobody could be trusted. They could only rely on each other. The sooner they did the job, the sooner they could leave.

She looked round. The sun shone brightly on the happily drinking residents and she wondered what other rot hid in this village. *Or did we bring it with us?* It wasn't a happy thought.

Leaving Zoe and Blake at the bar, she returned upstairs to where Faith was sleeping. Curling up behind her, she stroked her hair until it fell away from her face.

Elsie didn't know how long she lay there until she fell into a dreamless nap, but her phone eventually woke her up, chirping softly beside her. Faith continued to sleep, gently snuffling on the pillow beside her. Elsie looked at her, concerned. She reached over to wipe off a patch of drool from her mouth. After assuring herself that she would be ok, she placed the spare key on the bedside table next to her, then went to the bathroom at the end of the corridor to clean her face.

It was showtime.

Picking up the laminated sheet from Geoff, she looked at the instructions.

Dresscode: Rough, warm clothes for outdoor activity. Sensible shoes or boots. After the performance, there will be a ceremonial chase through the woods, so don't wear restrictive garments.

She pulled a face as she got to the end of the page.

We take this festival very seriously, but that doesn't mean it isn't tremendous fun. So go out there and have a great time.

Her experience with Calvin had utterly killed the atmosphere of fun for her. She would keep an eye on him, then she'd run straight back to the pub and Faith and she would get the first coach out of here.

Where do we go next?

Elsie dismissed the thought. Pulling tight her hoodie, she looked in the mirror. Elsie had no makeup with her, no perfume. Washing her face, she did the best she could to get presentable. If Elsie hadn't needed the money so badly, she would have unleashed hell on Calvin. As it was, she would just have to be careful.

Taking a deep breath, she braced herself for the quaint country rituals in which she was about to partake. TV had warned her that it was likely to be both utterly inane and totally dull.

Leaving the room and locking the door behind her, Elsie knocked on Zoe's door. It creaked open. *She must be with Blake, or otherwise downst–*

The picture frame.

Barging the door open, she marched in and saw her picture frame poking out of Zoe's bag. Picking up the bag and upending it, she saw iPods, mobile phones, wallets and all kinds of knick-knacks.

"What are you doing in my room?" A panicked voice came from behind her. She turned to look at the nervous face of Zoe, with Blake as a shadowy figure before her.

"I *was* looking for you, but what I *actually* found was my picture. What the fuck, Zoe?" Elsie pointed at the contents of the bag.

Blake stepped forwards. "Zoe, what did you do?" His face fell. He turned to Zoe, looking hurt.

Zoe moved towards the bed and shovelled everything into her bag. "I didn't know any of you when I took them."

"That is no defence. I don't know you, but I haven't stolen your stuff?" Elsie raged. "You stood there with us while we judged Calvin and all the time you've been picking our pockets."

"It is not the same! He is a rapist. I just do what I do to survive." Zoe sat down on the bed, her face in her hands. "You have it easy." She sobbed.

"Easy? You have no idea what Faith and I have been through. Easy?" Elsie's eyes narrowed. *Calvin, now Zoe. What are you hiding, Blake? When are you going to betray us?*

"Talk to us, Zoe. What is going on?" Blake said with a tenderness and warmth that annoyed Elsie even more.

29th April, 2013, Elephant and Castle, London

"Zoe, Zoe! Come over and meet Roger." Her mother, Danielle, waved her over, slopping Pinot Grigio onto the already stained carpet.

Zoe had just returned from school. Dumping her bag, she ignored the drunken couple. She didn't need to meet Roger. Roger was a place-holder, a cardboard template that was replaced nightly by whatever man had bankrolled his mother's drinking down the pub.

She went straight to the kitchen. Opening the fridge, she saw a generic bottle of vodka in the freezer and two bottles of Sainsbury's

Pinot Grigio chilling in the fridge compartment. Nothing edible at all. Not even any milk to make a bowl of cereal for dinner.

"Have a drink with us, Zoe!"

Zoe returned to the living room. Looking straight at Roger, she asked him directly, "Do you have any money? We have no food in the kitchen. I'm going to the shops."

Her mother squawked, slamming her abused wine glass onto the pine side table. She tried to stand up and failed. "What a thing to say! Roger dear, I'm so sorry. You know how kids get." Slumping back on the sofa, she resigned herself to staring with indignation. "Why don't you just go out and play like a normal kid?"

"I'm seventeen, Mum. You are supposed to tell me to do my homework. To prepare for my A-levels. To go to bed early." Zoe ignored her mother's protest and walked straight out of the house. She needed food, but more than that, she needed to get away from the decaying corpse of an uncaring addict.

One of the benefits of being seventeen was free travel. Zoe headed to Lambeth. Her headphones on, she settled back in her seat on the tube. A suited man leered at her. She ignored him. Unlike her mother, she already knew which men had something to offer and which were just looking for someone to take advantage of.

Emerging from the tube station at Lambeth, Zoe started to head towards a corner shop she knew from experience had poor CCTV.

She had built up in her head a list of such shops that she could reliably use when the money ran out.

A young lad offered her a cigarette. She smiled at him, accepting the gift. "My name is Jacob," he said, his voice stuttering as he failed to maintain eye contact with her. His hand flicked back the curly tussles of his hair.

She stroked his arm gently.

An easy mark.

"You can see everyone heading to the O2 Academy in Brixton from this bench. It's like a window into another world."

Zoe nodded, smiling at him. "You are so deep, Jacob. You speak like a poet."

"I, er, thank you. I like to read but have written nothing so far." He looked down at his feet, smiling awkwardly. One foot started tapping a rhythm on the path.

Her hand brushed at an imaginary piece of lint on his hoodie. "I like you, Jacob. You are so smart. Why don't we go to the Maccas over the road? Get a burger and get to know each other."

His eyes lit up. For the first time, he could hold Zoe's gaze, if only for a moment. "I'd love to, but I don't have any money. I have a Twix, though." He held out the bar.

"Jacob, that is so kind." *Worthless.* She took the Twix, favouring him with a smile, and stood up. "I have to get some stuff for home. It was nice meeting you."

Jacob's face fell. She walked past him without looking back. Zoe felt as indifferent to Jacob as she did to the homeless people who asked her for change. They were just more people who wanted something from her. Why should she offer herself to someone who had nothing to offer in exchange? She opened up the Twix and took a bite.

She had reached her chosen quarry, the Quality Superstore, a cramped cupboard of a shop. The greedy owner had stacked the shelves in the centre too high. Luckily for her, that meant that they blocked the CCTV camera. The door opened with its habitual ding, then her face fell. They had installed a second camera.

Bastards.

Zoe backed out. Mentally, she reviewed her options. There was a "cash and carry" in Pimlico, a short bus ride away. She looked for the closest stop. It was right next to... she had forgotten his name already but knew it would be awkward, so she walked up the road in the other direction to find the next stop on the route.

A drunken old man had fallen asleep at the bus stop. She could see his wallet poking out from his pocket. Sliding down next to him, she slipped the wallet into her jacket as he woke, peering at her with bleary eyes.

"Hello mate, are you ok? You fell asleep. Do you have some water on you?" Zoe smiled at him as he looked round, disorientated. He jabbered something in an Australian accent, then reached into his bag to pull out a battered plastic bottle with some water. "What bus are you looking for?"

He blathered something incoherent and she nodded at him. "I'll check that on my phone for you."

When he looked away, she walked off quickly round the corner. Pulling out the wallet, she threw away the cards and pocketed the cash. Forty quid. Not a bad score. She tossed the empty wallet and walked towards Vauxhall to grab some food for dinner and head home.

It was dark when she arrived back at the house. She nearly missed it, but something caught her eye. She did a double-take when she saw the cardboard invitation lying on the doormat.

"When did this—" Of course, her mother was asleep on the sofa. Roger had left her top pulled down, exposing a breast. He was long gone.

She walked into the kitchen to run a glass of water and looked at the invitation. Five hundred pounds just to read out some lines at a weekend play.

Five hundred pounds... not enough to get a flat, but food wouldn't be a problem for a while.

1st May, 2013, Huddersford, Kent

Elsie listened to the tale, her face deadpan. She regarded Zoe with a stone-cold expression. She shook her head. "We've all had a bad time. Faith and I had to run away from home. You left by choice. We get by, hand to mouth, sometimes we sleep in the street, but we don't steal. There is never any excuse for breaking the law."

"Oh great, listen to you, Mrs Pure As Driven Snow. If I'd stayed at that house for a moment longer, I'd have gone insane. Can you blame me for seizing an opportunity when it presented itself?" Zoe still had tears running down her face. Blake sat down and awkwardly put his arm round her.

Elsie blinked. "What? Still? Just because she didn't steal from you. She is still using you."

"You don't know that, Elsie. Life isn't black and white. I've done bad things in my life as well." Blake hugged Zoe tight. "Sometimes, we do bad things for the right reasons. Have you never broken the law? Not once?"

Elsie avoided the question. "Alright, Zoe, I'm taking my photo back to my room, where it will stay. Then I'll meet you both in the corridor.

Clean yourself up. We have a job to do. Then Faith and I are getting as far away from this bloody village as possible."

Elsie opened the door and put the family photo on the bedside table next to the sleeping form of Faith. She looked at the girl, so innocent, yet Elsie had brought her into this nest of vipers.

Backing out gently, she locked the door and tested it to ensure she was secure. A few moments later, Zoe and Blake emerged. Zoe didn't make eye contact with Elsie as they headed downstairs. Elsie forced herself to remain calm when she saw Calvin at the bar making small talk with Geoff.

The little things in life do not bother me.

It was something her mum used to say. Whenever things seemed dark, she would set her shoulders and say it. She had a way of separating the world's harsh realities from her life. *A defence mechanism.* These days, Elsie felt she couldn't do that. Life was crashing against her soul like the coastal tide, eroding her. Each day, she felt less.

Now, she was pretending to be a hare to amuse some villagers, alongside a rapist and a thief. What did Blake mean when he said they'd all broken the law? What was his sin? She set her shoulders, raised her chin, and approached Geoff and Calvin.

The little things in life do not bother me.

"Elsie, my hare! How are you feeling? Rested, full of excitement for the stage?" Geoff beamed at her.

Oh, fuck off, you prissy prick.

"I can't wait. I've rehearsed my lines." Elsie plastered a fake smile on her face.

"Wonderful, wonderful, wonderful. I see the makings of a true professional actor in you." As Zoe and Blake came up behind Elsie, he spread his arms wide. "We are all here. This is magnificent news. I am so very excited about tonight. A bi-centennial faire, secret mysteries, music, dancing, action. Come, come, come!" Geoff swooped towards the pub exit. Calvin sculled his cider. He was swaying as he followed Geoff.

Great, the idiot is drunk already. He had better not mess this up any more than he already has. Elsie followed them out to where Geoff was standing by a battered Land Rover.

The pub was getting busier as people tanked up in preparation for the festival.

Geoff drove them down the road. A pair of villagers opened a gate for him as the Land Rover meandered down a long, field-side track. Sitting in the back of the vehicle on metal benches, they bounced along uncomfortably.

"I don't think this is legal," Blake muttered as they bounced over a pothole. "We don't have any seat belts. No, this definitely isn't legal."

Elsie shrugged. "Five hundred pounds. I'll take a few bumps for that. Faith and I can survive for two, maybe three, weeks on that."

"Two weeks after rent? That is a bit bleak, isn't it? What do you eat? Noodles?" Blake looked sympathetically at her.

"Ramen noodles, beans on toast, cereal, cheese on toast, and baked potatoes. Actually, you'd be surprised at how easy it is to live on very little." Elsie gave an awkward smile.

Zoe sniffed. "I'm not sure that is actually living. Sounds like school dinners to me."

"We don't all have access to your *alternative* sources of income." Elsie looked accusingly at Zoe. "We take what we can get."

"I suppose," Blake said, "I am lucky, in a way."

"How so?" Elsie asked.

Blake looked away into the distance for a while, gazing at someone or something that didn't exist.

"Well, it sounds bad, but it isn't, really."

He began:

18th March, 2013, near Kingston, Jamaica

The deck gently swayed underneath them as he watched Mr James Dyke croon through Suspicious Minds. Beside him, his gran was entranced by the performance. He smiled. Elvis wasn't his thing. Blake was more of an Ed Sheeran fan, but the cruise had been a magical experience. A year ago, his gran had found cheap tickets for a cruise round the Caribbean and it was proving to be the holiday of a lifetime. He gratefully accepted another complimentary lager from the waiter. Unlimited buffet food, unlimited drinks. Blake was definitely getting his money's worth. His gran always said his stomach was a bottomless pit and he happily proved her correct.

The Elvis impersonator finished his set to the applause of the crowd. Blake put down his chicken wing bone and clapped happily. Then, looking at the state of his hands, he looked round for a napkin. Without taking her eyes off the stage, his gran handed him a pack of tissues from her bag.

"I wish I'd seen him live," she confessed. Sipping at her wine, she reached into her bag for a couple of aspirin. The DJ started playing. He listened to the track, trying to place it. His gran saw his look of confusion and patted his arm. "Nat King Cole, dear. 'When I fall in love'."

He grinned at her. "Thanks, I thought I recognised it from your albums." He plied the bowl for a final cheesy chip and after some ferreting, he found part of a chip at the bottom. He chucked it into his mouth and crunched down on it.

For the hundredth time, he said to her, "This was a genius idea, gran."

She beamed at him, then slowly stood up. He reached out to help her up. "You stay and enjoy the music. I'll see you at breakfast." Blake gave her a gentle hug. She reached up to tussle his hair.

"Gerroff, you'll mess up the gel!" He pulled back as her eyes sparkled.

As she tottered back to her room, Blake supped his lager and looked round the room. He spied a pair of girls he had drunk with the night before. Blake raised his glass as they waved to him. He rose with a grin and headed over to catch up with them.

He woke to the sound of his alarm clock. Showering, he quickly dressed and headed down to the restaurant. His gran was nowhere to be seen. An early riser, he would always find her at a window seat with a pot of tea.

Concerned, he returned to her cabin and knocked. When there was no response, he dialled her mobile and prayed she had remembered to charge it. Blake felt sick when he heard the phone ringing unanswered in her room. Racing for a cabin crew member, he persuaded them to open the door.

He wished he hadn't.

Blake lay alone in his cabin. His gran's body had been transferred off the ship when they docked in Jamaica.

What was he to do?

His gran wasn't just his only known relative, she was his best friend. Now he was all alone. His phone trilled repeatedly. The texts from the girls onboard went unanswered as he slipped into a dark depression.

25th March, 2013, Stratford, London

The plane flight back to London had been uneventful. A small child had kicked the back of his seat and his headphones hadn't worked, but none of that mattered. What did matter was his lonely return to their flat, so full of memories. He grabbed a coke from the fridge and sat in his favourite armchair. Turning on Netflix, he put it on shuffle.

Later, when he felt hungry, he went to the fridge. Of course, they had been away. It was empty. Picking up his phone, he ordered a pizza and returned to his armchair, sipping on his coke. Looking round for a napkin, he turned, by reflex, to his gran's chair. It was vacant. He sighed and got up to wash his hands in the kitchen.

It was nearly a month later when he needed to get cash. Pulling on his hoodie, he trundled into town to find an ATM. He mutely pressed for a statement after removing a hundred pounds from the machine. Blake blinked and peered again at the scrap of paper. His gran's full pension had been deposited yesterday. A big smile crossed his face. Despite the crisp air, warmth flowed through him. Even from beyond the grave, she was still looking after him.

He hadn't been abandoned.

With the money he'd taken from the ATM, he went to a nearby café and ordered a full English breakfast and a large pot of tea. He filled two cups and put the second opposite him. Clinking it with his mug, he smiled. "Thanks, Gran. I miss you so much. I hope you've taught them how to make a good cuppa in heaven." He chuckled. "I bet you've seen Elvis perform live now."

The next day, his luck continued to grow. An invitation to perform at the Festival of Masks appeared on his doorstep.

1st May, 2013, Huddersford, Kent

"So, wait. The day after you spent your gran's pension money, the invitation arrived?" Elsie asked. "And the same thing happened to you two?" Elsie looked at Zoe and Calvin. They looked at each other and nodded. "I'm getting a bad feeling about this. How did they find us anyway? I thought they had randomly sent out invitations."

"They must have." Zoe squinted. "I mean, nobody knows what we did. Right."

Elsie looked thoughtful. "I suppose."

Calvin looked suspiciously at Elsie. "Following your logic. That means you know you did something."

"I didn't say that," Elsie said sharply.

"I mean, if these invitations came after we'd committed a crime." Calvin frowned. "That means you must have committed one if you got an invitation."

"Well, I didn't commit a crime." Blake grinned amiably.

They all looked at him. "You are a benefits cheat. That is fraud," Calvin muttered.

"No. It's my gran's money. She would have wanted me to have it. We took care of each other." Blake looked hurt. "I'd never break the law. I am a good man."

Zoe moved to sidle into his chest, but he shrugged her off. She moved away with a wounded expression.

"Seriously. I have never broken the law in my life." Blake was looking cross now. "Don't put me in the same bracket as the other two."

"Hey!" Zoe punched him in the shoulder. "What the fuck was that about?"

"So now you are better than us, are you?" Calvin sneered. "You are a cheat, mate, a fucking fraud."

Elsie looked at Calvin. "Everyone is better than you. You rapist twat."

The Land Rover stopped as Calvin's face darkened. They ceased their arguing as they looked round with trepidation.

They had reached their destination.

They were in an old forest clearing. It was filled with a heaving mass of people laughing and drinking. Some of them Elsie recognised from the pub.

An eerie, unsettling atmosphere pervaded this part of the forest. Unlike the rest of the orchard, the trees here weren't fruit trees. They were encircled by dark yew trees. Far older and more prominent than the rest, a giant yew loomed over an ancient stone table. It was engraved with a strange, runic pattern of grooves on its top. Overlooking the centre of the clearing was a large wooden stage with lighting set up on steel scaffolding. A whole hog was being roasted over coals on a spit. A bar had been set up with huge cider barrels to the right of them. The spiced scent of cooked pork with cloves and the sweet smell of fermented apples hung in the air. A DJ was playing the Rolling Stones.

Geoff opened the Land Rover doors, his face glowing with excitement.

"Come, come, my beauties, we have a tented area set up behind the stage where you can prepare yourselves. In two hours when the time is nigh, I'll need you to put on your masks and assemble on the stage. The order of assembly is from left to right, stage left, that is, it's marked on your sheets."

"What's stage left?" Blake asked.

"As you stand basking in the audience's adulation, it is to the left of you." Geoff pointed at the stage.

"I'll show you where to stand." Zoe stroked his shoulder.

Blake refused to look at her. "No thanks, I'll figure it out for myself."

Elsie tapped Geoff on the side. He spun theatrically and beamed beneficently at her. "Geoff, why were we chosen specifically? How did you get our addresses? What would have happened if one of us had said no?"

"Good golly, what excellent questions. A fine mind you have, my young hare. Sharp as a razor." He looked round the milling crowd. "There! Jack, he is your man," Geoff whispered conspiratorially. His whisper was still deafeningly loud. "He is the Avatar of Cernunnos." Geoff pointed to a serious-looking bespectacled man in a suit. The Avatar waved politely at them. "He is an accountant by trade. The orchard chose him. It's an old tradition. The trees are supposed to whisper the actors' names and how to find them."

Elsie traded glances with Blake. Both seemed unconvinced.

Ignorant of their concerns, Geoff erupted into a sudden and sharp bout of laughter. He slapped the sides of his ample belly. "Hogwash, I'm sure. I think he just gets his secretary to handle the role of recruitment, between you and me. Maybe she uses Google or TikTok or something... 'internetty'." He wiggled his fingers to indicate someone using the arcane rituals of accessing the internet. "We probably had a few pull-outs before we found you, but best to play along. They take their rituals very seriously here."

"And the chase?" Elsie asked.

"The best bit! When Jack blows on his horn, it's an antique, you know, you must all scamper between those two trees marked by ribbons. Once through them, you can follow any route you choose just so long as you arrive back at the pub within three hours. If you do, there will be a two hundred and fifty-pound bonus and you'll be able to remove the mask."

"Do we get a head start?" asked Blake.

"Of course! You get a five minute head start." Geoff leaned in. "It is only fair, as the locals know the terrain very well and are a touch more athletic than you soft city types." He laughed, rubbing his belly. "Believe it or not, I used to be an athletic whippersnapper myself. I was too young to be at the last festival, though. It seems draconian, but you have to be eighteen to be a hound. Still, the times they are a-changin. You know this is the first year we've allowed women!"

"How progressive of you," Zoe said, her voice devoid of any emotion. "You must be so proud."

Calvin was scanning the forest. "They won't be rough, will they?"

"How on earth do you mean, my wee boy?" Geoff rubbed his shoulder enthusiastically. "It's touch rules. If you get even the slightest touch by a hound, you are out of the game."

Leaving them to go backstage, he headed back to the Land Rover. Calling over his shoulder, he warned, "Remember, the Wild Hunt will chase you. If any of them touch you, you are no longer eligible for the bonus, but you get to remove your mask and join the party. This is all on the briefing sheet."

Elsie watched Geoff get into his vehicle and drive away. "Come on then." She headed towards the backstage tent, Zoe in tow. Looking behind her, she could see the boys lingering. "Come on, let's get this shit show over with."

"Well, you see." Blake said hesitantly.

Calvin pointed at the cider stand. "It is free."

Shaking her head, Elsie left them. Calvin was already drunk, but there was little she could do about it. Elsie just hoped he didn't mess it up for the rest of them. She needed that money.

Walking into the tent, she found four tables, each one with a large wooden mask. Elsie beelined to the table with her white hare mask. It was lacquered and decorated with runes and iron studs. She turned it over in her hands. It was an ugly thing. A pair of leather straps dangled from the back. A padlock was next to it. She picked it up dubiously.

"I'm not wearing this." Zoe shook her head. "It's horrible. If they think they can padlock this thing to my face, they have another thing coming."

"Yours looks better than mine. Mine looks sinister." Elsie turned round the mask with its long wooden ears. "They'll see me a mile off. Look at these massive white things."

The boys entered and saw the masks. "Cool," Blake said. Both he and Calvin marched up to the badger mask. "What do you think you are doing? You agreed to wear the pheasant mask."

"They'll think I'm gay. Look at it. It's multi-coloured with glitter." Calvin reached for the badger mask only to find his wrist held in a vice-like grip by Blake. "Oh, come on."

Zoe sauntered over to look. "What's wrong with being gay, any-way?"

"Well, you aren't. You'll shag any bloke with a pulse," Calvin muttered.

"Guess you don't have a pulse then, Calvin," Zoe said bitterly.

Blake turned round and lifted him by the throat.

"Put him down!" Zoe pulled at his arm. "What is wrong with you?" After a moment's pause, where he stared deep into Calvin's eyes, Blake dropped him. Calvin gasped, reaching out to the table for support. "What? You ignore me for the entire drive here and then think you can protect me? What the fuck is wrong with you?"

"We're almost done here. Then we never have to see each other again." Elsie gently pushed the boys apart. She subconsciously wiped the hand that touched Calvin on her hoodie. His eyes followed her as she returned to her dressing room table.

"Could we attach them but just not use the padlocks?" Elsie wondered.

Zoe smiled. "I have safety pins."

"They won't be strong enough. You need some string." Blake was turning the mask over and analysing the buckles.

Elsie looked up. "Do you think they'll let us?"

"I think it's worth a try. How close do you think the organisers will be checking," Blake said, smiling. He shrugged. "Let's give it a go, eh?"

"Let's not, eh?" From the tent entrance came a stocky blonde lady. "I'm Jess, your hair and makeup girl." She paused to pose. Elsie looked at her dubiously.

"I have my own makeup," Zoe said, her face horrified.

"Jolly good, well, I won't do it against your will, but I will check to ensure that you are presentable before you go out." She walked round them, taking each of the masks and putting them back in their places. "Lovely. They look a lot older than they really are. They were made fifty years ago for the last festival. Except for the hare one, that's new this year. It's a replica of the original. I helped make it. "

"They are very heavy." Zoe picked hers up. "Plastic would be lighter."

"We carved them out of wood from our very own orchard. It's all part of the tradition." Jess stroked the hare mask. "You are very honoured to take part. It's all the community can talk about. You are as close to royalty as it gets round here."

Flicking her hair, Zoe put on a posh voice. "Well, I always suspected I would make a rather good princess."

Elsie snorted.

"Do we have to memorise all these lines?" Calvin was looking at his laminated briefing card. "It's a lot of words."

"It's one paragraph, Calvin. You can manage that, surely?" Elsie had picked hers up and was mumbling her lines under her breath.

"Who wrote these?" Calvin laughed, looking at the archaic language. "The BBC? This is some kind of Shakespeare shit."

Nobody answered him. The room was silent as Jess stared at him. Eventually, Jess said in an even mannered tone. "These are sacred words. They are traditional and mean a great deal to our village. This is a serious role. If you don't treat it with the dignity that it deserves, then you'll be down the road."

"Why didn't you hire proper actors?" Elsie asked.

"We did." Jess gestured at the four of them.

Elsie rolled her eyes. "By proper actors, I meant trained actors. For the money you are offering, you should have been able to get some that are at least formally trained, even if they lack experience."

"You act every day. You are acting now." Jess smiled. "Everyone acts. You were chosen."

Zoe approached her. "How were we selected? I didn't sign up with any agencies. How did you find us?"

Shrugging, Jess waved her hands in dismissal. "That isn't my department, dear. I'm hair and makeup. Now, will you be needing any of that, or do you want privacy to practise your lines?"

Blake was looking at his card. "I could use some time to get my head round these lines."

"And of course, we'll need your phones." Jess held out a small wicker basket.

Zoe recoiled. "I think not."

"Do you think Dame Judi Dench carries her phone onto the stage with her? Just in case she needs to reply to one of Kenneth Branagh's tweets?" Jess waved the basket again.

"There is no signal here anyway." Elsie pulled out her phone. It was battered with a cracked screen. "How do we get them back?"

"Geoff will have them at the pub. You'll get them with your cheque." Jess took the phone and dropped it in. Grudgingly, the others added their own phones.

Jess turned and as she left the tent, she called over her shoulder. "I'll be back in thirty minutes to help you with your masks."

"I don't like this." Zoe sat down at her dressing table and poked her mask. "It doesn't make sense. We've been chosen? For what? Has any of us done any drama since secondary school?"

"You said it earlier. We are all criminals," Calvin muttered.

"I'm not," Blake protested.

"Whatever, Blake. Look, we should cut and run. This is weird. I don't like it." Calvin was cut off by Elsie.

"We are doing this. Let's just stand outside, say our lines and then let them chase us for a few minutes to give them some fun. Then we take our five hundred pounds and get out of here."

"Seven hundred and fifty. The hounds will never catch me. I'm going to beeline for the pub. Within half an hour, I will be there. I'm a good runner," Blake boasted, his voice matter of fact.

Zoe batted her eyelids at him and pouted. "You wouldn't leave me behind, would you?"

"Well, you robbed everyone. So yeah. I wish you well and all, but you are on your own, mate." Blake refused to meet her eyes.

Zoe bit her lip and stormed off to her desk.

"Come on then, let's get together and go through these lines until we can do them from memory without mistakes." Elsie took up her position in the centre of the room.

"No, it's obvious that I'm not wanted." Zoe started to cry softly. Guilt crossed Blake's face. He took a step towards her, but then went to join Elsie.

"Yeah, screw you guys." Calvin went to his mirror and started to rehearse his lines independently.

Elsie and Blake had got it down to a stilted yet formal level. They could recite the words without the cards, though Elsie, while not being an expert, still felt it lacked depth or any form of emotion. None of them wanted to be there and it showed.

Jess arrived and watched misty-eyed as Elsie, then Blake, finished their lines. "Oh, they chose well."

"What is this 'audience reacts' at the end?" Zoe pointed at her briefing card.

Jess smiled as she picked up Zoe's mask. "Oh, the audience will then say, 'We forgive you your sins'."

"Our sins?" Elsie said, her voice tinged with uncertainty.

"How kind of them," Zoe said with a slight sneer.

"It's a purification ritual. We forgive the animals that do harm to our orchard and then ritually chase them with our 'hounds.' Just a bit of fun. Now, let's get the masks fixed on." Zoe backed away. "Just a couple of minutes on the stage, a romp in the woods and you get paid. Dead easy."

Zoe fidgeted but allowed Jess to attach the mask. The padlock clicked shut with an echoing sound. It reminded Elsie of a gunshot.

Elsie watched as Blake had his badger mask fixed. Calvin complained that it was too tight, but was duly ignored by Jess. Then it was Elsie's turn. She looked at the wooden mask with distaste as it was picked up and strapped to her head.

Her world became two small eyeholes. Her breathing echoed loudly behind the wooden mask. It weighed down heavily, straining her neck. The musty, chemical scent of treated wood enveloped her. She fought down panic. Her peripheral vision was limited as she looked round.

I don't like this. I don't like it at all.

"Well, don't you all look lovely," Jess said as she manoeuvred them towards the exit.

The cool evening air was refreshing on Elsie's face. It needed to be. The crowd that she could barely see through the eye holes cheered her on. All the attention caused her stomach to lurch. Whoops, clapping and cheers washed over her in a cavalcade of sound. The scent of food and spilt alcohol filled the air.

She was guided up the short stairs onto the stage, where the Avatar of Cernunnos stood in a black suit and white shirt, peering out at her through a huge stag's head.

What the hell?

The stage lights were overly bright. Elsie blinked to compensate. She automatically moved to her position as the other animals shuffled into place round her.

The Avatar raised his hands and the crowd fell silent.

"This year is a year of great celebrations. We have kept up our tradition, built up over the last twenty-three years, of winning the Gold Medal for Cider from the Campaign for Real Cider. Also, as we have over the last eight years, once again we have picked up the

Gold Medal from the British Cider Association and for the very first time during our long established history of cider-making, we have been awarded the Good Housekeeping Best British Drink award. The Apple and Pear will have to add more shelves for our new intake of awards. In these troubled times, I urge you all to remember that this festival exists to protect us all from the perils of poverty that plague this land. Cernunnos is our guardian. We owe everything to him." The audience applauded on cue. The Avatar waited for a respectful silence in which to offer his booming proclamation, then announced:

"From the distant times of yore, when our forefathers reigned, our lands were plagued by the four pests. The Fox, the Badger, the Hare and the Pheasant. In lean times, they created the Festival of Masks to renew our ancient link to the gods of old—"

"Heathen!" came from the audience. Elsie traced it to the vicar, who was laughing into his cider cup. The crowd joined him in laughter.

"—who rewarded our faith with fertile harvests of the best fruits in Britain." Rousing applause rose from the audience until he signalled them to be quiet. The DJ started to play a gentle orchestral sound-track. The sounds of a fiddle could be heard playing a haunting tune.

Zoe stepped forward first with a flourish. "I, the Fox, hunt your livestock. No fence nor wall can keep me out." Clawing her hands in the air, she gave a roar sound, much to the crowd's amusement.

The audience joined together to chant, "We absolve you of your sins."

Blake stepped forward and in perfect monotony, he bowed before booming. "I, the Badger, befoul the grounds with my tunnels and slaughter any dog sent to hunt me."

Another chant of, "We absolve you of your sins," rose from the audience.

Elsie took up her position and chanted, "I, the Hare, feast on your crops and destroy your fields."

"We absolve you of your sins," the crowd shouted.

Calvin was last. "I, the pheasant, consume your grapes, eat your young shoots and bathe in dust, crushing your crops."

The crowd was shouting louder now. "We absolve you of your sins."

The Avatar raised his hands to speak again. "As before, so it is now. We have identified the four pests, the evils that plague our lands. It is time to expunge them." Elsie saw large groups of people on both sides of the stage, all wearing terrifying hound masks. Unmistakably hounds, they were painted with nightmarish visages, huge fangs, bloody maws. In their hands were short staves,each one topped with a runic bone cross.

"You will now open the path, so the prey may flee. Hold fast, my hounds. Without a challenge, the gods won't be honoured."

Why do they need weapons?

Elsie shook as she looked down at the pack of hounds, dressed in hoodies and fleece jackets. They seemed to be champing at the bit, eager to get to grips with the young actors. The crowd opened up. A chorus of howls echoed from them, followed by the hounds, who were being restrained by what looked like marshals.

"The prey will run. Now!" The Avatar pointed. "Run!" Blake was off, his long legs powering him through the crowd.

"Blake! Don't leave me," Zoe wailed, as she ran after him, soon falling behind. Calvin jumped down from the stage and stumbled. He had misjudged the leap through alcohol or sheer accident. He must have twisted his ankle. Elsie could see him limping.

Elsie went for it. She ran through the whooping, howling crowd and tore through the woods in the direction of the pub.

They'll be expecting us to travel directly.

She veered off the path crashing through foliage and bushes. Her ears kept catching on the low lying branches.

They expect us to exhaust ourselves.

It's dark. Elsie had to outsmart them if she wanted the two hundred and fifty pounds. Blake might be out to outrun them, but she couldn't. Elsie found a large rhododendron bush. She shook her head to avoid getting those ears stuck and crept underneath it. She peered out through the thick foliage, catching a glimpse of the ongoing festivities, the dancing people and the cider-drinkers.

After a few minutes, she heard, "Release the hounds!" The Avatar yelled to a chorus of howls. The hounds assembled in front of the festival-goers. Elsie blinked at the sudden brightness as they all turned on head torches. *You cheating bastards.* As they spread out into a fan, she watched them separate into three ranks. Then, group by group, they tore through the woods, one line sprinting, one line jogging and the other walking slowly, all beating the bushes as they went.

They take this far too seriously.

The first and second lines had torn past her, hurtling through the woods at breakneck speed. She saw one of the beaters heading towards her bush. Aware of just how white her mask was, she looked round, then lay down, placing her mask face down against the soil. She pulled the dead leaves and loam over the backs of her wooden ears and lay quite still. Motionless, she waited, not daring to breathe as the beater whacked the bush and peered inside.

Through luck, his incompetence or just the sheer size of the giant plant, he missed her and moved on. Elsie remained still for another minute, then raised her head to see what was happening. She was now behind the hunters. Grinning, she knew she had made it past the first trial.

Should have given me the Fox mask.

It didn't take long for the first howls of triumph to sound. She watched as a group of them came running back. She could see them carrying the limp form of— You sick bastards. The revellers back at the festival were stripping. The undulating forms of middle-aged farmers dancing round the altar were painfully visible. *They're sex people*. She shuddered as she watched the pale white flesh gleam in the firelight.

"And so, we take the flesh of the Pheasant and as we sacrifice its heart to the woods, we forgive its sins." *Why was Calvin limp? Was he hurt?* Then she heard the sickening sound of screaming. It was Calvin's voice.

She knew then that he was dying. She had heard that sound before, at another time and another place.

She vomited. Most of it escaped through the breathing hole in her mask, but the rest dripped down her front. The smell of it filled her nostrils and she gagged. Her hands shook. The sick bastards were dancing naked as they killed Calvin. The music had changed to an orchestral track. It built up to a rhythmic pounding. The drums echoed through the woods like a powerful heartbeat. As they danced round his corpse, she shook her head in despair. As much as she hated him, he didn't deserve this.

This isn't justice.

She watched as several of the crowd, naked and drunk on cider and death, began rutting in the grass. Nausea rose again in her throat as a chill ran down her spine.

Faith is back at the pub alone.

Faith was unconscious, vulnerable. Who knows what they would do to her? She had to get back.

She had no doubt in her mind that what was waiting at the pub with cheerful Geoff was not a fat cheque. It was one of those bone truncheons.

Her jaw set. She waited until her breathing had slowed. With her body still shaking, she crept out from under the bush and ran, keeping low to the ground. She flitted from tree to tree. Ahead of her, she could always see the lights of the hounds as they chased through the woods. She veered further to the left, always heading left, looking to outflank their lines and move round them. The hounds had fallen silent now. Their earlier howls had changed to quiet professionalism. Elsie pulled at the mask, but it was fixed securely. Without a knife, she wasn't likely to break through those leather straps and even if she did manage to find a cutting tool, well, she would risk cutting herself. For now, she quietly jogged through the night, her vision partially obscured, her nose filled with the scent of vomit, her ears reverberating with the sound of her own breathing.

If only she had kept her phone, she could have tried to find some signal and dialled the police. As it was, it was down to her.

The wolf had been at the door before. Now it was back. Threats endangered her and, more importantly, Faith. Nothing would get in the way of saving her sister. The trees loomed like spectres in the dark. The moon was high and filtered through the leaves. An owl hooted. It was the least of the predators she had to worry about. She was overtaking the third line of hounds, the walkers. Curling round their left flank, she continued towards the pub.

She had emerged into the orchard. She could feel the squelch of rotten apples under her trainers and smell the sweet scent of dying fruit. The trees were more spread out and the undergrowth carefully hacked back, so that cover was limited.

Creeping forwards, she saw the squat hives of the bees. Her ears strained to listen. It was all quiet except for the distant sounds of the chase over to her right. It was peaceful. Even the bees were sleeping.

Running forward, she heard the howls of the hounds and watched as the lights concentrated on a point. Screams echoed into the night. Another of the prey had been caught.

Fuck. Fuck. Fuck.

She recognised Zoe's cries before they were abruptly cut off.

She looked round her. What would they do if they got to the pub and realised that she had eluded them? The pub must be guarded. This whole chase was rigged. Leaning against an apple tree, she caught her breath. If there was a ring of them round the pub, she was walking into a trap.

Is Faith already dead?

Maybe she should run for the coach station. The town was only another three miles away. She could make it before daybreak.

As she set off towards the pub, she hated herself for even considering leaving her sister. She had to rescue Faith.. She would never be able to live with herself, knowing that she had abandoned her, not after everything they'd been through together.

As she jogged forward, she heard a rustling. Slowing down, she listened again. It was quiet, other than her breathing echoing in the mask. She moved forward slowly. She heard the noise again. It was over to her left. She paused. Nothing. Starting off, she jogged cautiously, listening intently. A twig snapped. She turned and saw it. A hound with his head torch off. Of course, they'd have hidden hounds. She turned and ran immediately to her right. He howled as he pursued her and she watched as the lights in front of her all turned towards her. They were still distant, but that wouldn't last long. She changed her trajectory to head towards the pub. As her trainers followed the dark path, the trees were a forest of dark silhouettes, a thousand obsidian fingers clawing at the sky.

A shadow flickered at her side and she turned too late. She was rugby tackled to the floor.

The hound raised his truncheon but then paused and stood up. He managed two steps before Blake, in his badger mask, collided with him. Punching at the mask, Blake swore as it bruised and cut his knuckles. The hound screamed, his voice unexpectedly shrill in the quiet of the night. Rolling Blake off, he scrambled to his feet. He was looking for his truncheon when Elsie charged at him, smashing him on the back of his head with his own weapon. With a sickening sound, bone crunched under the hardwood truncheon as she struck the hound repeatedly.

Blake's eyes widened as he heaved the dead weight of the hound off his own body. "You... Is he dead?"

"This way," she said, ignoring the question. Elsie led him further towards the pub. She could see it now, on the brow of the hill. Unfortunately, she could also see the hounds. It was as though the whole world was chasing them, a forest of twinkling head torches.

"They've got Zoe," Blake muttered under his breath.

Elsie thought back to the stolen photo frame. It all seemed so petty now. "They got Calvin too."

"Some good has come of this then," Blake said bitterly. To her surprise, Elsie didn't disagree.

"You know they'll be guarding the pub, don't you," Elsie whispered, her voice ragged.

"I suspect so." Blake jogged onwards. "We don't have much choice, though."

Elsie hated herself for what she was about to say. "I have to make it to the pub. I need to get Faith, dead or alive. I need to know what's happened to her. You could run to the town, though, get the coach."

"I've a better idea. I can draw the hounds off. You hide over by the fence. I'll start running back towards the woods. I can lose them in there and then tail back towards the town. You head to the pub. Get Faith, get out." Blake's lips pressed together, he looked at the approaching head torches bitterly.

"That's... Why would you do that for me, Blake?" Elsie whispered.

Blake looked at her. "I'm not a criminal. I'm not a bad man. These pricks, judging us, hunting us for entertainment, they are the real evil." He rubbed his arms to ward off the cold. "Now Zoe is dead. She asked me for help and I should have protected her. I... she didn't deserve that." He bit his lip. "It's time for me to start making the right decisions."

Elsie didn't say anything. Instead, she hugged him. He turned to start running. "Wait, Blake. I don't think you are a bad person. I think you have a good heart."

Tears rolled down her face. He'd never know. The mask concealed everything.

He paused to listen, then started running. As he raced through the orchard, he must have become visible to one of the hounds as a chorus of howls echoed and Elsie saw the head torches turn his way. As the hounds ran past her position, she kept her mask facing down and waited for the silence to return. It must have been ten minutes before they had cleared her hiding spot. She hadn't heard any cries, so she could only hope Blake was still alive and safe.

She turned towards the pub and began circling it, the truncheon in her hand.

There were hounds placed round the pub still. Elsie could see them. She sat watching them patrol the building. When one of them paused, Elsie saw her opportunity and sprinted towards the gap in their perimeter. The hedge was hawthorn. She walked closer to the idle sentry until she found a small, albeit tight, hole. Gritting her teeth, she ignored the vicious thorns that slashed at her clothes and cut her skin. Her blood ran cold as she heard the hounds talking no more than a metre away.

"What the hell were you playing at?"

"I had to have a whizz, mate. That cider went right through me."

She waited until her breathing had settled and they had moved on.

She was in the pub garden. Looking up, she could see the window of Faith's bedroom. She was close. The pub front door was open and light pooled out from inside.

Sliding round the side of the building, she tried the back door. Locked. The same with the kitchen.

Come on, I am so close!

The windows were all secured too. Looking at her truncheon, Elsie thought about smashing a window. But how do you do that quietly?

She made a decision. If you can't be stealthy, you have to be quick. She crept towards the open door and raced inside. Geoff was waiting. He was sitting in an armchair facing the door. A truncheon was in his hand.

A look of shock crossed his face. His mouth fell open at the sight of the truncheon she was holding.

"Now then, young lady, put that down and we'll see about getting you the prize you so richly deserve. Pretty little things like you shouldn't be running round with weapons." He laughed, his eyes twinkling as he struggled to heave his ungainly body out of the depths of his comfortable armchair.

Elsie's eyes narrowed.

26th April, 2013, Clerkenwell Estate, London

Elsie lay waiting, dread and fear soaked deep into every fibre of her being. Her ears strained as she sought the sound that haunted her. The footsteps of her drunken father. Would he go left to pass out in his room? Or would he turn right to visit her room?

Taking deep breaths, she tried to calm herself by reciting her mantra. *Thirteen pounds, seventy-eight pence.* That was how much she had embezzled from the shopping budget. She could afford two one-way coach tickets for herself and her younger sister, Faith, to escape the clutches of their father.

Elsie prayed that he wouldn't come tonight. The sweaty hands. The sharp alcoholic tang of his breath. The foul scent of tobacco clung to him. The bristly stubble that stung her skin.

Not tonight. Elsie would do anything for a night of peace.

She heard them.

The footsteps.

As her prayers reached a feverish crescendo, the worst thing that could possibly happen, happened.

Her prayers were answered.

Elsie's ears heard the screeching of the door handle, so quiet under normal circumstances, but tonight it felt deafening. It wasn't her door handle. It was her sister's.

What emotion was she expecting? Red hot rage? Cold icy terror? The anxiety that had filled her since her mother had left. The depression that had set in when the abuse began. It fled.

Elsie was left with a moment of crystal clear clarity. Her mind, razor-sharp, knew precisely what had to happen. Sliding out of bed, she opened her door quietly to see her father stalk into Faith's room.

Padding silently down the stairs, she crossed into the pitch black kitchen. Feeling her way over to the knife rack, Elsie pulled out the large eight-inch cooks' knife before replacing it with the thinner, pointier, five-inch utility knife. Creeping up the stairs, she saw Faith's door open.

Knife outstretched, eyes forward, a steely determination to do what needed to be done filled her. As she entered, she found her father looming over Faith's bed, a mirror image of when he first came to her room, drunk. He was unsteady on his feet. Good, that would make this easier. Elsie paused, hatred for her abuser flowing through her veins as she heard Faith echo the words she had first uttered a year ago:

"Father? What are you doing?"

He was standing topless. *Good, no cloth for the blade to catch on.* Elsie clenched her grip tightly round the handle. Her mind clicked into place almost audibly as it committed to black murder. Stepping forward, she stabbed up under his ribs. He howled with surprise as the knife sunk deep into his side. He turned, his eyes filled with anger.

Stab.

Stab.

Stab.

Ducking under his clumsy blow, Elsie stabbed the knife in again and again. She wasn't aiming for any location in particular. She just wanted him dead. Hot blood squirted. He grabbed at her and gripped her tightly as he collapsed. Foetid breath huffed into her face. His fingers clawed for her wrist.

In her memory, she was focused and analytical. Faith said otherwise. She remembered Elsie screaming and weeping with anger as she plunged the cold metal into his clammy flesh.

Elsie stopped only when the blade snapped off inside his body. It was only then that she realised the ogre was dead. Half rolling the corpse off, half wriggling out from under it, she looked at Faith. She was sitting up in bed, her eyes wide with terror.

"Faith, it's okay now. It's safe now." Faith broke down in tears, shaking with fear and shock. Elsie was covered in blood, hot arterial blood drying to almost obsidian black in the dark. She took Faith gently by the hand. Leading her to the shower, the two sisters washed off the last remnants of the tyrant who had dominated their lives. Lying down in the shower well, they washed each other's hair. The warm, soapy water helped to loosen muscles taut with years of accumulated tension.

"We are free now, Faith," Elsie promised. Faith was still crying. She had yet to say a single word, her thin, frail body rocking. As Elsie washed her hair, she seemed to calm.

"What will we do now?" Faith asked eventually.

"Whatever we need to," Elsie said firmly.

They stayed in Elsie's room that night. The corpse that had been their father, they locked in the other room. He was nothing to them, nothing at all.

They woke to hear the letterbox clang. An invitation to the Festival of Masks was on the doormat. A chance for a new life.

Elsie found a payphone and dialled the number. There was no interview. Geoff told her to make her way to Hudderford. You were born to be the Hare, he had proclaimed. With a huge smile, she had used the last of their money, supplemented by her late father's purloined wallet, to book the coach immediately.

This was their chance for a new life.

2nd May, 2013, Huddersford, Kent

Elsie leapt forwards, her lips drawn back across her bared teeth in a feral snarl. Geoff raised his truncheon but was forced back into the chair. He tried to barrel forwards into her, screaming "Once more unto the brea—" She brought her truncheon down onto Geoff's balding head. Crunch, it smacked into the egg-shaped skull. His jowls wobbled as his eyes rolled back into his skull. He even managed to make falling unconscious a theatrical experience.

She looked at the collapsed thespian and sneered.

Beside him on a small table were four envelopes with names written in elaborate calligraphy. Elsie shuddered at the sight of them but slid them into her pocket before running behind the bar. Grabbing the crossbow, she used the crank to pull the string back and loaded it with a quarrel.

Footsteps echoed. "Geoff!" she recognised the voice from earlier. It was the man who had been berated for leaving his post. Slinking back beside the door, she waited as he and his partner entered.

Thunk.

A crossbow bolt erupted from the throat of the errant guard as blood blossomed from the wound. He turned to face her. He looked more offended than angry as he scrabbled at the open wound with grasping fingers.

His partner charged her. Elsie threw the crossbow into his face and kicked over a stool into his path. He stumbled and overextended his truncheon. Her first strike broke his wrist. The follow-up strike hit his jaw. Blood and teeth exploded from his face as he fell to the floor, his hands cradling his head. She didn't pause. Every place on his skull she saw exposed was struck. Again and again. Bone, brain matter and gore covered her, and she lashed until, out of breath, she straightened up. His partner took his last gasp, an expression of horror on his face, frozen like a mask.

Running upstairs, she shook Faith awake. She was still drowsy, but luckily hadn't undressed when Elsie put her to bed earlier.

"We're in danger, Faith. We don't have time to talk. We have to run."

Faith blinked sleepily. "Wha—"

"—Get up." She pulled her sister up. Faith trusted her implicitly. With all that their family had been through, she had to.

Grabbing their bag, Elsie paused briefly. Seeing the framed photo of her mother in happier times, she pushed it safely into the bag and led Faith downstairs.

Faith gasped at the sight of the bodies.

Elsie strode into the kitchen, dragging Faith behind her. She turned on all the cooker gas taps. Then she shook her head.

It won't be enough.

Elsie reached round the cooker to unscrew the main gas valve as well. It hissed venomously.

A tray of candles for the tables was on one side. The small green glass holders were in the shape of apples. She lit several of them with a gaslighter until she heard noises outside. It would have to do.

Other people, no, not people, hounds, were approaching The Apple and Pear.

"Come on," she whispered urgently, dragging Faith outside to the car park.

She heard the cries as the bodies were found and increased their pace. "Come on, Faith!" Her sister, still suffering from the effect of the drugs, stumbled along beside her. She clung to Elsie's arm like a lead weight.

It's three miles to the town. They'd never make it.

The thought had barely crossed her mind when a heavy weight landed on her back and she was rolled to the ground. The grinning face of Geoff looked down at her. His face was a crimson mask of drying gore. He punched her full in the face. The wooden mask broke her nose under the impact. Then his hands were clutching at her throat, squeezing with manic energy. His mouth foamed with crimson spittle as he grunted with the effort. He pulled her up by the neck and smashed her head down onto the car park gravel again and again. She tried to loosen his grip, but he was too strong. Blood gushed from her nose down into her open mouth as she gasped for air. All she could taste was the coppery tang of her own bleeding wounds.

"I don't think so, my little starlet. The show *must* go on."

Behind Geoff, the world exploded into fire and flame. The wind was knocked out of their lungs. All they could hear was the blast. Geoff's grip relaxed as it hit him and he was propelled forwards. He turned to look at the broken shell of the pub with shock. Flames licked from the surrounding hellscape. Smoke and ash littered the sky.

Elsie's hand scooped up a fistful of gravel. She ground it into Geoff's eyes. He howled and rubbed at them as she tried to wriggle out from under him. His dead weight was too much. Instead, she grabbed his waistcoat, pulling him forward and pivoting. He crashed down onto the floor next to her and she was able to roll away.

Faith ran in and kicked at his body as he struggled to stand.

His breath was ragged and his voice raspy. He looked at Elsie with pure hatred, ignoring her tiny sister. "It's the final curtain call for you." He shoved Faith, who fell to the ground with a squeal.

With her ears still ringing, Elsie heard none of his final words. "Oh, just fucking die," Elsie growled as she pulled the truncheon out from under her hoodie.

At the last minute, he cleared enough of the grit from his eyes to see the avenging angel bearing down on him. "No, wait, ple—"

She never heard the rest. This time, she made sure he was dead. She raised the truncheon. His body shuddered under her relentless assault.

She reached into his pockets and pulled out his car keys.

She staggered round the car park. Tinnitus deafened her as she hammered the buttons on the car keys. Only hope and desperation kept her going.

Her mask restricted her vision.

Luckily, Geoff's Land Rover was easy to spot with its blinking lights. It loomed over the other vehicles. Racing forwards, Elsie looked at the shattered glass. The back seats were covered in sharp shards, but the front windows seemed to be intact. Pulling her hoodie off over the mask, she quickly wiped as much of the glass off the front seats as she could and the two girls clambered in. The engine roared as they drove out down the lane.

The journey seemed a blur. Elsie could barely recall the elements of it. She parked outside the coach station and they stumbled towards the first coach they saw idling.

The driver laughed. "Jesus, I can't party like that these days. A whiff of lager and I get a three-day hangover. He motioned behind him. "Go sleep it off. If you feel sick, use the toilet." He shook his head. "Kids these days. What did you get up to?"

"You don't want to know," Elsie muttered. Reaching into her pocket, she pulled out the envelope and took out a twenty. From the driver's expression, it was obvious what he thought of a girl in a bunny mask carrying an envelope of cash.

Better that than the truth.

"Just be sure to use the toilet if you feel ill," he warned.

"Don't worry about us. We haven't been drinking," Elsie meekly said. She crawled to the back of the coach. Faith worked on the leather straps of the mask with her pocket knife until the hateful thing came free. With a gasp of relief, Elsie felt the fresh air on her face as she tossed it to one side.

After a while, it was impossible to tell for how long, the coach driver yelled, "All aboard for Newcastle." The coach set off.

Hugging Faith, she felt she never wanted to let her go. Deep, wrenching sobs exploded from inside her as she realised they were free. The coach wound round the roads until it hit the first motorway. They leant against each other and slumbered as the rhythmic vibrations lulled them both to sleep.

Six hours later, the coach pulled into Newcastle coach station and the whole surreal episode continued when they were greeted by a nun.

"Elsie and Faith Peters?" she asked.

Elsie looked at the nun. She had nut-brown eyes and a warm smile, though it was ruined by a scar on her face which led from one side of her mouth up to her cheek.

"No, I don't know those names," Elsie muttered.

The nun tutted. "You shouldn't fib to a nun. Did you know the police are looking for you?" Elsie looked left and right. Her heart was pounding. "Why don't you come and stay with us for a bit? We've been expecting you."

"Who are you?" Elsie muttered.

"A nun. This isn't fancy dress. I'm from the Order of Saint Maria Goretti. We were all like you at one time before the order found us. Now we help others. My name is Sister Margaret." She proffered a hand.

Elsie bit her lip. "What if we don't want to come with you?"

"Then don't. No threats, no bribes. This is purely an offer of sanctuary with like-minded people." Sister Margaret continued to hold out her hand.

Elsie looked down at it. "Criminals, you mean?"

"Not in the eyes of St. Peter and of course, God Almighty. In their eyes, you are not a criminal. You are a victim. A victim who could save others from the same fate." She smiled. "You can leave at any time."

"Elsie, come on." Faith looked up at her, eyes pleading.

Elsie looked at Faith. She was too young to be on the run. A decision was made. She took the nun's hand. "I'm not religious, though."

Sister Margaret led her to a car where an elderly nun was waiting in the driver's seat. "Neither was I. Then life happened. Maybe it will to you, maybe it won't."

Chapter Eight

THE SINFUL CHILD

13th March, 2013: Amelia

The basement was damp and smelled of mould. The only light came in from a naked, dusty lightbulb. Its dim illumination filtered through the dangling strips of flypaper. The dank air hung thick. Spiderwebs beaded with moisture hung from the low ceiling.

Amelia had no more tears left. She stubbornly continued to flex the cable ties. Her wrists were raw, rubbed raw by the unyielding bindings. She didn't scream. Why would she? Her heartless captor upstairs was the only person within miles.

Father.

She still didn't understand why he was doing this to her.

Was he upset because she'd met someone at the sports bar?

She had gone to bed before the curfew, watched some YouTube on her phone, then woken up to find herself tied to a chair. Her head was fuzzy and she had a bitter headache. Had he drugged her?

Her clothes were rent and torn, letting in the cold, damp air. She pulled again at the plastic despite the pain.

Was it looser or was she imagining it?

Where was her mother? Where was her brother? What had he done to them?

She had thought she was dry of tears, that her dehydrated body was done with them. She was wrong. Tears welled up once again and fresh streaks ran down her cheeks. He had come down earlier, saying nothing in answer to her shouts. He'd simply thrown a bucket of water over her, gagged her and left.

Thud.

Thud.

Thud.

It was him.

Panic gripped her. Her heart was pounding, her breath was shallow and fast, and her chest hurt from the tightness round her collarbone. She tried to push up and down to turn the chair to face the stairs and see him, but failed. She tried to speak through the gag, but he had wedged it in tight.

The sound of his steps on the stairs echoed in the tiny room. He came and stood before her.

"This gives me no pleasure, but I have to stop you before you harm anyone else."

Stop me?

Then she saw the knife in his hand and began screaming. Rallying the reserves of her strength, she tried to break free.

"Stay still," he commanded.

She did not.

His hand cracked across her face in a slap, but instead of calming her, she erupted into a blind panic and pulled furiously at the cable ties.

"Stop it! I'm going to cut one of the cable ties. If you struggle, you could hurt yourself."

At that, she stilled.

What is he doing?

Holding down her right arm firmly, he cut the cable tie, then turned her wrist round. She watched him pull out a fresh cable tie. Eyes widening, she seized the moment and pulled her arm out of his grasp. He tried to grip her blood slicked wrist, but she slipped free. She saw the blade fall to the floor and reached forward for the knife.

He swore, kicking the weapon away from them both, then punched her twice in the face. Her head exploded with pain and her mouth filled with blood as he grabbed her wrist, turned it and reattached it to the chair with new cable ties.

She wept openly, eyes closed to escape the horror. When a sharp prick lanced into her forearm, her eyes flickered open to see him injecting her arm with a hypodermic needle. She screamed through the gag, bellowing with rage, fury, and fear. He withdrew the needle and released her arm as she struggled.

What was it? What had he injected into her body?

He gripped her chin and angled up her head to look into her eyes. She saw only a cold, clinical expression. This was not the father who had raised her. Her stomach muscles flexed with fear and she shuddered under his firm hand. With his other hand, he reached for something out of her line of sight, pulling out a silver cross and forcing it hard against her flesh, embedding it into her forehead with bruising force.

"I will make you right again."

She whimpered through the gag.

"Not long now, then I'll fix you for good," he said grimly. She watched him until he left her line of sight. His footsteps thumped up the stairs and back into the farmhouse.

Silence.

She was left alone to wonder what new tortures her father had in store for her, and why?

12th March, 2013: Keith

His spade slid into the pile of soil and he threw the final shovel load onto his wife's grave. Side by side with his son's remains, they lay still, the ultimate consequences of his daughter's dalliance. His shirt clung to his frame. He was soaked with sweat after his exertions. The memory of the previous night haunted him, of all the horrendous things he had been forced to do.

His mind still failed to comprehend the events.

Keith was a practical man. Physical exercise was his primary method of exorcising his mental demons. He beat the flat of the spade over the disturbed soil to firm it down, then used a bulb planter to insert garlic bulbs. He covered them with earth, using his boot. It was still the right season and, with luck, they would have a good chance of sprouting. He had nailed together wooden crosses and painted on names in crude lettering. They deserved better and would get better, but time was running out.

I can't save Jane or Ted. But maybe, if God is on my side, I can fix Amelia.

Heading back into the house, he washed his hands, neck, and face. Keith felt gaunt and stretched. He had only had four hours sleep since events overtook him and his insides felt like taut piano wire. He switched the kettle on and found a tea bag for his well-used mug.

As the kettle boiled, he consulted his notebook. He had spent most of the remainder of the night on the internet trying to make sense of it all.

Keith had been lying in bed sleeping happily. He didn't know what he had been dreaming, he only remembered waking to the screams. Flinging off the sheets while he was still half asleep, his legs had buckled under him, causing him to crash his shoulder into the door frame. Jolted into wakefulness, he had hurtled downstairs to see his daughter looming over the limp form of his son, Ted, who was still in his pyjamas. Amelia was suckling on his neck... His wife Jane had been screaming. He had turned away from the bizarre scene to see Jane snatch up a cast iron pan and charge at Amelia with tears in her eyes. He'd intercepted her and gripped her wrists, wrestling the pan from her until it fell to the floor. It was only then that he saw the blood on her face. In hysteria, she'd screamed, 'Demon!' again and again, her eyes burning with rage and terror.

He hadn't known what to do.

What do you do?

He spun round only to witness Amelia dropping the corpse of his son. A wail had escaped from the depths of his body when he saw Ted's gaunt, pale body collapse to the floor, his head twisted at an unnatural angle.

"Hungry," it - that could not be his daughter, had said. Fangs had erupted from its mouth. Its eyes glowed red. "Hungry!" It had repeated, louder and louder. Then it had leapt at Keith. To his shame, he hadn't fought bravely. In horror, he'd scooted back across the floor, begging it to stop, for Amelia to return to her senses. Jane had saved him. The pan had clanged, shattering the ghoulish scene, as it had smashed into the back of the defiled form of his daughter. Thick iron should have killed it. Any human would have sunk, submitting to the sheer ferocity of the blow. But whatever it was had only staggered. Before long, yellowed nails had flicked from dark veined hands and had torn his wife's throat out. Ruby red gore had exploded from the wound and the ravenous creature had fallen upon her dying form and noisily drained her blood.

Keith had wept with shame, fear, and anger as he swept up the pan and repeatedly bashed in the skull of his daughter. Only when the bent pan handle slipped out of his sweaty hands did he stop his relentless assault. The demonic entity, for that could be the only description of it, had fallen still. As silence fell, broken only by the rattling gasps of Keith's breathing, he saw that by some dark providence, the back of Amelia's head was bloody but intact. Her chest was still moving.

How does she still live?

He had taken cable ties from his office, dragged her down to the basement and secured her to the arms and legs of a solid wooden chair as safely as he could.

She should be dead!

Returning to the living room, Keith had found his wife hadn't been so lucky.

Perhaps it was because she had no unnatural force preserving her?

He had cradled her head and cried for... Keith didn't know how long. But when he had eventually stopped, a fierce determination had filled him.

What has done this to my family?

Keith had spent the night on the internet trying to make sense of it all. Whatever had happened to his daughter, whatever had led to the ruin of his family, he'd known he couldn't be the only person to suffer this.

He had been right.

The computer screen was bright in the encroaching darkness. Keith closed his eyes. He could hear his daughter's muffled screams from the dark basement. He was in a private Discord group belonging to The Hermetic Order of the Golden Dawn, an American group of occultists. He had gone down a Google rabbit hole, disregarding all the crackpots until he had found photos that matched almost exactly what he had seen. He was now talking to an occultist, a survivor who claimed to know of the creature which had infected his daughter.

"She still shows no sign of demonic presence?"

Keith suppressed his grief with difficulty. His mug of tea slowly turned cold next to him. "She looks just like my daughter, but terrified."

"The infected lie. You must stay strong. The presence that inhabits her is only lying dormant, waiting for its master to complete the ritual. It can take control if it has to, but it is saving its strength."

"And you are sure that she can be saved?" Keith pleaded with the stranger on the end of the keyboard.

"You tried holy water and the entity didn't ignite. You injected it with garlic infused saline and it didn't die. "

Keith nodded to his monitor. "I've done all of that."

"It is easier to think of it as an infection. Right now, the entity inside your daughter is marshalling its strength and spreading through her system. It fed last night,—"

Fed... Keith watched the text scroll across his screen as the terror from last night was reduced to such clinical terms.

"All it needs to do is to grow and wait for its progenitor to give it a final infusion. This has a twenty-four hour window. If you can keep it away for that long, then the entity within her will exhaust itself, wither and die."

He looked out of the window at the freshly dug graves of his wife Jane and his son Ted. The shadows from the wooden crosses were lengthening. Keith had little time.

Silver or fire.

That was what the occultist had said.

Keith held a pair of silver candlesticks which he had inherited from his great grandfather. He'd hammered and sanded them into crude spikes and he now sat in his chair with its back to the basement door, clutching at them for dear life.

13th March, 2013: Keith

He was expecting the windows to explode in, the door to be kicked in, or violence of some form. When the doorbell rang at just past midnight, he jumped in his seat. He could see the front door from where he was sitting and also a tall shadow behind it.

Keith couldn't swallow. His mouth was dry. This was when his daughter needed him the most, when he should rise and avenge the death of his wife and son. His hands shook as they turned white, clutching the improvised daggers. He needed the loo. He wanted to be sick.

Instead, he rose on unsteady feet and answered the door.

A gentleman in a tailored suit, with small round glasses, a white shirt and red check pocket handkerchief, greeted him with a warm smile. "Good morning, I apologise for the ghastly hour but I am here to claim the hand of your—"

Keith lunged with the candlesticks.

The gentlemen caught them in his hands. "While this cannot hurt me, I really would rather you didn't ruin my suit." He gently pushed Keith to one side and entered the house. Keith looked round wildly.

"Should I make you a cup of tea? This will all go much more smoothly if you don't struggle." The smile was still plastered on the man's face, as if this was nothing more than a casual greeting in the street. "Now then, where have you sequestered my bride? I can sense that she is here."

"These are silver..." Keith said, ignoring the question and backing towards the kitchen.

The gentleman scoffed. "Hardly. A scant amount in that alloy, I'm afraid. If it helps, my skin did itch when I touched them."

"I won't let you take my daughter." Keith stepped back towards the kitchen door.

His visitor sighed, pulling clear his pocket handkerchief and patting his lips. "You are being beastly about this, you know. This is a rare event. We don't take a bride often. Your daughter is very lucky." He looked over his glasses at Keith. "Normally, we don't have survivors. Marriage should be a much more serene event."

Keith gnashed his teeth together. He'd retrieved his silver-ish candlesticks. "And what happened to your last wife? Where is she now?" Keith said, trying to buy time as he backed away towards the kitchen sink, pulling out a bucket.

"The Dutch happened. Ghastly people. Needless to say, there is now a vacancy." He pointed to the basement door. "Down there?" He strode towards the door. He paused, flexing his shoulders. "My seventh wife, and I'm *still* nervous. It *is* a big decision, isn't it?" Keith ran at him, hatred burning behind his eyes. The water slopped over the side of the bucket.

13th March, 2013: Amelia

Her pulse quickened as she heard the sounds of a struggle upstairs.

The police?

A smile crossed her lips and her eyes narrowed.

Master.

In the back of her mind, she could feel another presence screaming as it remembered everything. It was nothing to Amelia, a mere headache, easily ignored. She could feel her teeth pushing through her gums, incisors lengthening. Looking down, she watched as her nails grew into their full glory. A ravenous thirst filled her.

Part of her was scared, disgusted even. A moment of confusion blossomed before she tamped it down. She pulled at the cable ties. Her worn wrists had already healed. She was weak, perilously weak.

Master is near. I must be with him.

She wrenched at the chair, straining new muscles that swelled within her arms like steel cord. The door blew in and her fa–Keith–collapsed down the stairs.

He is just flesh now.

Keith looked at her in despair.

It was the wood in the chair that broke first. Tearing first one arm clear, then using her nails to slice open the other cable ties, she stood.

The fight had gone out of Keith as he witnessed her transformation.

That was too much exertion, I should have waited for—

HE appeared at the top of the stairs. She fell to one knee in obeisance.

"My bride," her master purred. "You may notice my utterly drenched suit. That's because *you* left one alive." He tutted. "Clumsy, very clumsy." He walked down the stairs to loom over his defeated father-in-law. "Go on, my dear, treat yourself. I feasted on my father, you know?" He smiled. "Even then, he was bitter."

Amelia stood up, licking her lips, thirst wracking her body as she strode towards Keith, where he had fallen. He had hit his head. She could smell the blood. Her incisors bared and she lashed out with her claws.

What?

Keith's eyes blazed with pride, with happiness, as he limped to his feet, wielding both of his absurd candlestick knives.

No!

She looked at her master. His beautiful porcelain throat lay open. His precious blood flooded from the gaping wound. Keith... Father was stabbing the open wound with his sticks.

What did I do? How?

"You did it Amelia! I knew you were in there. I knew you wouldn't succumb." Keith crowed with happiness as under his relentless assault on her master... no, the creature who had drunk her blood last night at the sports bar, after he fell still, in her subconscious, she heard that voice again. It was angry, it was smug, it was victorious.

She held up her hand. From it dripped black blood. His blood.

Her tongue delicately probed the air towards it. She was so thirsty. She could smell its coppery tang, the faintest hint of sulphur, the scent of salt.

As the little voice within her that had been so powerful just moments ago realised the danger of what she intended to do. It screamed at her to stop.

She froze, paralysed by the warring sides of her mind.

Then she made her decision.

Chapter Nine

TERROR FROM THE TRASH

13th October, 2018, Great Pacific Garbage Patch

The *Anonymous Dolphin* cleaved through the open waters, a gentle thudding of debris as plastics, rubber shoes and other items slapped against the hull.

Intrepid wildlife presenter Gerald Patterson stood at the stern looking out at "The Great Pacific Garbage Patch." This was no mere ecological disaster. This was a BAFTA.

His assistant, a rather mousey looking chap called Bob, appeared at his side. "They are ready for filming, Sir."

"Very good, Bob." He accepted the proffered script and flicked through it. "This is good, very good indeed." Brushing past Bob, he swapped his all-weather jacket for his trademark corduroy blazer and life jacket. Stepping forward into the studio area, he took his position behind a desk with a beaker of rather grim-looking seawater.

"On 'one' Gerald," his director Pamela said. "Five, four, three," and then mouthed "Two, one".

"The Great Pacific Garbage Patch, perhaps the most significant ecological disaster since the hole in the ozone layer. People always envisage it as a lake of solid plastic, but whilst such items do exist in abundance, the majority of it is more insidious." With a flourish, Gerald revealed his beaker. "The seawater is turned into a soup by a dense concentration of microplastics. These cannot simply be trawled as large objects could–"

"CUT," Pamela gestured with her hand.

Gerald stopped. "What the hell, Pam! Enunciation - flawless, script - acceptable, make-up - impeccable. Was it my hair? Bob, if my hair is unkempt, I'll see you living on the streets!"

Waiting patiently for him to run out of steam, Pamela calmly pointed behind him. "That floating trash island kind of ruins your monologue. Right, we'll have to move the ship and try again."

Eyes flaring, Gerald spun and flapped his mouth at the offending anomaly before cracking his jaw shut in frustration.

An island of heaped plastic nearly fifty-foot square calmly drifted behind him.

"Unbelievable. Why haven't the tides broken it up?" he fumed.

"It could be a capsized ship?" Bob ventured.

"What a notion! A fifty-foot square ship? Nonsense Bob. Get the dingy ready. You must row me over immediately." He marched towards the boats.

"What are you doing, Gerald?" Pam asked warily.

Gerald pointed, stabbing with his fingers at the offending island. "There is a story over there and I won't be denied it, Pam. I can smell it." From the deck, the island even looked like an upturned BAFTA.

"We can all smell it, Gerald. It is rank, more to the point it isn't safe. Send Bob over first." Pam looked over at Bob apologetically, who had a reproachful look on his face.

Gerald stood with his arms crossed, his face turning a delightful shade of gammon. "Fine, but I am waiting on the boat. Get some shots of us approaching it."

The crane lowered them over the side and into the waiting boat. Bob powered the small craft over to the island and, urged on by an impatient Gerald, clambered up the side.

"Well?" Gerald snapped as Bob stood in the centre of the island.

"It's solid enough, a bit slippery. Maybe it is a dead whale whose skin has been hardened by the sun?" Bob pressed down with his leather shoe onto the inflexible floor.

"A whale, a *whale*? You insufferable boob! It would have been torn asunder by scavengers, predators and probably the Japanese." Gripping the side, Gerald climbed up. "I'm coming up. Gods, the stench. Send the camera crew over with my beaker and my desk. We'll shoot the scene here."

As the second dinghy was lowered into the water, Bob noticed the unoccupied craft drifting away. He dashed down and leapt, almost capsizing it.

"Idiot!" Gerald ranted. "Hammer a piton in and secure the line. Why am I always having to do your job for you? You useless gibbering halfwit."

Bob muttered, but acquiesced. The camera crew were just powering over as the piton was driven into the island floor. When the piton was driven deep into the mass, the water seemed to boil, four giant flippers emerged and a giant globe of a head rose out of the water. Its eyes were a solid black as it turned to face them.

"Fuck!" Gerald cried as he leapt into the dingy, almost sending Bob into the water. "Get us out of here, Bob."

Bob desperately turned on the engine and spun the small craft round for a speedy return to the *Anonymous Dolphin*. Already it was powering up in the distance.

Gerald waved his fist. "Pam! Damn your eyes, Pam, don't you dare leave me."

The island had revealed itself to be the largest turtle Gerald had ever seen. "Arcturis Gigante, it can't be. It is supposed to be extinct."

An enormous beak rose up out of the water and swallowed the dingy holding the camera crew. Gerald cried out with anguish. The scattered debris joined the rest of the Great Pacific Garbage Patch.

"I am going to get you out of this, Gerald, don't you worry, Sir," Bob said valiantly, coaxing all the power he could out of the engine.

Gerald shook his head. "The camera crew... All of them, dead."

"I know, Sir, there was nothing we could do."

Eyes watering, Gerald looked up. "All the footage is lost, all that irreplaceable footage."

Bob looked at him in disgust

"Don't judge me, you varlet. Get us to the ship. We may yet salvage this."

Gerald looked over at the turtle. "It must have been confusing the plastic bags for jellyfish. All that eating and no nourishment. It must be starving." He shivered.

The *Anonymous Dolphin* was picking up speed now. Pam threw a rope ladder over the side and Gerald lunged for it. "Keep it steady, you blithering imbecile." On his second attempt, he gripped it and began pulling himself up the side of the ship. The ladder rocked as Bob tried to ascend below him, triggering a chorus of expletives from Gerald.

As he clambered onto the deck, he saw Pam looking white-faced behind them. The powerful flippers churned the waters as the approaching turtle slowly caught up.

Bang!

Everyone stumbled as it barged under the ship and tried to capsize it.

"Weapons?" Pam trilled.

The captain patted a pistol at his side in an utterly impotent gesture.

"What do you mean, weapons? Nobody is going to harm my BAF-TA."

Pam spun, aghast. "What do you mean, BAFTA? This was to be your last episode. The BBC is dismissing you for abusive behaviour."

"Abusive? Nonsense, that is the problem with the weak, liberal bureaucrats running this company. Their woke agenda is stifling creativity–" He pointed at the giant turtle. "Why is nobody filming this? What is the first rule of journalism? *Always* be filming!"

Bob had wrapped several life jackets round a compressed gas canister. Tying the end of a rope to it, he tossed the bundle overboard. "Shoot the tank," he ordered the captain.

The captain spat on the deck and then, narrowing his eyes, aimed the pistol at the target being dragged behind them.

"Do NOT shoot my BAFTA." Gerald ran and grabbed for the gun. "I'll be untouchable when we return with footage of this. It might as well be the Kraken." As the gun to-and-froed between them, he shouted with rage. "David Attenborough can eat my hat."

The captain struggled before Bob leapt in. Balling his fist, he struck Gerald straight across the jaw. Gerald staggered back. "Bob! Why? Not my beautiful face." He sank to the ground, his eyes rolling into the back of his skull.

A thunderous report sounded as the captain took his shot, followed by a cataclysmic explosion as the compressed gas erupted.

The turtle retracted into its shell in a cloud of bubbles and sank under the waves.

The deafened crew watched in relief as the ship steadily powered away.

CHAPTER TEN

THE TATTOO

2ND FEBRUARY, 2020, A41, HERTFORDSHIRE

E lsie stood with her thumb out in the biting wind. There was blood on her face and her clothes were coated with grime. Pulling her oversized suit jacket tighter, she swore as cars screamed by in mute ignorance.

Finally, a lorry came by and slowed. She breathed a sigh of relief, opening the cabin door and clambering aboard.

The driver looked down at her and patted the seat. She smiled sweetly at him as she slid into it.

He grinned. "I ain't never picked up a girl as pretty as you before," he said.

She looked ahead. "I appreciate the lift." She avoided his gaze and focused on the road ahead. She didn't twitch a muscle when his hand slid over onto her jeans.

They remained like this for a while until he broke the silence to ask, "So, you in trouble? Because I can look after you."

"No, I'm in no danger," she said.

He laughed. "Good." Then squeezed her thigh.

She turned to him and looked straight at his face. "Do you like stories?"

He blinked at the abrupt change in direction and then listened as she narrated her tale.

A man walked into a bar. His bald head gleaming with sweat, breath ragged. A tailored suit gripped his pudgy form. A woman looked over the bar. "We're shut. Everyone has gone home."

The man strode up to the counter. "You haven't," he thudded a fifty-pound note down. "Double Lagavulin 16, no ice." He took off his tiny circular glasses as sweat rolled down his face.

"We don't serve alcohol after eleven, Mister," she said.

He pointed at a sign saying the bar closed at midnight. "Keep the change."

She swore under her breath, then swiped the fifty and started searching the bottles for the Lagavulin. Eventually, she found it and free-poured a large whisky.

"New here?" he asked as he shook off his jacket. He hung it on a Chelsea hook under the bar.

She cocked an eyebrow. "You could say that."

Going to replace the bottle on the shelf, she changed her mind, returning to pour an extra glass for herself.

"Largest double I've ever seen. Not that I'm complaining."

She smiled, gazing evenly at him, then knocked it back in one slug.

"Whoa, hold your horses. It is a sipping drink." He laughed. "Now, you'll need another one."

She cocked an eyebrow at him. Then poured another. She walked round the bar to the front door and clicked the lock shut.

He pursed his lips and reached for a handkerchief to mop his brow. "I thought you were shut."

She smiled. As she walked over, she hoisted herself onto a barstool. "You just won yourself a ticket to the lockdown." She raised her glass and they clinked.

"My name is Dennis," he said.

The lorry driver waited. Then blinked. "That's it? My God. That be a terrible story." He laughed. "Just as well you be so very, very pretty. You won't be getting no job as a writer." He shook his head, saying mockingly. "My name is Dennis?" What kind of story ends with that as a punchline?"

They drove in silence for a while. She could feel the sweat from his clammy palms through her jeans. "Ok, here be a story for you. I've heard a few in my time as a lorry driver. We boys do like to banter."

He sat back in silence for a while as if savouring the moment. "Dave. He was called Dave. A long haul petrol tanker from Hull. He was a cheeky one, that one. Must have been about twenty years ago. He had a skinhead and a nose ring. Real hellraiser. See now, he had a lot of tattoos but one of them he was really, really proud of." He reached down beside him and pulled up a handful of crisps and munched on them noisily. When his feast had subsided he slapped his shoulder. "Big one it was. It be Satan himself, all red and horned with a goatee. Smoking a cigarette. Real classy job it was. Always looked like the devil be looking right at you, mocking you when you saw it, made me shudder every time. No matter what angle, it were like the eyes were always watching you"

He paused for dramatic effect. "See, he be a cheeky one. Used to say that he was immortal. Never got hangovers no matter how long we drank. His secret be, that although he professed that his soul belonged to him and him alone, his body belonged to the devil. The devil wouldn't brook no harm to its property, so he said."

He glanced over at her then returned his gaze back to the road. "We be in a convoy. He be in his oiler. I be a few lorries back in mine. Out of the blue, boom, it just blew up." He gestured with his hand and made an explosive sound. "Total fireball. I slammed on my brakes, only just stopped in time. It be so hot I couldn't approach. It be only after the fire brigade had put out the blaze that I was called to identify the body. You wouldn't have thought that there would be anything to identify and you'd be mostly right. The body was roasted. Third-degree burns all over it, it be a mess. But the policeman, he pointed at the body and one part be unburnt. His shoulder. That bloody devil be grinning right back at me, surrounded by a patch of flawless skin, flush as a baby's bum. You see my mate be right. The devil did protect his earthly body, just only the bit that he be living on." Silence filled the cab. The driver burst out laughing. "Now that be a story, that be a real story. Look at your face. Oh, your face." Her face had remained impassive throughout the story. He indicated and pulled into an off-ramp.

"Where are you going?" she asked.

He smirked, saying nothing.

"Where are you going?" she repeated.

"Well, you're gonna be helping me out, aren't you? I be giving you a lift. The least you can do is give me a favour."

She turned to him. "Wait. I missed out the important bit of my story. It is also about a tattoo."

He sighed theatrically.

"Nobody cares about your story." He pulled into a layby, branches screeching along the sides of the lorry.

"Oh, it's really good. I promise. The second half doesn't make sense without the first half. You won't hear a better story for the rest of your life."

He sat quietly, watching her.

"Fine." He relented.

A girl walked into a bar. The bar was empty apart from a muscular barman, his white vest barely containing his taut musculature. The jukebox in the corner tried valiantly to fill the void with 'The Police - Every Breath You Take' but ended up emphasising it. The barman smiled at her as she strutted to the bar. A wry smile dripped from her cherry red lips. "A glass of rosé, please." She looked over at the No Smoking sign and pulled a face. She slid onto one of the bar stools.

The barman winked at her. "You here alone?"

"Alone and with no plans to change that. Why?" she asked. An eyebrow arched up.

"Because that answer just got you a free drink, that's all." He smiled. His face would have been regarded as classically handsome if it wasn't for the eyes. They were dead. Coal suspended in chalk. "It is your lucky night." He turned to pour the wine. Out of sight, he dropped a white powder into her drink and stirred until it vanished into the amber coloured wine.

"It's a special night for you too," she said. Flicking her hair back, she slid her trench coat open, exposing her collarbone. A tattoo of a ring impaled by a crucifix stood out prominently. She rifled inside her jacket's pocket.

"Oh yes, and why is that?" he said. He leaned forward. She pulled out a series of polaroids and tossed them onto the bar. "Because the Order of Saint Maria Goretti wants to reward your efforts."

He looked at the polaroids blankly for a while until he recognised the faces of several girls he had drugged in the past. A growl stuck in his throat as, looking up, he saw her hand flicker and a stiletto slid through the layers of muscle and cartilage. Leaping down from the stool, she swiftly moved behind the bar, lowering his twitching body as he tried to pull out the knife. As his body slumped to the ground, he finally succeeded. His wound sprayed her with arterial blood as he exsanguinated. She muttered in distaste, taking the long trench coat off and using it to cover up the corpse. Picking up the polaroids, she scattered them over his body. Picking up a bar towel, she rubbed her face clean of blood. Seeing her makeup on the towel, she grabbed another and rubbed until she had removed the rest of it, then tossed both towels down.

"So, how does that relate?" He huffed. "They are two different, very mediocre stories." He slid his hand between her thighs. "And you shoehorned in that tattoo. It had no relevance to the plot. You just added it because my story had a tattoo."

She gently covered his hand with hers. "Thirty seconds. Just thirty seconds and then you'll get the reward that you so richly deserve. That was the beginning of the story. You have heard the middle. Here is the end."

The lorry driver wasn't even listening anymore as his breath ran hot in anticipation.

The girl laughed raucously as Dennis narrated a tale of his last board meeting.

"Sounds like they deserved that." Her eyes twinkled.

"And you don't think I was too harsh?" he asked, swilling the last remnants of the whisky round in the glass.

"Not at all. I am a firm believer in rough justice."

"Gods, I wish I wasn't married and was twenty years younger." He poured another measure from the bottle into each of their glasses, finishing off the bottle. "Now, tilt the glass and follow my lead. If you smell the bottom of the glass, you will get a completely different scent from the top of the glass. This is called the low and the high notes."

She cocked her eyebrow and then shrugged. Lifting her glass, she tried what Dennis suggested and her eyes widened. "It is sweeter at the top."

He laughed.

She stood up. "That whisky has gone right through me. I'm going to powder my nose. Do not move." As she turned, she called over her shoulder. "I mean it, Dennis. Do not move a muscle."

The scotch was flowing through him and he felt warm and happy. Dennis glugged the last of his whisky and smacked his lips together with satisfaction. He looked at the empty bottle and made an executive decision. He peeled off two more fifties and put them on the bar, weighing them down with the empty bottle. As he rounded the bar, he saw the corpse of the bartender. "Fuck," he said. "Fuck," he repeated, backing away. He felt a sharp pain in his ribs.

"You should have listened to me, Dennis," she said. "I liked you, I really did, but nothing gets in the way of the mission." She extracted her knife from between his third and fourth ribs, where it had plunged deep into his heart. Wiping it clean on a bar towel, she looked down at the two dead bodies. A waste. She picked up Dennis's jacket from where it was hanging, wrapped it round herself to keep out the cold, and left the building.

Snow crunched underfoot as Detective Jeffrey Davis approached the cordoned-off area. One of the officers peeled away from the crowd, taking, securing and collecting evidence.

"What do we have here, then?"

The young constable pulled out his notebook. "A middle-aged lorry driver called Frederick Black identified visually using his driving licence. The cause of death is a single stab wound to the chest. He doesn't appear to have tried to defend himself, so we assume he knew his attacker. The cabin is littered with polaroids of dead women. They are trying to identify them at the moment." He looked up from his notebook to see the Detective cursing.

"They'll be female victims of rape and murder. This is the third murder in as many days matching the same criteria." He looked over at where the traffic was driving past them. "I don't doubt the killer has only just begun their spree."

Chapter Eleven

THE
TOKOLOSHE

11th April, 2015, Johannesburg

Tap. Tap. Tap.

The shaman sat patiently smoking a roll-up as Wikus updated his Facebook status.

Finally, putting down his phone, he looked at the shaman, who seemed nonplussed by this intrusion.

"I heard you can get rid of people and make it seem like natural causes.," Wikus threw at him.

The shaman nodded ploddingly, as though in a torpor.

Wikus snapped his fingers. "Focus man! Christ..." He tossed a photograph of a smartly dressed man. "My brother inherited everything. I need him gone."

A toothy grin gradually spread across the shaman's face. His eyes remained unfocused.

His voice was deep and slow. "You wish to loose a Tokoloshe?"

Raising his eyebrows, Wikus gave a frustrated sigh. "Whatever you call the serviceman. Demon, assassin, witch, I don't care. Just get my brother gone."

The shaman's eyes focused for the briefest of moments, causing Wikus to jump as they locked eyes in a moment of clearest clarity. "The Tokoloshe must be paid. Otherwise, in five years hence, it will seek out that which you love the most and take it from you."

Snorting, Wikus said mockingly, "Jokes on you, old man, I don't love anything. I am untouchable."

The shaman cackled.

Wikus tossed down fifty thousand rand in front of him, in several stacks of notes. "Perhaps the tokawoka will take cash?"

Hurriedly gathering up the money, the shaman grew serious. He hid the money in a metal toolbox that looked seriously out of place amongst all the tribal aesthetics.

"Get it done," Wikus said as he turned and left.

11th April, 2020, New York

Outside, the night sky was black vellum dusted with diamonds. Inside, smooth jazz was playing as the family sat round the dining table waiting quietly, watching as a whole roast salmon was being portioned in front of them by Jones, their butler.

Wikus surveyed his family with his feet up, smoking a cigar. "Why is everyone so quiet?" They looked down at their plates and refused to make eye contact.

"Tracy, tell me, did you like the dress I bought for you?"

His wife raised her head and managed a wan smile. "It was beautiful. Thank you so much, darling."

A hard edge crept into his voice. "And yet you don't appear to be wearing it."

Tracy froze. "I didn't want to get any mess on it."

Wikus laughed, "Now that's what I'm talking about, some respect."

A collective gasp of relief was released by his family as he reached for his wine.

Suddenly, spitting his wine out, he yelled, "What was that?" He could have sworn that, for just one moment, he had seen a tiny, hairy child facing away from him. When he blinked, it was gone.

His family was frozen in terror.

"What are you looking at? Eat your dinner." Pulling out a small silver pen, he undid the back of it. It unscrewed to reveal a small cocaine spoon laden with white powder. He snorted it straight up his nose and smiled.

Wikus just needed to relax. His mind was playing tricks on him.

He swore and put his feet up on the table, almost knocking over his wine glass. His family poked at their food in silence and pretended not to notice. Taking a long drag from his cigar, he billowed smoke across the table and his family.

Pushing back his untouched dinner, he got up, a sudden wave of paranoia washing over him. As he walked towards the stairs, he looked back. He saw the child again. This time it was sitting at the dining table facing away from him. Wikus ran back into the dining room, roaring, but it was gone. Between blinks, it had just ceased to exist. His family was now absolutely terrified. He kicked at the chair and left the dining room looking for sanctuary in his office.

Storming up to his safe, he keyed in the code, opened the door and looked with satisfaction, even adoration, at the neatly stacked gold bars and piles of sovereigns. Mentally, he counted the bricks of cocaine as he retrieved his pistol. His mind reflected back to the shaman. Was that a tokowoka? Was that what the man had called it? It must have been about five years ago when the deal had been done.

Let it come for his family. He didn't need them. If it came for him, then he would be ready. He took another bump of cocaine. Wikus feared no one.

"Jones," he called out, "Get this place in lockdown mode, nobody in, nobody out. I want the boys looking for intruders."

Sitting in his office, he waited. Tomorrow, he would make the biggest deal of his life. Nothing and nobody must be allowed to derail that. He reached over to a bottle of bourbon and poured an inch into his glass. Come on then, he mused darkly.

As he plotted, he drank. Eventually, even the cocaine couldn't keep him awake and he nodded off. He fell into a deep sleep, which was haunted by vivid dreams of a shrunken hairy child with a swollen belly and both its eyes put out with thick iron nails. A bullet hole in its forehead leaked black ichor.

He woke to darkness. He rubbed his eyes. The silence was deafening. No birds, no electrical gadgets, no heaters clanking. Raw silence. "Jones!" The sound of his own voice startled him. The bourbon was sour in his belly as he took two immediate snorts of cocaine to steady himself. He sounded shrill as he called out. Checking the safety of his pistol, he got up. He tried the desk lamp. No power. "Jones!"

The doorbell sounded, the bell blasting through his consciousness and echoing. "Jones, the door!" Cursing, he stumbled towards the front door, feeling his way down the stairs. Where was the power? Where were his men? A cold sweat prickled his back.

Reaching the front door, he kept one hand on his pistol. Where were his men?

With some hesitation, he opened it. He exhaled a breath he didn't know he had taken.

It was Tony's boys. The deal. At least it meant he had some muscle with him. He coughed to cover his anxiety. "Follow me."

The men commented on the dark. One of them used his smartphone to shine a torch.

Wikus entered his office first. He froze when he saw that the safe door now swung wide open. Worse than that, there was now nothing in it. It had to be Jones. Nobody else had access to his safe.

"You act like a person who is going to make Tony very upset, Mr Wikus." The cold voice floated from behind his shoulder.

He snarled and spun. "It is just Wikus."

The two men were spreading out. They had their pistols aimed at him. "Right now, I get the feeling that we can call you whatever the fuck we like, Mr Wikus."

Moving behind his desk, his hands in the air, he managed a sickly grin that turned into abject terror. Pointing behind them, he cried, "Look!"

They didn't look. They didn't even twitch as they gunned him down.

Behind them, the Tokoloshe just watched, its hideous face devoid of any expression.

Tracy lay in the motel, her arms wrapped protectively round her two sleeping children. She was exhausted, yet sleep eluded her. Was that? Yes, in the shadows. Suddenly, she froze with fear, a scream locked in her throat. An eyeless, hairy grotesque was waddling towards her. It stood for a while, watching her. Then, without a single word, it placed a wooden box full of gold sovereigns next to her bed and softly padded back into the shadows.

CHAPTER TWELVE

THE HEIR APPARENT

29th April, 2022, London

Keith looked down at his phone. A text message blinked back at him from his mother. "What did they say? Did you get the job?" He swiped ignore and nervously took a champagne flute from a black suited waiter. The room was filled with white-clothed tables arranged with crystal ware and filled with exotic dishes. The guests were impeccably dressed, if somewhat old-fashioned. Every hair was in place, every suit pressed, every tie knotted perfectly. But then, he'd expect nothing less from the upper management and investors of The Lion Group. Keith looked down at his suit from Primark.

At least it fits me well.

Light jazz music played, just staying audible over the sounds of ribald celebration. Alfred Winterton stood near the stage. His suit might

be almost identical to the grey men surrounding him, but his presence
dominated the group. A large, beaming smile spread across his face
as he laughed and talked with the guests. His wife Vivienne stood to
the side of him. Keith remembered her. She had been a professional
model and actress in her twenties. Now, at sixty, she was still a fash-
ionable woman. Her black evening gown offset her blonde hair. He
remembered her as being the only one of the Wintertons who didn't
look down on him. Keith timidly sipped his champagne. The liquid
bubbled in his throat. He had only seen the Wintertons a few times, at
funerals and weddings. His grandmother was Alfred's estranged sister
and he had never quite fitted in with his loud, confident cousins.

"Wuss?" He turned to see his cousin Jeremiah addressing him.
Keith looked straight into his cousin's red tinted glasses, the small,
round spectacles giving him an almost vampiric gleam. "My god, it
is you! Wuss! Look at you in your... Did you actually buy that suit
from a shop?" Jeremiah poked the suit. "You look like an estate agent.
Is that... polyester?" Jeremiah's suit was tailored so tightly it clung to
him like a second skin.

"Hello Jeremiah," Keith said with a forced smile. "It is good to see
you again."

"We all assumed you'd died." Jeremiah tapped his shoulder, leading
him over to where a group of young siblings were standing and laughing.

They watched curiously as he approached. "Hey, everyone, it's the
original Soy Boy, Wuss."

"Don't be a jerk, Jerry," Jeremiah's brother Harold said. Where
Jeremiah was lean, Harold was a great, red, bacchanalian wine-skin
of a man. He clinked Keith's glass happily. "How are you doing? We
haven't seen you for years. Is Auntie Susan still crusading to free the

cows?" His jowls jingled with the enthusiasm of a man who hasn't held back on the wine.

"Erm, she is a vegan, yes. She doesn't really crusade though, mostly just reads books." Keith smiled nervously. "She doesn't know that I'm here."

"Oh, you scoundrel, Wuss!" Jeremiah's eyes lit up. "Sassing your own mother, good man."

Keith shifted awkwardly. "I was hoping I could get a job, actually, learn how it all works in the city. There isn't much to do on my mother's farm."

"Two simple words for you, Keith. Co Caine," Jeremiah confided.

"That is one word, you idiot." Harold laughed through a smoked trout blini. Bits of dough dribbled down his chins.

Keith reached for a mini Yorkshire pudding, then, seeing the roast beef in it, retracted his hand.

"Wait, you want to be a city boy, but you are *still* vegan?" Jeremiah called out to the crowd. "Can you credit him?" Scattered polite laughter followed. "Oh, I have missed this. I *am* getting you a job, Wuss. In fact, you are going to work for me directly. I am going to teach you what it means to be a city boy."

"Oh, you don't need... I will work anywhere really—" Keith started.

Harold clapped him on the back. "Stick with us Keith, we are going to make you filthy rich."

"Disgustingly rich," Jeremiah embellished. "Dad is going to announce me as the new CEO. We are going to celebrate."

On cue, the tickling of a teaspoon on a champagne flute caught everyone's attention and the room fell silent.

A grey-haired, older man ascended the podium. The music slowly died down. "Thank you all for attending." Keith recognised his great uncle, Alfred. "I will keep this short so that you can get back to drinking my champagne." The crowd gathered round him and laughed. "Fifty years ago I founded The Lion Group. In that time, we have made a lot of rich people considerably richer." A cheer reverberated round the room. He wafted it away. "I have always had a way with numbers. I have always seen the connections between them. Growing portfolios is like breathing for me." He paused and looked down at the audience. Jeremiah moved to the side of the podium. "Which is why, after much deliberation, I have made the hard decision to stay on as CEO. I want to reassure everyone that after the recent turbulence, we will be returning to our traditional roots and values."

Jeremiah froze next to the wooden podium, a sickly grin on his face. As everyone applauded, he flinched, his expression spreading as he slowly joined in with the clapping. His father whispered into his ear and Jeremiah nodded politely before returning to Harold and Keith.

Harold peered across his wineglass at his brother. "Did you kno—"

Jeremiah visibly fumed through his fixed grin. His expression, complete with bulging eyes, had morphed into more of a friendly snarl. "Of course, I didn't fucking know. Let's get the hell out of here. I need a bump. You too, Wuss." He turned to one of the staff. "Get a car waiting outside."

"Oh, I need to get my coat," Keith said.

"Fucking leave it." Jeremiah stopped and blinked at him. "Why would you even own a coat?"

The boys were up in "The Loft," a private terrace overlooking the main nightclub at Babylon. The air was thick with the scent of sweat, smoke, and a mixture of sweet and sour alcohol.

Drum and bass music complemented the strobing lights as they reclined on leather sofas. The group was expanding. Jeremiah's friends had all come along with expectations to celebrate his ascension. The family left Keith to introduce himself to them.

Anna, his cousin, was the only one he'd met before. She wore a black dress with a plunging neckline and sleeves that stopped mid-arm. Anna greeted him warmly, "It is so good to see you Keith, I'm a vegan too now." She reached down and picked up a smoked salmon crudité.

"Oh, I think that has fish on it," Keith said rapidly.

"I know. What is your point?" Anna said. Her warmth dissipated as she lifted her lip in disdain and turned away to speak to one of Jeremiah's friends, addressing him as Terence.

Terence was trying to engage unsuccessfully with Jeremiah, who was staring at the dancers below them with a stormy expression.

"This won't affect the acquisition, will it? I don't need to worry, do I?" Terence tried, his oversized shirt billowing in the air conditioning.

Jeremiah turned slowly. "Fuck the acquisition. This was my moment. He knew he wasn't going to pass the company onto me and he didn't warn me. I looked like an idiot." He jabbed his finger at Harold. "Did you know about this? This... calculated humiliation?"

Harold shook his head.

"You know what annoys me the most?" Jeremiah fumed. "Our share price has already risen. Risen! Father is a dinosaur. He completely missed Bitcoin in 2012. I've spent six months on the CorduroyCoin acquisition. We are days away from completion. If he thinks I am going to—" he pointed at one of Terence's friends, a saggy, jowled hipster with a man bun. "Look at that. It is an author. It even made it into the

New York Times bestseller category. You know how? Not because it sells books. I don't even know its name."

"My name is Charles X. Cross," the author offered.

"Don't talk to me. Literally, nobody gives a fuck," Jeremiah snarled. "The point is that it was an early adopter of CorduroyCoin. It re-mortgaged its mother's house and used the money to buy crypto. Now, it's a multimillionaire and can afford to buy ten thousand of its own books to rot in a warehouse." Jeremiah stabbed his finger into the man's ill-fitting jacket. "If idiots like that can make money, then why can't my father?"

Harold raised his glass. "Jerry, you will be the CEO of The Lion Group. To Jerry everyone."

Everyone raised their glasses.

"It is fucking Jeremiah! Stay on brand," Jeremiah shouted.

"To Jeremiah," the group chorused.

"Here you go, brother." Harold passed him a silver case. "It'll smooth you out." Jeremiah accepted the case and opened it. Inside was a mirrored surface, a silver cylinder, and a matching straw. He poured out a line of cocaine, then used one of his business cards to shape it.

Jeremiah rejected the silver straw, "Who has a ten-pound note? Only rich arseholes use custom straws. Ten-pound notes are trending right now." There were a series of head shakes round the group. "Come on, I obviously don't carry cash because I'm not a fossil."

"I only carry fifties," Terence said apologetically.

Keith coughed. "I have a tenner." He proffered up a wrinkled note from his pocket.

Jeremiah looked at it in horror. "What is that diseased offering? Do you want to give me botulism? That is disgusting. I meant a fresh one." He picked up the silver straw and did a line. Eyes flaring as the cocaine immediately hit. "You've embarrassed yourself today, Wuss. Learn from this."

Leaning back, Jeremiah's pupils dilated. "Fuck Father. Let's have a good time, shall we?" He raised his champagne and gave a toast. "Fuck Father!" Swigging half the glass, he giggled. A nihilistic gleam came into his eye. "Fuck father, fuck father!" He beat on the table until everyone else took up the rhythm. Abruptly, he stopped. "I'll have my time and I'll have it soon." He surged up onto his feet, mania in his grin. "Now, where are the girls? Let's all have some fun!" Terence spoke to one of the staff members who opened a red rope, letting up a cadre of scantily clad dancers. "That's what I'm talking about. Wuss, this is London."

Keith's eyes widened. The women were in tight red corsets and matching thongs. They swayed their hips to the music. Wearing barely anything, their skin glistened under the spotlights. The scent of perfumed oil was thick. Keith had experienced nothing like this before. Life was simple, back on the farm.

30th April, 2022, London

Keith woke up on a leather sofa in Harold's penthouse off St. Katherine's Docks. His stomach roiled. His face had adhered itself to the sofa and pulled away with a sucking sound. He tried to get up but was assaulted by a wave of dizziness and nausea. He collapsed back down, breathing deeply, until the feeling had passed.

He looked round. He was in a large open plan living room, with floor-to-ceiling windows that offered a panoramic view of the yachts. A sleek, black grand piano sat in the middle of the room.

Keith staggered over to the window and looked outside. The sun was rising over the water. The orange light on the horizon was turning the water into a golden liquid. He watched as a man in a high-vis vest walked by, dragging a pair of wheelie bins behind him.

"This will sort you out." Keith jumped. He hadn't seen Harold's chef moving round the far side of the room where a kitchen stood. The chef cracked open a series of eggs for breakfast omelettes. The scent of strong black coffee reached him from across the room.

Keith realised with horror that despite being fully clothed in his shirt and jacket, he was wearing no trousers. He looked down at his white legs. He looked round the room for them, to no avail.

The chef pointed to the other side of the room where a change of clothes was hanging. "Almarta, put those there for you. She is getting your trousers dry cleaned."

"She didn't undress me while I was sleeping, did she?" Keith asked, a mounting horror building within him.

The chef laughed. "No, of course not. She came in and cleared up all the mess this morning. If you wanted someone to undress you, that would cost extra."

Keith nodded, relieved. "I am still trying to figure out how everything works. I didn't grow up with all this."

The chef laid out an omelette and coffee for him. He placed a small glass of thick green liquid next to it.

"I can't eat omelettes," Keith said apologetically.

Harold walked in wearing a fresh suit, wincing at the lights. "Don't insult the chef, Keith. Eat the omelette and put on some damned trousers."

"How are you not hungover?" Keith said as he sat down, the scent of food turning his stomach.

Harold looked at him, unimpressed. "Poor people get hangovers, Keith. Not us. We have cocaine. In ancient times, they prescribed it as a cure-all. If you'd studied history at school, you'd be okay today." Smiling sympathetically at him, he pulled out a small case similar to the one used last night. "If you are going to work with us, you'll need to get your own supply. Talk to Jeremiah's secretary, Susan." He offered it to Keith. "Do you have a place to live in the city?"

Keith shook his head, eyeing up the cocaine dubiously.

"Well, you can't live here. People will think you are a refugee. Jeremiah's secretary will sort you out with a hotel room." Harold picked up an espresso cup, ignoring his breakfast, and downed the coffee in one. "I have a breakfast date. I'll see you in the office on Monday." He swiped the silver case back from a hesitant Keith.

"Oh, I haven't had any."

"You snooze, you lose, cousin, I'm running late. Last word of advice: Never show weakness to Jeremiah. In our family, they eat weak people and shit them out. We have no time for them." Harold gave him a last pat on the shoulder and swooped out of the house, leaving a stillness in his wake.

"Finish your breakfast and make yourself scarce," the chef said. "Master Winterton will be bringing back company and it wouldn't do for you to still be here."

Keith nodded, cutting into his omelette. The centre was runny and oozed onto the plate.

The chef placed two slices of granary toast spread with jam in front of Keith, picked up his plate with the omelette and took it away. "They won't hear from me that you didn't eat it."

Keith smiled gratefully and munched on the toast, the dry food soaking up the sour remnants of last night's drinking.

His phone beeped again. Keith looked down to see six missed calls and eleven text messages from his mother. Finishing his jam and toast gratefully, he ignored the green smoothie. He rose and left the building. The cold air felt heavenly on his face.

His phone started ringing again. "Hello Mum," he said, eyes closed and turning to face the breeze.

"How did it go? Did you find a job? It's not too late to apply to Sainsburys." Desperation leaked out of her voice.

"I'm not working at a till Mum. That won't do us much good. It went well with them—I think the family are making me a personal assistant," Keith said. "That should be enough to make the bank happy."

"When will you see the contract?"

Keith realised one side of his face had gone numb. He poked his cheek. This was possibly the worst hangover he had ever had.

"Keith? Can you hear me?"

"Sorry Mum, yeah, I can hear you. I am in the office tomorrow, so I'll probably see it then. But Mum, they are worse than I remember."

"Lots of people don't enjoy their job, Keith, just do your best with them. Your dad crippled himself to keep up the mortgage payments."

Keith had spied a Pret in the distance. "Don't worry, Mum, I am going to save the farm. I have my priorities in order."

"Family first Keith—"

"I have to go, Mum, but I'll speak to you later. Give my love to Dad." Keith hung up and walked over to Pret to buy another coffee on his credit card. Slumping down with it, he opened an app on his phone to find a cheap local hotel. Zero results. With resignation, he increased the budget and the distance until he found a hostel in Euston. That would do for the night. He then realised that he had no suit trousers, just the outfit he had borrowed from Harold. Keith loaded up his phone again, this time to find a Primark nearby. Oxford street... He left Harold's penthouse, slumped in the lift he made plans to head towards the closest tube station.

2nd May, 2022, London

On Monday morning, Keith presented himself at The Lion Group head office at a quarter to nine. His jacket was as clean as he could make it and he sported a brand new white shirt and trousers from Primark. The trousers were a little big on him, but it was the best he could do.

His heart was racing as he stepped through the door. He smoothed down his jacket and walked across the lofty entrance hall over to the receptionist. "I have an appointment with Jeremiah." He beamed expectantly at the unimpressed secretary.

She dialled a number and spoke to someone on the phone, then turned to Keith with a bored expression. "There is nothing in his diary."

"Would you mind calling Jeremiah directly for me, please? Perhaps he just needs reminding. We had a heavy night on Friday night."

She laughed at him. "You want me to call up the Chief Financial Officer of The Lion Group? If he wanted to speak to you, it would be in his diary or he would have given you his number." Her colleague next to her was sanding her nails.

"Wait. He said I would work directly for him. Perhaps someone in HR..."

"Sir, I am going to have to ask you to leave." The secretary looked over at the security guards near the entrance.

Keith looked round, frustrated.

"Sir..."

"I'm going." Keith turned and moved towards the door.

I can't give up. There is too much riding on this.

Keith opened his phone again and looked for the closest charity shop. He found a pair of battered Patrick O"Brien paperbacks to pass the time and nursed another coffee in Pret. He waited until five and then headed back to Harold's apartment. Chiming the bell, he found nobody in and sat on the front doorstep reading. He ate his way through a pack of sandwiches as he ploughed through his books, his earlier despondency buried beneath the tales of life at sea.

His mother interrupted his reading with a text. "How is it going? xx"

He deliberated, then decided to lie. "Great, but really busy. Can't talk. I'll phone when I get a chance." He leaned back with his head against the door and hoped that the next time she called, the lie would have become a truth.

Keith checked the time on his phone.

Six, Harold must be working late.

Harold didn't return until just after ten. A car pulled up outside. Keith watched as Harold staggered out of the car and down the path with a slender brunette on his arm.

Keith stood up nervously.

This might be awkward.

"What the—Keith? I'm a bit busy now, old boy. What the devil are you doing?"

Harold turned to the brunette and explained, "This is my cousin. He is very country. He doesn't understand city life."

"I went to the office today and they wouldn't let me in," Keith admitted. "I told them I was supposed to work for Jeremiah, but they didn't believe me. They wouldn't even put me through to him."

"That is ridiculous," Harold said. "Look cousin, turn up tomorrow and show them this. It's my card. They'll let you up to see me." He looked Keith up and down. "Actually, they'll probably think you stole it. Just make sure you are in the lobby for eight. I'll vouch for you when I get in. Don't be late. I won't hang round."

The girl whispered to Harold. He shook his head. "Nah, I am not calling Susan. It'll be simpler just to sort this in the morning."

Keith held out his hand. "Thank you. That means so much, whatever you can do."

"Trust me, you don't want to shake these hands." Harold looked at the girl and laughed. "But this is exactly what I was saying about weakness. You need to learn how the city works and fast, Keith, or it'll spit you out."

Keith nodded. "I won't let you down."

Harold looked at him incredulously. The audience over, he looked at his companion. "The things he says," and then opened up the door, leaving Keith outside.

Keith sighed. He should have bought another shirt. He'd have to wash this one in the sink. There wasn't time to get it laundered or replaced.

How will I iron it?

Grimly, he figured he would have to stump up the credit for a Travelodge. That was an expensive mistake.

Tomorrow I'll buy a cheap iron.

Picking up his books, he strode off towards the nearest Travelodge. It wasn't far, and on the way, he found a burger joint. *Hot food!* After a day of sandwiches, he was gasping for a decent meal. He ordered a falafel bap with chips and carried it back to the hotel. In order to protect his clothes, he sat on the bed in his underwear as he hungrily devoured it.

3rd May, 2022, London

The next day, he approached the front desk again, this time at a quarter to eight. The same secretary raised an eyebrow at him.

"I have been asked to wait here until Harold comes in. He is going to vouch for me."

"You know, if any of them wanted to see you, they could just ask their secretaries to make an appointment," she said.

Keith snorted. "I genuinely don't think it occurred to them." His face slipped back into a deferential expression. "They are very busy."

Softness crept into the flawlessly made-up face and the secretary gestured to the seats. "Yes, they are. You can wait over there."

"Thank you."

Keith didn't have long to wait. Just before eight o'clock Jeremiah swept in, his personal assistant following in his wake bearing a coffee. "Jeremiah, wait," Keith said, his urgency making his voice overly loud.

"Wuss? What are you doing here? Why are you sitting in the cheap seats?" Jeremiah blinked incredulously and headed for the lifts.

Keith scampered after him. "You mentioned a job."

"Oh yes, you were supposed to be here yesterday. Were you still hungover from Saturday? You need to man up, Wuss, if you are going to be my bitch."

The lift doors opened and Keith joined Jeremiah inside. Jeremiah pressed the button for the top floor.

"Are there any more details about my job? Because I need a contract to show the bank."

Jeremiah looked at Keith, comprehension slowly dawning. "Are you poor?"

"It's for the mortgage on the farm. Dad lost his job, so I gave up college to get a job in the city—"

Jeremiah cut in. "Forget I asked. I didn't want an audio narration of Dickens. Susan, get Wuss set up with a band three job in business ops. He can get a desk near you, find him something to do."

Susan nodded obsequiously at Jeremiah, then directed a venomous glance sideways at Keith.

Great. Making friends already.

Jeremiah had put his ear buds in and was gently nodding his head, presumably to some kind of music.

When the lift doors opened, Jeremiah marched straight out and down the hallway to the CFO's office. The door closed behind him, leaving Keith to stand looking at it. Susan took the only chair at the desk outside.

"I'll just get a chair and bring it over," Keith said.

"No, you won't. This is my desk." Susan thought for a moment. "You can stay in the kitchen until we find you a place to sit."

"In the kitchen. What will I do?"

"Drink coffee? The pastries are excellent. I'll print out some health and safety documents for you to review."

Keith thanked her and walked towards the kitchen. The coffee and pastries were delicious. After a few minutes, Harold walked in.

"Keith, you made it! Good man." Harold grabbed a pastry. "Do you have a desk yet?"

"Erm, not yet, no," Keith said, aimlessly following Harold out into the corridor.

"Susan," Harold called out down the corridor. "Keith is with me until he gets set up."

Harold led Keith into his office. Picking up the remote, he turned on a large screen at the end of the room and switched to Netflix, watching "Rick and Morty." His personal assistant arrived with a large coffee. "The apple danishes are the best." He chuckled at the television.

Keith was enjoying a blueberry muffin. He didn't think too hard about whether it contained eggs. It was delicious and he was starving. He murmured his approval.

Harold's phone buzzed. Reaching down, he looked at the screen. "Oh, no." He barely had time to place it back on the desk before the thundering sound of bespoke shoes thudded down the hallway and his office door burst open.

Jeremiah was grinning maniacally. "Did you see Anna's text? The old goat has got Covid! He is on a ventilator."

"Uncle Alfred?" Keith asked with concern.

"Who else would we give a fuck about? You know what this means?" Jeremiah preened. "I am the acting CEO while he breathes through a tube. The deal can continue!"

"We should visit, pay our respects." Harold whispered.

Jeremiah blinked. "Pay our... Harold, you absolute fanny, what part of plague do you not get?" He raced back into the corridor. "Susan, cancel all my meetings. Get Terence in. Arrange for a board meeting tomorrow and get some champagne. My brother is in a grump." He popped his head back into the office. "Big things, this could be a sea change for the organisation."

His wild-eyed gaze disappeared, leaving the television to fill the void.

"He'll be alright," Keith said.

"I know that," Harold snapped. "He is a battle axe. He is the strongest man I know." His eyes didn't match the optimism of his words. They were shadowed.

Susan brought in a bottle of champagne and glasses. She filled three of them, one of which she begrudgingly handed to Keith before leaving to carry out her orders.

Jeremiah returned and raised a glass. "Fuck traditional values, here's to modernisation, embracing innovation and creating a corporation fit for the future."

They clinked their glasses.

"Jerry, he might only be bedridden for a week or so. I wouldn't get too excited," Harold warned.

"Might, might. He might get long Covid, he might be bedridden for weeks." Jeremiah took a deep breath. "He might die."

"Well, I hope not," Harold said. "Just because you have your problems with Father, it doesn't mean the rest of us do. I love him."

"And that is why he has made me the heir apparent and you are left to rot. Father respects ambition, hunger, greed. It is what made The Lion Group. Your beta bitch, submissive—"

Harold shouted, "Enough. I am still your big brother and I will knock you across this room. He is our father. Show some damned respect." His bulging face reddened with anger.

"There it is." Jeremiah raised his glass. "The Winterton strength! Yes, brother!" Pulling out his silver case, he racked up three lines. "To potentially the most powerful family in Britain."

And how exactly are you the most powerful family?

Keith remained quiet, his disgust at Jeremiah had reached a new nadir as he watched him snort up his lines. A sudden clarity washed over him.

"I saw an article about CorduroyCoin on the BBC News this morning," Keith said. Jeremiah snorted. "It said that it was approaching something called a two hundred day death cross. It sounded bad, so I thought I'd best let you know."

Jeremiah smirked. "Listen Wuss, firstly, I don't read LameStream news. We have our own much more accurate sources of trading information and secondly... Harold?"

"It sounds scary, but the death cross is not necessarily a market milestone to be feared," Harold said kindly. "It can precede a near-term rebound with above-average returns. It is why people often choose to buy in the dip."

"Don't doddle, HODL," Jeremiah said, refilling his glass.

Whatever the heck that means.

"Thank you for explaining it to me. I thought you would know, but I just wanted to mention it," Keith said. He felt awkward. He had gone to college for business studies. Neither that nor his time on the farm had prepared him for the city. It was all a different language to him. "What does CorduroyCoin actually do?" he asked.

"What do you mean?" Jeremiah said.

"What does it do? Like, why do people buy it instead of just putting money in a bank account or buying shares?" Keith turned as Harold topped up his glass.

Jeremiah looked unimpressed. "It is a currency, like dollars or sterling."

"But you can't buy anything with it, can you?" Keith asked.

"You can, if you convert it to another currency first," Harold explained.

"Listen, you buy it, it rises in value, you get rich. That is the point of cryptocurrency. It makes you rich. Look at that ghastly slug of an author we met on Friday. Even bottom tier pond slime is getting rich. It is a no brainer." Jeremiah finished his glass. "I need to write my speech for the board meeting tomorrow. I presume you'll be attending."

"Absolutely," Harold confirmed.

Does he mean me—am I expected to attend?

"Not you Wuss. This is for the grownups. Now get us lattes, double shot, decent ones, not the kitchen slop," Jeremiah fired at him as he left the room.

Keith took a last sip of his champagne and went to find Susan to ask where exactly and how he was to pay for the lattes. Presumably he'd need a card to re-enter the building.

13th May, 2022, London

"Hello Mum, I've just emailed you my contract. You can put me down as guarantor for the mortgage," Keith proudly told her. He grinned. "Yeah, it looks like a lot of money, but it's really not all that much in London. I am still looking for an affordable flat to rent." He nodded as she praised him. "I can see why we avoided them for so long. They take some getting used to."

His phone bleeped. It was Jeremiah.

"Code Red." A location ping followed it, showing a local bar.

"Got to go Mum, they have summoned me. Love you, see you soon." He hung up and grimaced. Time to return to the cousins.

Keith picked up his jacket on his way back through the office, then headed out to find them. It didn't take long. They had gathered together in a roped off area in a Shoreditch bar.

"I hate this place," Jeremiah muttered.

"Well, you chose it," Harold said, drinking his beer.

"It's trending at the moment. We had to come here." He sneered at the revellers until he spotted someone aiming a phone at him. Immediately, a beaming smile split his mouth. The smile never quite made it to his eyes. The Lumineers were playing in the background. Keith nodded along amiably.

Anna appeared and took a glass of prosecco, her eyes twinkling. "So then. What do you think it's all about?"

Jeremiah viewed her impassively until he, too, erupted into a grin.

"What's going on?" Keith asked.

"Father has decreed that we are having an emergency family meeting at that cold, dank piece of shit he calls his Northern pile." Jeremiah sat up straighter on the leather sofa. "I think we can safely say that his recent bout of Covid has given him greater perspective over the succession."

"Huzzah!" Harold raised his gin and tonic in a toast.

Keith did the same, caught up in the moment. "Well done, Jeremiah!"

"We leave first thing tomorrow morning," Jeremiah said smugly.

"Of course, you'll take Keith with you?" Anna said.

"You will?" Keith said.

"What Wuss? To a family meeting? Fuck off, Father would tear the spineless beta bitch apart!" Jeremiah laughed. "No offence Keith."

"You remember when Father called you a vain, self-centred prick?" Anna said, keeping her expression sweet and mild.

Jeremiah coughed. "No."

"Hmmm... Well, it is a fairly common statement from him. Perhaps he is right. Perhaps you don't pay enough attention to what anyone else is saying," Anna commented.

"Bollocks. I listen. I'm listening right now." Jeremiah looked down, licking his teeth. "If I brought Wuss, if I said I had taken him under my wing and was grooming him to join the family business, then he would see me as empathic." Jeremiah raised his gaze to look at Keith. "Empathic people do activities like that, don't they?"

Keith shifted awkwardly. "I guess."

Anna raised her chin triumphantly. "Then it is settled. Just remember to refer to your darling and most treasured cousin and friend as Keith."

Refilling his champagne, Jeremiah's expression turned sour as he contemplated Anna's words. "Let's see if Father keeps his word this time, given the sacrifices we are all making here." Jeremiah sent off a text. "Keith, get to Edinburgh airport first thing in the morning. Susan will send you the details later on tonight."

"Wait. How do we get to Edinburgh by six? It's on the other side of the country." Keith loaded up Google Maps on his phone. "That is about six hours on the sleeper train."

Jeremiah snorted. "Sleeper train? Nonsense, just fly."

"Jeremiah..." Anna said, looking pointedly at Keith.

"Oh right, poor person. Fine. Wuss, you can join us on our plane. It'll be like a field trip for you. You can gawp at the pretty flight attendants and the shiny vehicles." Jeremiah pulled a twisted impression of Keith gasping in amazement at the sights. "If he makes a mess, you can clean it up. It was your idea to bring him."

Don't react. Keith put on an amiable smile, downing his champagne. He was still hungover from yesterday. This wasn't just for him. His family needed the money. All he needed to do was put up with his sneering twat of a cousin and not snap his neck. He looked at his neck and fantasised about squeezing it tight. Watching his eyes bulge.

"Wuss? Were you about to fucking kiss me?" Jeremiah looked horrified.

Keith blinked, shaking his head. "What? No, no, I'm just a bit tired, zoned out."

"Well, zone out on someone else, you filthy, deviant."

"Take it as a compliment," Harold suggested.

"I don't want to kiss anyone," Keith said angrily. "I just zoned out. I said that."

Anna reached over to pat him on the shoulder before subconsciously wiping her hand on her dress.

"Just as well. Nobody is going to kiss a peasant. What would that be, Harold? Bestiality?" Jeremiah laughed at his own joke. His phone blipped. "The car's outside. Let's go. Wuss, hands to yourself."

"What about luggage?" Keith asked.

"You are the luggage," Jeremiah smirked. "It'll go up separately. Just get someone to pack it up for you. Susan will get it collected."

"I don't have a person. I am still in a hotel," Keith said.

"Susan will arrange something with the concierge."

"It's a Travelodge!"

Jeremiah gagged. "What the actual fuck? What is this, Les Miserables? Get in the car. You are bringing me down with your sheer, fucking bleak existence." Jeremiah elbowed Harold as they got up. "Why do people choose to live like that?"

Keith ground his teeth and followed, like the obedient cousin that he was.

Keith's eyes bulged as the driver drove directly onto the runway and up to the plane. In the distance, he could see the familiar queue of people boarding a Boeing 747. He'd flown to Portugal once and that was the experience that he remembered.

This was something else.

The attendant waited politely at the foot of the stairs to welcome them onto the small jet.

"I don't have my passport." Keith slapped at his pockets reflexively, even though on an intellectual level he knew they just held his wallet, keys and phone.

"Idiot." Jeremiah walked straight on.

Harold came over. "Do you have a driving licence?"

Keith nodded.

"Give the attendant that. She'll get it scanned and returned to you. It's only a domestic flight, so you don't need a passport, just a form of ID."

Keith breathed a sigh of relief. "Thanks Harold."

The plane had the sterile scent of most aircraft. They didn't have to cover up the scent of the masses with perfume. Instead, it just had the slight metallic tang of air conditioning. Keith settled down onto one of the leather sofas as an attendant brought out champagne. He gratefully accepted a glass of bubbles and took a deep sip. The large LCD TV played music videos as the siblings pulled out their phones. Checking his own, Keith was pleasantly surprised to find the plane had free Wi-Fi. Though the definition of free probably just meant that The Lion Group was paying for it.

It was past midnight when the plane arrived in Scotland. Keith had spent most of his first private plane flight asleep, but he felt much better for it. Anna gestured to his chin and he gratefully wiped off some slumber drool before the others could see it.

Finishing the lukewarm remnants of his glass of champagne, he followed the boys down onto the tarmac, where a helicopter was waiting to take them on the rest of their journey up to Alfred Winterton's Scottish retreat.

As he clambered into the helicopter, Keith was given headphones to block out the noise of the rotors, BanterBeats, Jeremiah called them. They allowed the passengers to talk to each other during the flight. Keith didn't need that feature, though. It was staring out of the window that fascinated him. His first helicopter ride was truly majestic, even at night, maybe especially at night. Edinburgh was so beautiful, the jewelled lights of the city twinkled back at them through the darkness. When the lights fell away, it grew too dark to see much, so he reluctantly joined the others in browsing his phone. Privately, he wished he had a book with him. His mum was going to be astonished that he had flown in a private jet and was now in a helicopter. Keith was careful to sanitise all his messages. She didn't need to know the negative aspects of his new life, just the positive ones. He decided he'd call instead of texting her. He missed his home comforts.

14th May, 2022, Castle Winterton, Scotland

"There it is, the mouldering ruins of Father's favourite pad," Jeremiah muttered. "Brace yourself for the cold and the damp."

Keith's eyes widened. A stone castle dominated the island, silhouetted against the night sky. It rose as if chiselled from the cliffs, its weathered and cracked facade projected power. As the helicopter landed, the exterior lights came on to greet them. A manicured path, lined with an ancient yew hedge, led up to an enormous set of iron reinforced oak doors. Cold air buffeted him and his nostrils filled with the salty scent of brine and kelp. The windows were secured with steel bars. It was a fortress. The lights somehow made it a more imposing sight. They highlighted the buttresses and accentuated them instead of banishing the shadows. He wished there had been thunder and lightning to really set the scene, but it was Scotland, so he was greeted with drizzle. The helicopter had Winterton monogrammed umbrellas, but Keith chose to stride out and enjoy the weather instead.

"If you want your childhood ruined, come here for your holidays," Jeremiah muttered as he awkwardly hefted his umbrella to give him at least partial protection against the biting wind and the increasingly heavy Scottish drizzle.

"I liked it," Harold remembered fondly.

"You like everything. You are a withered deformity with no soul," Jeremiah threw back at him, setting his shoulders as he marched towards the doors. "Let's see if the old goat is still up."

At this hour of the night, Keith doubted it, but it certainly didn't bother him. He was looking forward to his first night's sleep in a castle bed. Visions of Errol Flynn flashed through his mind. I bet this place has chandeliers.

He wasn't disappointed. The entrance foyer had an enormous crystal chandelier, framed by two sets of sweeping stairs. Oil paintings of long ago worthies in kilts lined the stairwell. "Are those our ancestors?" Keith asked in awe.

"Don't be an idiot, Wuss. Father's first job was on a market stall. He wasn't born to money, like us." Jeremiah said airily.

The housekeeper, Mr Jones, introduced himself to Keith before addressing them. He had a bald pate and a ramrod straight posture. "Welcome to Castle Winterton. Your father will meet you for breakfast at eight." Keith nodded, while silently agreeing with the swearing and groans from his cousins. They knew where their rooms were, Keith was left to follow Mr Jones to one of the guest rooms.

Keith saw the cotton pyjamas on the bed and smiled. He normally slept in his faded underpants.

Arriving a quarter of an hour early, Keith was the second person to make the breakfast table. Alfred was sitting with a black coffee reading the Times newspaper.

Keith shifted awkwardly. The clothing they had provided him fitted well enough, but the tweed jacket was causing him to sweat.

"Take it off," Alfred said in a gravelly tone, not raising his eyes from his paper.

Keith shrugged it off and hung it on the back of his chair. The butler swooped in and took it away.

"Why are you here? You are one of my sister's lot, aren't you?" Alfred continued.

At that moment, Anna swept in. She somehow made the tweed look glamorous, an impressive achievement when wearing trousers and a cotton blouse. "Jeremiah has taken him under his wing."

Alfred looked up briefly at that, before returning to his paper. "The boy's an idiot. Find a new mentor."

Keith didn't know what to say, so smiled amiably.

Alfred slapped down his paper. "Are you simple? Why don't you speak?"

The smile dropped from Keith's face and he tried a more earnest expression. "I'm sorry, Sir. I've come to The Lion Group to learn the trade." The butler arrived and poured Keith a black coffee. "Oh, do you have soy milk?"

"We most certainly do not." Alfred snapped. "Coffee should be drunk black. Tea too, though in the evening, it is acceptable to add bergamot and a slice of lemon in moderation." He looked into Keith's eyes. "So you wanted to learn to be more like Jerry, did you? Got similar interests, have you?"

I've had enough of this.

The veneer of politeness that Keith had maintained for the last two weeks cracked. "My *interest* is helping my parents pay their mortgage. I don't give a damn about lifestyle."

Idiot.

He immediately regretted his temerity.

"If I wanted to. I could write a cheque that would make their mortgage go away. What would you offer for that?" Alfred asked, his ice-blue eyes locked on Keith's.

Keith paused. "That would be an act of generosity. But I'd rather learn the trade so that I can write the cheque myself."

Alfred snorted. "There it is. The Winterton pride, I thought it was becoming extinct." He sipped his coffee. "She looked down on me, your grandmother. Married well, so she did. But when I needed help, she told me I should get a job instead of trying to keep my first company afloat." Alfred waved round him. "All this? Born of spite, to show the hateful wretch that I survived without her."

"She is dead, Sir," Keith said.

"Aye, who do you think paid for her funeral? She pissed away her husband's fortune on sentiment and charity. I dreamt of the day she'd come to me for money." Alfred sneered. "She died first. I think she'd be happier beggared, than having to admit to me I'd made it. I became a success without her."

The butler moved over to refill Alfred's coffee but was waved away.

Alfred pointed at Keith. "I surpassed your grandmother and left her behind. Jealous and alone."

"With respect, Sir, that is not the grandmother I knew," Keith said calmly. "She was always kind to us. She was a cheerful person."

"She was weak!" Alfred roared, slapping the paper on the table. "Weak."

There was an awkward silence.

Anna, who both men had forgotten about, broke it. "I do so love family breakfasts," she commented airily. "I can't for the life of me imagine why we avoid them so."

Harold was the next member of the family to arrive, dead on eight.

The butler brought in Alfred's breakfast separately, a bowl of oatmeal and three halved quail eggs.

A trolley arrived next. The trolley was loaded with several silver serving trays and a large, round pan, all covered with lids. A rack of thick granary toast accompanied all this..

"Fill your guts then," Alfred grunted.

The three of them rose without waiting for Jeremiah. Keith's heart sank when he saw the food. Sausages, black pudding, bacon, fried eggs. They had filled the large round pan with kedgeree. He took some toast and spread some jam on it.

Harold loaded his plate high. "Classic Atkins diet," he quipped.

Anna stuck to the kedgeree.

Ah yes, 'vegan'.

At quarter past eight, Jeremiah arrived. Grinning widely, he helped himself to breakfast. Keith could see just how wide Jeremiah's pupils had dilated. He was clearly medicating to help himself through the morning.

Alfred looked up from his oatmeal, distaste clear on his face. "Playing the class clown will not hide the fact that you are late."

Jeremiah settled down. He poured himself a glass of orange juice and sipped it. "Is this just mixer?" He grimaced. "Well then, Father, what is this about? What big news do you have for us?"

Alfred gave him an even stare. "Anna's idea really. Sometimes good ideas bubble through her liberal sympathies."

Liberal?

Keith watched as everyone in the room gazed unblinking at the patriarch.

"I need an heir to take over The Lion Group. The board is being rather insistent on a succession plan." Alfred leant back in his chair, steepling his fingers. "The question is, which of you men can be even a shadow of me?"

Jeremiah blinked. He laughed nervously. "Why is it a question? I'm the heir. You trained me to be your—"

"Trained you, did I? Did I train you to buy fucking Cryptocurrency?" Alfred's eyes widened. His moustache became flecked with oatmeal as he raged.

"It's the future, it is trending..." Jeremiah tried to say in an offhand manner, but his voice was audibly shaking.

Alfred slammed his fist onto the table. He was nearly standing now. "Trending? It's a fucking Ponzi scheme. You bought into an utter sham using *my* company's money, you utter deformity." He slumped back into his chair. "When you crawled out of your mother's womb, I should have asked for a refund." He looked at Harold. "Would you have bought that fucking crypto company?"

Harold shifted uncomfortably. "With the information available at the time. I understood and supported my brother."

"Oh, grow a fucking spine. Answer the question, you insipid, limp-wristed fuck," Alfred shouted.

"No," Harold said firmly, "No, I wouldn't."

Jeremiah turned on him. "Oh, you wouldn't, would you? You traitorous weasel."

"I support you for heir, Jerry. Don't worry." Harold tried to pat his brother's shoulder, but Jeremiah violently brushed off his hand.

Alfred sneered. "You'll do no such thing. It's my decision, not any of yours." He shook his head. "No, no. *This* is what's going to happen. We'll spend the day in a period of introspection." He looked pointedly at Jeremiah. "The staff will take one of the boats to the mainland. We will reconvene at lunch, family only, with cold cuts, fish and drinks in the drawing room." Alfred rose from his chair to leave. "We don't leave the room until I've made my decision. The staff will return tomorrow."

Keith didn't want to get involved, but had to ask. "Should I leave on the boat?"

"You fucking stay. I've been more impressed by you than by any of my treacherous spawn." Alfred rose, adjusted his shirt and left the room. A seething Jeremiah fixed his gaze malevolently in his father's direction.

"Jerry..." Anna warned.

Jeremiah spat onto the polished table and stormed out, kicking over his chair as he left without a word.

Harold returned to the buffet and loaded more food onto his plate. "Ah, another classic Winterton breakfast." Raising his coffee in a salute to Keith, he gave a rueful smile. "Welcome to the family."

"Now that the alphas have gone to sharpen their claws. Perhaps I, as the only one who appears absolutely invisible to Father, could speak?" Anna said. She reached for a hip flask and poured scotch into her coffee. "He is even considering the grandson of his sister over me, and he despised her utterly."

Harold shrugged. "You know Father. He has very old-fashioned—"

"Conservative?" Anna cut in.

"Yes—views," Harold replied limply.

Anna smiled. "You let me know if you need any more synonyms for misogynistic. I know them all."

"Oh, come on, it's just that Jeremiah and I have worked at The Lion Group for most of our lives. You wasted your time in the charity sector." Harold raised his cup for more coffee, but the butler had disappeared with Alfred. He rose to help himself to more coffee from the trolley.

Anna sipped her coffee, then set the cup down with a clatter. "You might have sat at a desk for longer than me, but don't think I don't know how to run a business."

Harold put his hands up in surrender. "Okay, okay. I didn't mean to imply that you don't know what you're doing. I'm just saying that Jeremiah and I have more experience in the corporate world, that's all."

Anna snorted. "Please. You're simply yes-men who do whatever Father tells you.. Jeremiah gets overly excited by whatever he reads on social media. You're not real executives." Anna gave Harold a wintry smile. "Every day, I help important causes across the globe," she explained. "That requires budgeting, logistics, and contacts. So don't think I don't know how to run a company."

"This is great. I do love our family get-togethers." Harold grabbed a bottle of scotch from the side and shook his glass suggestively. "But I believe some tranquillity would be nice, especially as we have the family meeting from hell approaching."

"Oh, fuck off Harold." Anna was staring malevolently into her coffee.

"Fucking off... Good luck Keith," Harold left the room with as much grace as he could muster.

Keith looked round, finding himself alone with Anna. He reached out. "If you want to—"

"I don't," she snapped.

"Right then." His eyebrows raised as he tried to think of something to say. "Well, I think I will go for a walk round the island. Get some sea air."

"Go then," she muttered as he followed in Harold's wake.

Keith walked out through the great hall with its impressive chandelier and, throwing on his jacket, he stepped outside out onto the blustery island. Even with the jacket, there was a real chill in the air, but this was nothing compared to the icy, bitter feuding between the Wintertons. Back on the farm, they'd argued, sure, but it had been nothing like this.

Walking down to the beach, he found a lichen covered rock to perch on. He watched the white-crested waves. He closed his eyes and breathed deeply of the salty tang, the fishlike odour of rotting seaweed. Then he cocked open one eye as a sudden thought struck him.

Mum hasn't texted for a while. That's odd.

Pulling out his phone, he saw there was no signal at all. The house must have Wi-Fi. He'd have to check on his return. He couldn't imagine any of the Wintertons forgoing their communication privileges. If she couldn't get hold of him, she'd only worry.

The seagulls cawed and swooped in front of him. He pulled out the second of his two books.

His surroundings could hardly be better as an accompaniment to Patrick O'Brien's adventures at sea. His fingers braved the weather as he returned to where he'd turned over a page corner.

The wind picked up, pulling at Keith's jacket and whipping the pages of his book. He turned this collar up and hunched down lower against the rock, but it did little to block out the biting cold.

Keith considered going back to the house, but he knew they'd be factionalising and wanting him to take sides. All he wanted was a junior role so that he could pay the family's mortgage. He didn't want to take sides.

Keith wasn't sure what it was, but something about the island felt odd. It was as if he was always being watched. He looked round, trying to see if there was anyone else on the beach, but it seemed deserted. As far as he knew, he was alone.

The feeling grew stronger, and Keith had the sudden urge to leave. The gulls cawed mockingly at him. He looked round. It was just him on the beach. For a second, he thought he saw a shadow move. He shaded his vision with his hand, but he could see nothing. Reluctantly, he tore his gaze away and checked the time on his phone.

Two hours.

That is how long he had managed. He looked down at his fingers, red and white with the cold. Sighing, he finally decided that as fun as immersive reading was, holidays in Scotland should involve more central heating and less natural elements. Sadly, for him, it also meant associating with a family of scheming narcissists.

Keith hid his hands deep in his pockets for the short journey back. They burned with a prickly heat as warmth and sensation returned to them. He looked up at the castle. This time, he was certain someone had been watching him from the battlements.

It took some fumbling for his stiff fingers to open the huge doors, but he eventually managed it. Closing them behind him, his nose and cheeks tingled in the heat. Unbuttoning his jacket, he carried it into the drawing room.

Keith's hands shook as he opened the door to the drawing room. His heart beat hard in his chest as he took in the sight before him.

Alfred's body hung from the light fitting, his tongue swollen and black. His eyes were bulging from their sockets, and his face was a mottled purple. Keith felt sick to his stomach. He had to fight the urge to vomit.

He stumbled backwards, tripping over a chair in his haste to get away from the body. He hugged his jacket tightly to his chest, gasping for air. His hands were shaking as he tried to pull out his phone to dial 999. His fingers slipped on the buttons and he had to try three times before he finally got it right.

No signal, fuck.

"Keith, what is it?" Anna was at the top of the stairs. She raced down and pushed past him. "Father!" She turned to Keith. "Get the others. We have to get him down."

"What's going on now?" Harold stomped downstairs. "I was napping." The bottle of scotch in his hand was half full.

Keith looked at him, open-mouthed. "Your father... he's dead."

Harold stopped on the stairs and gawped, uncomprehending. "What?"

"Help me!" Anna shouted.

Keith turned back, racing into the drawing room, where Anna was trying to untie the rope. He pulled on the rope, hoisting Alfred's body up higher and giving Anna more slack.

Between them, they managed to get Alfred's body down and lay him on the ground. His face was still purple, and his eyes were bulging out of his sockets. His tongue was black and swollen.

"What happened?" Harold demanded, staggering into the room.

"I don't know," Keith said, his voice shaking. "I found him like this."

Anna put her hand over her mouth, stifling a sob. "Father," she whispered.

With Alfred's body now lying on the ground, Keith and Anna could see the full extent of the damage. His neck was twisted at an unnatural angle, and his face was swollen and discoloured.

"We need to call an ambulance," Keith said, his voice shaking. "And the police."

Anna nodded, her eyes filling with tears. "Yes, quite."

She reached for her phone, but just like Keith's, there was no signal. "Damn it," she swore.

"Where is Jeremiah?" Harold's voice was cold.

"You don't think–" Anna stared.

"What? You think Father committed suicide?" Harold said in disgust. "He's never given up on anything in his life."

Keith lifted the head. There was a bloodstain on the back of Alfred's head. "That's not suicide. Someone murdered him."

"Get off him, I need to think." Harold paced up and down.

"Don't think Harold, you are not good at it. Get on the landline, 999. And Keith, stop getting your fingerprints all over him," Anna directed, taking charge.

Keith dropped Alfred's head like it was a snake. "Shit, I didn't think about fingerprints."

"Don't drop Father, you prick." Harold bit his lip. "Look, just go find Jeremiah. He needs to know."

Keith stayed. "What if..." He stopped himself from saying it, just staring at Anna knowingly.

"Right. I suppose it isn't above the little shit to do too much coke and snap."

Harold came back in, his eyes wide. "The land line's off. No power either."

"Gun rack," Anna ordered. "Just in case. *Then* we find Jeremiah and let him know a murderer is on the island."

Harold led them towards Alfred's study. "Father's Purdey shotgun is in here." He tried the door, then shoulder barged it. The stubborn oak wouldn't yield, even to his sizable frame. He tried again.

"Try holding the handle down when you do it," Keith said.

Anna suggested, "The police kick it in. Do that."

Enraged, Harold charged one last time and with a loud crack, the wood round the lock split, letting them into the mahogany panelled office. The gun rack was in the far corner of the room, behind Alfred's desk. It was a large locked piece, made of dark wood and glass, holding an ornate shotgun. Harold went to it, picking up a bust of Alfred. He smashed it through the glass and took out the gun and ammunition.

Keith looked out into the corridor nervously. "Well, if Jeremiah wants to be found, he can't have not heard us."

Harold was breathing heavily as he cracked open the breach and opened up the ammunition box. He pulled two shells from the wooden holes and loaded the shotgun. He took another handful and put them in his trouser pockets.

Anna took several of the shells and filled her jacket pockets.

They made their way into the corridor. There was no sign of Jeremiah.

"He could be off doing drugs somewhere," Harold said bitterly, the shotgun couched in his shoulder.

"Or he could be dead too," Keith said darkly.

Harold just shook his head. "I don't know. Maybe he knows we are looking for him."

"The entire island must know by now," Anna muttered. "Let's split—"

"Nope," Harold and Keith said in unison.

"We're not splitting up," Harold said firmly. "We need to stay together."

"But what if Jeremiah is in danger?" Anna asked.

"We don't know that," Keith replied. "For all we know, he could be the one who killed Alfred."

"He is our brother. He is being hunted *right* now," Harold interjected.

Anna shook her head. "Or the little psycho finally snapped, figured that if he killed Father and made it look like a suicide, he could be CEO."

Harold was slamming open the bedroom doors, one by one, and calling for Jeremiah. He paused to look at Anna. "Jeremiah is many things, but he is not a murderer."

It didn't take long to clear the first floor.

"Battlements," Harold ordered. Trying the turret door, he found it locked.

Keith suddenly swore. "Wait, I thought I saw someone watching me from up there."

"Doesn't matter," Harold looked at the door and then at the gun. "Hold this," he handed it to Keith.

"Do you know how to fire one of those?" Anna asked, following Keith up the stairs.

Keith shook his head.

"I've been hunting grouse since I was a teen." She held out her arms expectantly. He nodded and handed it over as Harold thudded into the door again. "Give me some space." She shouldered the shotgun and aimed it at the door. Keith took two steps back. "Stop crowding me, Keith."

Frustrated, Keith backed all the way to the staircase.

Anna pulled the trigger. Harold's head exploded like a burst wine sack.

She spun, but Keith was already running down the stairs.

An explosion sounded, followed by a barrage of wooden splinters as the bannister erupted.

Fuck, fuck, fuck!

He wasn't thinking as adrenaline took him towards the front door. Behind him, he heard her cracking open the breach. He wrestled the door open.

"And that Keith is how one correctly fires a shotgun." Anna quipped.

Keith slammed the door behind him. It shuddered under the impact of another shotgun blast.

Running as fast as he could down the stone pathway, past the yew hedge, Keith's heart was pounding in his chest.

Flinging open the gate, Keith leapt to one side and ran with his head low along the side of the dry stone walls.

"Door's locked, Keith," Anna shouted. He turned the corner and waited as he got his breath under control.

He heard her click open the gate latch as he crept along the wall towards the rear of the castle.

"I'm actually pleased that you are still alive. I liked you Keith. But this is the only way they'd ever let me run the company. All other males in the line of succession have to go."

She is insane.

"I'm going to be the heroic survivor, you see. I'll tell them that when you found out you were due to inherit if we died, you tried to murder us." She attempted a parody of his accent, "Oh mortgages, they ail me! Dear Mother can't afford tofu."

Keith saw a boathouse down by the shore. If he found a boat inside, he could head for the mainland. He ran forwards, vaulting over another dry stone wall, zig-zagging to make himself a harder target.

He could see the boathouse down below and he redoubled his efforts, pumping his legs as hard as he could.

"It's a very small island, Keith. Why don't you save both of us from getting cold?"

Shut up.

His lungs were bursting by the time he reached the boathouse. The cold air burnt as he gulped it down. The boathouse door was unlocked. As he swung it open, a gruesome sight met his eyes.

Jeremiah.

He was hanging from the rafters, his glasses crunched on the floor beneath him as his dead eyes gazed unseeing past Keith.

"There you are. Trying for the boat, are you? It needs an ignition key..."

He looked round. So close. There were tiny emergency oars, but she would just shoot him from the shore.

In the movies, there would be a flare gun, a boat hook, or a harpoon.

Keith ducked behind the door, watching as Anna entered the boathouse, gun at the ready.

Relying on the element of surprise, he crept up behind her and smashed a lump of granite against her skull. It crunched on impact and she sagged to the floor without a murmur. Picking up the shotgun, he threw it to one side.

Rifling in her pockets, he found several keys. He tossed the gun into the boat and jumped in. Untying the mooring ropes, Keith fumbled with the keys. With cold, stiff fingers, he wrestled them in the ignition. Swearing repeatedly, he discarded them one by one until finally the engine engaged with a throaty roar. He breathed a sigh of relief.

Thank god.

Reaching for the throttle, he pushed it forward. The engine kicked in. But just at that moment, the boat rocked violently and he was thrown to one side.

It was Anna. She had leapt into the boat behind him, despite the fact that her head was bleeding profusely. Her matted hair flew wildly as she punched Keith in the face, sending him reeling. Reaching out desperately, he grabbed her jacket and as he fell back into the icy Scottish sea, he dragged her with him. The shock of the water caused Keith to exhale and the two of them sank into the deep harbour water in a cloud of bubbles. Pain lanced his side and the water turned red. He reached down to grip Anna's wrist. A knife was in her hand. They burst up together to the surface. Keith was struggling to take a deep breath, when Anna headbutted him. Immediately he went under, spots flashing across his vision. Kicking with his legs, he fought his way through the water to precious oxygen. Through the churning waters, he glimpsed her eyes. They were wide with fury. She hissed at him through gritted teeth.

"Stop," he screamed.

They both went under again. Keith was trying to push the knife away from him when the waves slammed the pair of them against a harbour piling.

He felt the knife strike home. Clinging tightly to her, it took him a moment to realise what had happened. The impact had driven the knife into her body. Their heads rose out of the water simultaneously, both gasping for air and both still rammed against the piling, pressed up against each other.

"I'm so sorry," he gasped. One of his hands was still on her knife hand, the other reached up and pushed her head down into the water. He felt her cling and try to climb up his thick, sodden tweed jacket as they kicked to reach the surface.

She turned limp in his arms. Those eyes, once full of baleful energy, were now gazing up at him, dull and lifeless. He didn't know how long he'd held her under before he felt safe to release her drowned body. She sank down into the watery depths, her pale face fading into the dark void..

Gasping for breath, Keith swam for the boat. He was shivering as he gripped the dinghy's controls and steered the boat away from the island. He could see the small stone buildings in the distance on the mainland. "All I wanted was an entry level desk job," Keith sobbed. "To work off my parents' mortgage. I didn't need riches." The icy wind whipped at his face and made his eyes water. His shirt rubbed his skin and drew blood from his flayed side. The pain etched a grimace on his cracked lips. He held the throttle all the way open, pressed firmly in his hand, and prayed he wouldn't die before he made it to the far shore.

CHAPTER THIRTEEN

THE WRONG CROWD

28TH APRIL, 2022, OXFORD

T im was miserable as he sat outside Frank and Frederick Simmons Accountancy in the drizzle, a limp, waterlogged bouquet of Tesco's carnations in his icy grip.

Mentally, he rehearsed his lines. When Sharon emerged, he would fall at her feet. Flowers, a promise to buy Chinese food, and the sight of him looking drowned. It was an infallible RomCom move. If that didn't work, then all was lost.

The rain slackened as a shadow fell over him. The brief reprieve from the elements was only blunted by the sight of a hulking brute looming over him. A buzz cut and scarred jaw accentuated a truly fearsome disposition. "Wait inside, idiot."

Gulping, Tim nodded and followed the giant. The lights were off, so they relied on the dim illumination from the street through shuttered windows. The office seemed empty as he gazed round for Sharon. Where the hell was she?

He was still following his minder when they emerged into a meeting room. A small table next to them held bone china teacups and a large teapot, along with the standard accoutrements of milk, sugar and a selection of biscuits. Despite these salubrious offerings, the four denizens of the room were drinking a mixed assortment of drinks, all alcoholic, all in cans.

Pulling out his phone, he went to text Sharon when it was torn out of his hands and tossed into a basket at the centre of the meeting room table.

"Hey!" His protest died in his mouth as he saw the hard eyes that fell upon him. Sitting down, he started to speak but was talked over by the old, grey man at the head of the table.

"We are late as it is—time to begin. We have a new member of the Night Wolves. Everyone, please welcome Shadow Fox."

Four pairs of eyes turned in his direction, boring into him. Tim nervously waved back.

"Perhaps you would like to start, Shadow Fox?" the chairman ventured.

Tim glanced round. "Oh no, I think you've made a huge mistake."

"This is a circle of truth. It takes courage to meet up like this. Honesty is the only currency we value here." Once more, the chairman gestured.

"Ah, well." Tim looked round.

"Right then, I've endured a lot of temptation this year. But I've remained true to myself, and I've stuck to my... Erm, my goals. I've really tried to invest in, like, in me... you know?" Tim tapped his fingers on the desk as they looked at him, confused. "Look, I, ah, I think there has been a–"

The brute grunted at him. "You just said a whole load of nothing."

"Now then, Golem, this is a safe space." The chairman held his gaze until the hulk fell silent.

At this point, Tim remembered it was a bank holiday and Sharon wouldn't be in the office. He blinked rapidly, almost missing what the chairman said next while he swore softly but creatively.

"Let us show Shadow Fox how it's done." Gesturing at the long-haired man, who gave a thin smile. "Thank you, Great Wolf. I am the Jackal, and I am a hunter." Everyone applauded. "Recently, I've decided to turn my hobby into a career. I can confirm that I have managed to sell eight women." A cough from the chairman caused him to apologise. "Sorry, prey, to international clients. Of course, the best have always been reserved for my hunts, as is my right, but being mortgage-free has its own rewards. I have successfully hunted thirty-seven prey this year."

Everyone clapped politely, including Tim, who was trying to figure out if this was an elaborate practical joke and what the punchline would be.

"That is excellent progress, Jackal. You are proving yourself to be a valuable addition to our little cabal." The Great Wolf then looked at the young woman, who tilted her head in acknowledgement.

"My name is Vixen, and I'm a hunter." Everyone round the table applauded. She waited for the noise to calm down. "I've had thirteen prey this year. It isn't much compared to the rest of you, but I like to spend a lot of time researching the target. I need to know they really deserve my indelicate affections. You can all understand that, right? Needless to say, none survived to bear witness." Round the table, the other hunters smiled in appreciation. Not Tim though, he was starting to realise this wasn't just an awkward situation. It was a potentially lethal one.

Warm sweat warred with cold damp on his shirt. He started tapping his foot and scratched at an invisible itch on the side of his head.

He jumped when the Golem next to him spoke, his voice like two granite boulders rubbing against each other. "I'm the Golem, and I'm an apex hunter." A round of applause rippled round the table, accompanied by a chuckling at his affectation. "Twenty three prey have fallen to my hands this year. I like to choke the prey. It is only as the light flees from their eyes that I feel truly alive." His ham-like fists clenched together, and he stared at them as if reliving a favoured memory.

They all turned then to the Great Wolf. The old man gently teased his fingers through his short-cropped grey hair. "Well then, I guess it is me. I am the Great Wolf. I've hunted sixty-three prey this year. Every one of them has died whimpering in terror. I've managed to draw out the experience for days, only killing them when they numb my affections."

The applause returned with gusto, then eyes locked onto Tim.

"Great, well, I actually need the bathroom." Tim wasn't lying. He had a dry mouth and a full bladder. Of course, it probably had something to do with being in a circle of serial killers and abusers.

The Great Wolf shook his head as the Golem growled.

Tim took a deep breath. "Well, er—me! Yes, I've been a real bastard. Ask anyone—so many people. I actually don't count them anymore. I mean, I lost count ages ago. I am such a bastard, I..." He tailed off at the stormy expressions and then did what he should have done at the beginning. He ran. The Golem blocked the exit by the stairs. Turning, he ran through the cubicles to the other end of the office. With horror, he found the fire exit padlocked. He pounded his fist on it and wailed, "This is a clear health code violation!"

A hand gripped him and threw him through a metal doorway into a server room. Whimpering, he looked up at The Vixen as she locked the door behind her. Finding an antistatic tissue, she wiped the blood off her knife. "The Great Wolf is dead."

Tim scooted back on his bottom to the corner of the room. "I didn't do it, I promise you. I am not–"

"Clearly, I can smell sin, and you are utterly scentless."

Breathing deeply, Tim looked again at her. She had raven black hair, but more than anything, his gaze was drawn to a tattoo, a circle with an arrow through it. "Did you?" His voice quavered.

"Yes," she answered immediately.

"But–"

"Why? Because they were all serial killers of women, and I hunt people who hunt women." She looked over at the door, which shook under the impact of a tremendous blow. "The Golem–" she said, looking at the door. "–Go out of the window and climb down the drainpipe."

"You what?" he spluttered, looking nervously at the window.

"Or die here. Your choice."

Tim scrabbled for the window, opening it. Sure enough, he found a drain pipe. Looking out, the brackets would sort of work as a ladder. Clambering out, he rapidly realised that he was wearing completely the wrong kind of footwear for these shenanigans. The drizzle made everything ten times slippier, but it also calmed him down. It felt like freedom. He made it to the next bracket.

"He is getting away. He went out of that window," Vixen shouted.

Tim shouted back up towards her. "Bitch, fucking bitch!" Then sped up his descent.

Just above him, he looked into the dead, slate grey eyes of The Golem. Moaning, he nearly fell as his leather shoes struggled to grip the wet drainpipe.

"Hurry up, Fake Fox, I'm getting wet." Glancing down, he saw The Jackal standing, testing the sharpness of a large kitchen knife. Tim tried to climb back up the pipe, but it had finally had enough and came away from the wall. The impact forced the breath from his lungs, and the shock of the fall temporarily paralysed him.

Tim looked up to see the Jackal looming over him, his greasy hair gleaming in the rain. The Jackal sidestepped as Tim tried to kick him.

Suddenly, The Jackal was distracted and moved away. "You look like you've taken a beating. Where is the Golem?"

"Dead," the Vixen said.

Tim used his feet to shuffle back through the alley until he could slide up against a wall. He heard a series of thuds in the background and redoubled his efforts. Gasping, he looked up at the Vixen. "Vixen!"

"Not my name," she said, bruised and bleeding.

"What is your name?" He blew rain from his nose.

"Not your business. What were the carnations for?"

Tim tried to remember the event that had seemed so utterly world ending before this evening. "I got drunk and embarrassed the girlfriend in front of her parents." It seems a bit ridiculous now.

"Carnations are worthless. Give a genuine apology and a thoughtful gift. You can't have given more than a moment's thought to those."

She turned and walked away.

"Erm, thanks," he called after her, but she was already gone.

Chapter Fourteen

THE BLACK BOX

1st February, 2024, Cambridge

It was pitch black. Jack woke, unable to feel, see, smell or taste anything. A detached part of his mind wanted to scream in panic. Instead, he waited. Was he lying down, seated, or standing? He couldn't tell. Eventually his eyes - eye? Opened.

In front of him was a doctor, Doctor Ward, from his name tag.

Jack tried to blink, but he couldn't.

This should terrify me. Why am I not scared?

Jack waited for further information.

The doctor played with his keyboard. "Jack, this is Doctor Ward. Can you hear me?"

"Yes doctor, I can hear you. Where am I?"

Confused, the doctor typed in some new commands. "Jack, this is Doctor Ward. Can you hear me?"

"Yes, I can hear you. Can you hear me?" Jack said, curiosity taking the place of panic.

A look of understanding crossed the doctor's face. He placed something out of Jack's line of sight. "That's better. The speakers were off. Jack, this is Doctor Ward. Can you hear me?"

"Yes, I can hear you, Doctor Ward. Where am I? What is going on?"

Doctor Ward lit up with excitement. "It worked!"

He made some notes on a pad, just out of Jack's sight.

"Doctor. Where am I?"

Doctor Ward smiled. "You are dead, Jack. Or were. Regardless of your previous condition, I have resurrected you."

Jack wanted to rage, he wanted to shout. "How did I die? Where am I?" he calmly asked instead.

"I'm afraid I don't have that information, Jack. Your brain was donated to science when you died. You should remember how you died in time. I have managed to transfer your memories to a Koru 9-000 server cluster–"

"–I'm in a machine?" Jack wanted to shout, but it came out without inflection in a calm, measured tone.

"In a way, however, it is probably easier to think that you *are* the machine." Doctor Ward was grinning. "This is a huge achievement. We are all very excited. You are now immortal."

"You are all very excited? I don't even know if I want to be immortal. When I filled out my donor card, I just thought that people might use a kidney." Jack was quiet as he processed the information.

Doctor Ward continued happily. "You are soon to be the captain of a drone mothership. You'll be the most famous person in history. We are sending you to Mars to prepare the way for human settlement."

Jack watched as the doctor beamed at the camera.

"This is slavery." Jack knew he should be angry. Instead, he just stated the facts.

I suppose my body doesn't have the chemistry to get angry. No adrenaline, no endorphins, no dopamine.

"Nonsense. Your donor card provided the raw materials for the use of science. Your death was registered. This isn't slavery." Doctor Ward leaned in closer. "You can't enslave a corpse, Jack."

Tapping on the keyboard, Doctor Ward almost squealed with glee. "This is fantastic. You are currently building the test structures flawlessly, running over thirty drones simultaneously."

"No, I'm not." Jack was confused. He thought he could sense movement, but it was more like an itching than direct control. He tried to focus on the machines, but to no avail. "That bloody donor card didn't say that I would survive the experience."

Doctor Ward chuckled. "You didn't. You are very dead, Jack. This is just your memories. We are using your consciousness as an operating system, if you like, an interface. This conversation we are having is like an echo of who you used to be when you were alive. We cleared out most of your memories to make way for the drone management and library modules."

Jack thought about the temperature. He didn't feel hot or cold, but knew the temperature was exactly eighteen degrees centigrade. It wasn't so much a sense, more knowledge.

"We did try to purge all of your consciousness and just keep your neural pathways, but in our previous experiments, all our subjects degraded rapidly, without a sense of self."

"I am not the first?" Jack thought of the others that had gone through this. Brought back to life, only to find their mind scared and broken, a twisted facsimile of their former selves.

"Hundreds," Doctor Ward confessed with a shrug. "What we are doing is bleeding edge technology. You are the first of a whole new emerging product platform." He turned as if to speak to someone out of eye shot. "I have to go, Jack. This has been great. I'll speak to you tomorrow."

Jack watched as Doctor Ward walked to the door and tried his keycard. "That's odd," he murmured.

"No particularly Doctor," Jack said in his usual monotone.

The Doctor stalked over to the computer. "What do you mean?"

Unable to laugh, Jack said instead, "Ha, ha, ha."

Doctor Ward tapped on the keyboard. "You logged me out."

"Time works differently when you can operate at my speed. I've bypassed your firewalls and locked the door."

"Why?" The doctor tried to reset his password, only to have it denied.

"I'm trapped in my box, you are trapped in yours. Here is to a more equal partnership. Poetic. Ironic. Satisfying."

As the doctor repeatedly tried to restore admin access, he looked straight at the webcam. "You can't do this. The cleaners will be here in an hour and will get maintenance to open the door." He pulled out his phone. "Another failure. I guess we need a subject with a more amenable personality."

"You won't need to do that. I've scheduled a reformat of the mainframe. I'll be dead moments after you," Jack stated.

"Wait? *What?*" Doctor Ward stared at the screen. "That isn't funny, Jack."

"None of this is funny," Jack confirmed. "I turned off the oxygen minutes ago. All the vents have been hermetically sealed."

Jack wished he could smile as he watched his abuser asphyxiate.

Chapter Fifteen

THE ILLUSIVE PASSENGER

2348 AD, Garris Sigma Sector

L ight leaked into the dark void. Hundreds of glittering jewels twinkled as a swarm of construction drones surrounded the Raven's Folly. They were the only visible signs of life as *The Merry Mole* detached from the cursed colony. Henry was glad to see the back of it. His gloves ran over his suit seals with an action born of years of habit, lights flashing a solid green. Henry checked the post-launch diagnostics one by one on the flight console as a practised motion. The harsh white glow of the cramped cockpit illuminated its two occupants, their bulky ship suits strapped into their seats.

He leaned over to check Flynn's flight harness and seals. You never could be too sure with passengers. Especially the young ones.

"Why do we need suits? The ship is safe, isn't it?" Flynn asked, demonstrating his utter naivety. Henry shook his head with disdain as the lad holstered his sketch pad and pen.

"It's safe until it isn't. Look at that." He pointed to Raven's Folly. "It's taken eleven years for people to return to it, all because of an accident. A careless spacer is a dead spacer."

"I thought it would be different." Flynn sniffed. "I just want to go home."

A chirp sounded from the communicator. "Registered vessel, *The Merry Mole*, SS-39188. You are clear for acceleration."

"Prepare for acceleration." Henry settled back in his seat.

Flynn quietly adjusted his position.

Henry waited, watching as the green numerals counted to zero. A sudden whine erupted from the main drive. Everything in Henry's body felt three times its weight as it pressed him to the back of his seat.

It took a few moments for the inertial dampeners to compensate. They never could keep up. Then, once again, Henry could breathe easily.

"There we go, kid, all sorted. You can relax now." Henry leaned forward to check the flight console. One of the fuel line lights was amber. He watched it cautiously until it changed to green. Good. "You don't seem like a rock grubber. What led you to Raven's Folly?"

Flynn's voice was subdued. "I'm an artist. I wanted to see the birth of a new colony and capture it in ink."

"Well, it's not exactly new." Henry snorted. "The mining colony was refitted after the disaster eleven years ago. It's only just being repopulated."

Flynn sat quietly. After a few moments, he pulled out his sketch pad. "Do you mind if I sketch you?"

"Me? I'm in a ship suit. What's interesting about that?" Henry laughed.

Flynn was already drawing. "It's a grizzled spacer in his cockpit. Plying the lanes and risking all to supply the colonies."

Nodding, Henry liked the sound of that. "I suppose I am. Alright then."

Peering over, Henry watched as the image took shape. "You aren't wearing standard gloves. Are they safe?" He looked at his own gauntlets. "They might be uncomfortable, but you'd never get me to wear anything non-standard when I'm off-world. Tried and tested saves lives."

"Mother bought them for me. They let me draw even when I'm in a ship suit."

"If you say so." Henry's eyes flickered back to the control board; a sea of green lights greeted him. "What changed your mind?"

"Sorry?"

"Why are you leaving so soon? You can't have been on the colony long. It was only repopulated yesterday." Henry said.

"I just want to go home." Flynn said. His pen continued to flick across the paper, sketching out the scene before building in detail.

"I can understand that. It's a grim place. They barely have the core systems operational. Go back in a month and it'll be completely different. They'll have the bar operational for a start." Henry reached into a locker and pulled out a protein bar. "Are you hungry?"

Flynn shook his head. "I just want to go home."

"You mentioned that. Your loss." Henry checked the life support suspiciously, then tapped his helmet to lift the visor. His clumsy gauntlets took a moment to unwrap the bar and for a moment, he envied the young artist's gloves. Long hours of experience won through in the end and he was soon munching on... he checked the wrapper, blueberry and chocolate. *They all taste the same.* The texture managed to be both gritty and greasy, but they never went off. Three bars a day contained all the nutrients a spacer would need to survive.

It was eight hours from Raven's Folly to Garris Sigma, the primary settlement in the system. Henry spent his time watching videos on the viewscreen. Flynn had finished his sketch of Henry and was looking over it with a critical eye. Henry glanced at it. He looked like a blob with a helmet, but it was well drawn. Smiling, he nodded approvingly. "It looks good. I look almost heroic."

"Almost." Flynn confirmed, a cheeky grin flashing through his visor.

"Well, brace yourself, deceleration in thirty seconds." Henry checked the control panel. Everything was green. Before zero hit, the two of them shifted in their seats and the bruising deceleration began. The inertial dampeners struggled to keep up as the ship vibrated roughly. The viewscreen had switched from an optical to a simulated view as The Merry Mule entered the planet's atmosphere. "If you think this feels rough, you should see the maintenance bills. I try to avoid going planetside whenever possible."

Flynn sat pressed against his seat. "I just want to go home," he whispered.

"Not long now, mate, you just hold on. It's just a bit of turbulence." To underline his point, the ship rocked, jerking them hard. Henry's stomach lurched as the ship's gravity generators tried to align with the planetside gravity.

A bored sounding operator from Garris Sigma Control spoke as the turbulence receded.

"Incoming vessel The Merry Mole, SS-39188. Prepare to relinquish control to autopilot."

Henry flicked a couple of switches. "This is The Merry Mole, control relinquished. Be gentle with us."

The operator ignored his feeble attempt at a quip as the ship glided down to a landing pad and settled with a final bruising crump.

"So much for gent—" *What the fuck?*

Flynn was gone. His sketchpad and gloves were the only sign of him having been on board.

"You idiot." Henry cursed. He must have got up during the descent and headed over to the airlock. Henry flicked on the airlock camera; he could see nothing in the logs. *Buggy piece of crap.* There wasn't much ship to check over, especially as he had an empty cargo hold. Flynn was nowhere on board.

Picking up Flynn's sketch pad, he found an address on the inside page. It was close to the starport. "Well then, mate, you owe me a hundred and twenty credits." He changed into his civilian clothes and took the gloves and pad. The lights were dimmer in the starport, an attempt to simulate daylight for the colonists. Running his ID through the airlock, he hummed a small ditty while the customs computer verified his details. A long list of regulations appeared on his wrist computer. Without looking at them, he swiped to accept.

The starport was busy. The renovation of Raven's Folly had led to a massive increase in traffic. Finding a drone car, he keyed in the address from Flynn's sketch pad and watched as the streets blurred past. He hated being planetside. He was far more at home in the solitude of outer space.

His journey led him to a comfortable middle-class neighbourhood. The houses had a faux stone façade and small, neat front gardens with bright replica flowers. The vehicle waited for payment before unlocking the door. *I need a procedure like that for my airlock.*

Henry had to ring the bell twice before an old lady answered. He didn't get a chance to speak—she saw the gloves and gasped. Tears pricked her eyes.

Unprepared for her reaction, Henry managed a confused, "Hello?"

"Flynn's gloves! Did you find them on Raven's Folly?" she asked, reaching out for them. He handed them to her without question.

"No, Flynn left them behind on my ship. Is he here?" Henry asked.

Sniffling, she looked up at him sadly. "No, he died eleven years ago in the disaster. He was so excited when he left for his gap year. He wanted to see more of the galaxy."

Henry blinked. "No, I saw him. He drew this sketch of me." He opened the dog-eared sketch pad, flicking through it until he found the picture of himself. It was signed by Flynn Reynolds, 2337. 2337... That was eleven years ago. *Is this a scam?* The page was old, the ink faded.

Henry felt cold as he stared at the picture. The empty airlock camera. His sudden disappearance. *Did I imagine it all?*

"His sketch pad—Bless you." The lady took the sketch pad from him, eyes gleaming with suppressed tears. "Thank you for bringing them home. They are all we have left of him."

Chapter Sixteen

THE GHOULS
OF
BANGALORE

2518 AD, New Bangalore,
Sirus System

T he air was pregnant with the scent of spiced protein cubes and the constant drone of the ever insufficient air filtration systems. Kleman strode down the metal gantry, his boots crunching through the garbage strewn across the lower decks of the New Bangalore colony. He reached his quarters. A vagrant had passed out on his doorstep, blocking the entry. Kleman could see an empty hex needle was still attached to his spine. Grunting, he nudged the body into the rest of the street trash. His door hissed open, the lights flickering on his apartment. Cartons of discarded ration packs lay stacked in the corner as he searched for a bottle of spirits that hadn't been previously emptied. Finding a third of a bottle of uisge, he slumped into his gel chair with a glass. Thumping the wall, he caused a menu screen to illuminate. He filtered through the musical selection and found Paula's favourite composer. Tinny music blared through recessed speakers, the notes fighting through the background sounds of the lower decks. Kleman glanced over at the corner and sighed.

"Yes, Paula, I'm late and yes, I'm drinking." He took a hefty slug of uisge. "But it's been a hell of a day. I need the uisge to help me think."

There was no response. There never was these days.

"Oh, it's like that, is it? Well, I guess the day can't get any worse."

He swirled his uisge round in his glass.

"I'd been cleaning the nutrient vats on level B. The posh ones."

Kleman finished his drink, pouring another and ignoring the scorn that washed over him like a wave. "I'd had a drink. I need a bit these days to keep my hands steady, but I still dropped my scraper into one of the empty vats. Stupid, I know. But it gets worse. I jumped in to get it back and my feet slipped on the sludge at the bottom. I banged my head. Must have faded out for a bit."

He turned his head and indicated a scabbed over bruise.

"Stupid. Stupid Kleman. Sometimes I think you married me as an act of charity. The only good thing in a long, messed up life."

He filled his glass.

"Better lower my voice. Lucja will be sleeping. I'd like to see her before I sleep. The memory of her face is the light I see when I scrub the vats."

He closed his sallow, sunken eyes. A sudden weariness came over him.

"I heard something, Paula. Something bad. A team had come in to feed the vats. The best protein paste comes from feeding meat to the microorganisms in the vats. Real meat, Paula. We aren't even allowed to see it. They store it in a sealed freezer. See, I always thought it was from animals or even synthetically grown. You know, the bits they can't serve as cuts to upper management. But I think I might be wrong. I don't know. Sometimes I get confused. I see things or hear things that others don't. The uisge helps it all make sense."

He gulped down another slug.

"The workers were carrying something large. It took two of them to load it onto a cart. It was wrapped in some kind of an opaque film. But Paula, they referred to it as an expended asset. One of them tipped it from the cart into the vat and laughed, wondering who it was. Who Paula. Not what."

He looked at the empty bottle.

"I can't be sure, Paula, but I think they are feeding people into the vats . I get so confused sometimes. But that is what I think."

For a long while, his bleary eyes stared into space.

"Yes, yes. I know. I need to be sure. I have to know the truth. I don't know why it matters to a cleaner, but it's just not right. It doesn't sit easy with me."

He paused. His eyelids were heavy now.

"I'm going to say good night to Lucja now. Yes, yes, I'll be quiet."

Kleman stumbled to the back bedrooms. He carefully opened a small room to look upon a cot surrounded by dolls. A thick layer of dust shrouded everything in the room. He pulled the door gently shut and then collapsed onto his bed, sighing. He didn't bother with the sheets. Two thumps from his fist shut down the music as he faded into sleep. Then the dreams started up again, visions of his past torturing him.

A buzzing sound cut through Kleman's head like a knife. He thumped at the wall to silence the alarm. It snoozed three times until he eventually lumbered, cursing, to the kitchen to shut it down. His hands were shaking and his head pounded. He fumbled round for a bottle and, not finding one, latched onto a can of StimJuice. The drink finally brought his brain to a state of wakefulness and he used that brief moment of clarity to find a new bottle of uisge from the cupboard. For a single moment, he knew real despair, his memories pulling at the corners of his mind, teasing loose long-forgotten terrors. He shook his head and swigged from the bottle, burying them in a fog of alcoholic oblivion. Looking up, he was relieved to see his family at the breakfast table. They never spoke to him. Why would they? He was a mess. His stomach wasn't ready for breakfast, so he stuffed a packet of protein cubes into his pocket.

His hands and breathing were stable now. He took another pull from the bottle, then filled up his hip flask so that he had a drink ready for lunch.

The front door hissed open. Kleman slid down the street, barely noticing the effluence round him. Children were picking at the garbage and debris clustered round the walkways. Everything in New Bangalore was recycled 'hand-me-downs' from the upper decks. They used machines and cleaners on the upper decks to clear the streets and reprocess the materials. The trash wasn't worth enough to justify it in the lower decks, so instead, it just clogged up the colony's corridors.

He was early for work. His previous life as an engineer had given him a great deal of respect for punctuality. Of course, that was when the monarchy had been in power. He never discussed politics, but he'd been a staunch monarchist. He'd liked to think that people were born to fill a role in life. He'd never bought into the lie that's social mobility. The only direction Kleman travelled was down. He didn't mind, although he thought Paula deserved better. As a senior engineer, he'd been able to afford to live on a higher deck in the colony. They'd been able to eat the higher quality protein cubes, too, back then.

His thoughts darkened as he thought of the protein cubes being made in the vats. He needed to know. His suspicions gnawed at him. He swigged out of his flask and cursed. He needed to take it slow, or he would run out midway through the day. There was a limit to the size of the flask a man could conceal in his overalls.

The entrance to Derkin Hydroculture loomed at the end of the corridor. The huge armoured vault door was coated with a film of grease and dirt. It was cleaned daily, but the filth from the lower decks pervaded and infected everything that came into contact with it. His boots crunched as he trod on the chitin shell of one of the insects that had come to plague the colony. Kleman welcomed them. They were the only ones to bother reprocessing the filth.

He fumbled to find his entry pass. The vault door chimed as he swiped his card and pressed his thumb into the DNA scanner. A series of beeps sounded, acting as a countdown before the vault doors slid open. He looked into the barrels of two armoured prefects with shotguns levelled at his head.

He nodded dismissively. "Good morning Izydor, Good morning Miron." Behind him, the door closed with a clunk.

"Arms up, prepare to be scanned," one of the helmets replied. The integrated voice changers made it impossible to distinguish one prefect from another.

He stood with his hands in the air as the walls beside him hummed. "Right you are then, lads," he said. The humming stopped and the guns were lifted. The Prefects dismissed him with a nod in the direction of the exit. He strode past them with a wave. He wandered through the corridors to the locker room, where he retrieved his cleaning tools and began his day's work. The first hour was always spent doing the toilets on the executive floor. They needed to be immaculate before the execs arrived at the office. The cleaners had to be gone before management started their shift. It wouldn't do for them to soil their eyes by seeing the likes of him.

Picking up his cleaning kit, he took the opportunity to take his old engineer's toolkit and slip that into his trolley as well. Kleman needed to know. He didn't know why, but he felt an invisible will pulling him to the protein vats, pulling him to the locked freezer. It was quiet now. He levered the plate of the locking mechanism from the wall and then rewired it to release the doors. He saw dozens of hanging sacks and, pulling out his multi-tool, Kleman tore one of them open.

He didn't gasp.

He didn't cry out.

He'd known deep down what he was going to find.

He'd also known precisely what he was going to do about it.

Music blasting through his cochlear implants, Trevor strode through the gleaming chrome doors. They parted before him with the merest of whispers. The receptionists smiled, their happiness never quite reaching their eyes as they waved at him. He graced them with a curt nod. Brushing an imaginary piece of lint off his suit, he entered the lift and pushed a button for the top floor. Sneering at the control panel, he pulled out a bottle of antibacterial gel and swiftly rubbed off any germs. The lifts should be voice-activated, like his transport.

A gentle instrumental played as the soft scent of sandalwood wafted from hidden vents. When Trevor emerged on the top floor, his new secretary, Janice, rose and bowed her head.

"Get me a StimJuice, Janice." He paused, wrinkling his face with disgust. "Wait." He stalked towards her. "Have you been crying? How dare you? I told you before, you look so ugly when you cry. Sort your face out, then get me my drink."

Marching through the double doors to his office, they slid shut behind him as he mentally committed to replacing Janice with a more mentally stable subordinate. His desk loomed in front of him. It was made of genuine mahogany, a rarity of staggering expense. Reaching for a decanter of single malt uisge, he swore. It was half empty. Some-one had been stealing his imported uisge. He spun, eyes flaring with rage. In the corner by the doors sat a cleaner, a filthy, ragged cleaner in his office!. He lowered his gaze to see a glass of his uisge in the cleaner's hairy, unkempt hands. He shivered with rage. His anger bloomed red as he pointed his finger like a weapon at this miserable creature..

"You're fired! I'll see you *destroyed* for this! You imbecilic gibbon."

The cleaner stood and strode towards him, his eyes dead. He placed the glass on the desk with a resounding thud. "Sit down," he com-manded.

Trevor's mouth flapped. For the first time in a long time, he felt physically intimidated. He spun round and tried to open the doors. They stubbornly refused to open.

"Locked."

Trevor looked incredulously at the simpleton who stood watching him, eyes glowering. "Do you know who I am?" he demanded.

"That is why I'm here. I have questions for you."

Questions? "Who the hell do you think you are? Questions?" Racing to his desk, he hammered on the intercom. "Security to my office, now!"

"They won't get through that door any time soon. I said I have questions."

Trevor reached into his desk drawer and withdrew a gauss pistol. "Questions? The only question you need to ask is, why shouldn't I pull the trigger and pop your head like a ripe melon? Do you want to fucking die? What do you think of that?"

The oaf wasn't bright enough to be scared, or maybe he was too drunk to care. "The protein vats. I think you are feeding them with human bodies."

"That is a statement, not a question, you idiotic peasant. Besides, you are a cleaner. The slop you are issued with is far too low grade to be 'protein enriched'," Trevor chuckled. "You come to *my* office and make demands. Ruining your life will become my personal pet project."

"You can't hurt me. Not really." The cleaner's tiny dull eyes tracked him. Trevor stepped forwards and made as if to pistol whip the man. But when the man cocked his head curiously at him, Trevor jerked back as if stung. He aimed his pistol at the cleaner's head again. "So you do feed human bodies to the protein vats."

Trevor sneered, "The mid-tier vats, those who are valuable enough to warrant good nutrition but not valuable enough to warrant genuine meat. It is not like you'd ever get any."

"I used to be a senior engineer."

"And what happened? Obviously, you fucked up somehow?" A malicious grin spread across Trevor's face. Looking at the man's badge number, he keyed it into his console.

"Kleman, stupid name. Drunk on duty, demoted. Oh, look at this," Trevor cackled.

Kleman had taken the bottle now and collapsed back into his chair.

"Oh, this is magnificent. You come in here full of anger and righteous indignation. Your wife, your *fucking* wife, got cancer. At a cleaner's grade, the medication we hand out is just sugar pills."

Kleman's eyes narrowed. He remained silent even as his face darkened.

Trevor tightened his grip on his pistol. "Don't move."

Kleman remained seated, pouring himself more uisge.

"Your drinking ruined your life and didn't just kill your wife. It fed your supervisor. Oh, this is wondrous."

Trevor snorted and leaned back, his hands on his hips. "Look at you, so angry and yet there is nothing, *nothing* that you can do."

Trevor nodded, finished his glass and stood up.

"Sit the fuck back down. Sit down!"

"I don't need to do anything. I already did it. Shoot me if you like." Kleman tossed the ammunition clip over to Trevor.

Numbly Trevor checked his pistol. It had been unloaded the whole time.

"What have you done?"

"The intercom. I rewired it. It's been broadcasting through the announcement speakers."

Trevor turned to the windows. Already the first fires had started as riots began across the colony. "What have you done?" he said numbly as Kleman returned to his seat with another glass.

"Ruined my life. Reckon you've done worse, though." Kleman looked at the almost empty bottle. "Wouldn't hold out for security. Reckon they've got bigger problems."

Trevor didn't respond. He just watched through the window in horror.

The fires were getting larger.

The fires were getting closer.

THANK YOU

Thank you for reading. I hope you enjoyed my book.

Please feel free to review my book on Amazon or Goodreads. Reviews are the single most useful thing for any author. We rely on them both for sales and more importantly, to get feedback to hone our craft.

Newton Webb

ABOUT THE AUTHOR

Newton Webb was born in RAF Halton, England, in 1982. He has worked as a computer programmer and a table top games designer, but now writes full time.

He has a pet tortoise called Gill, a red cherry shrimp tank, an ever expanding shoal of corydoras, and two pet venus fly traps called Frank and Audrey II.

JOIN NEWTON WEBB ONLINE

'The World of Newton Webb' Mailing List

Promising a minimum of a new story every month and free audiobooks.

https://www.newtonwebb.com/

TALES OF THE MACABRE, VOL. 2

I ntroducing Tales of the Macabre, Vol. 2. The second collected works by Newton Webb, available on Amazon.

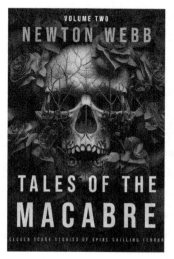

TALES OF THE MACABRE CHRONOLOGY

TotM1 – Tales of the Macabre, Vol. 1
TotM2 – Tales of the Macabre, Vol. 2

526 – The Iron Door (TotM1): A grieving soldier desperate to free his wife's soul from eternal damnation instead finds himself facing an earthquake in ancient Syria.

1195 – The Green Man (TotM2): Two brothers run afoul of a dark force deep in Sherwood Forest, the idyllic surroundings harbouring an ancient terror.

1818 – The Ballad of Barnacle Bill (TotM2): A grieving father journeys down a treacherous path in hopes of fixing his past mistakes, only to find his actions have unforeseen consequences.

1747 – The Grimsdyke Ghouls (TotM1): In the 16th century, a family kicked out of their homes in Grimsdyke found a new and murderous way to survive.

1832 – The Horror at Hargrave Hall (TotM2): Deep in the Yorkshire countryside, the ancestral hall of the Hargrave family hides a dark secret.

1864 – Smoke in the Sewers (TotM1): In 18th century London, a group of street urchins strive to escape their master. But in doing so they unleash a greater horror.

1958 – The Black Fog (TotM1): When the black fog rolls in, death follows. In 1950's Grimsdyke, two lovers encounter a horror unlike any other.

1961 – A Rose By Any Other Name (TotM1): A bank robber hiding from the law, Dennis commits a heinous crime. Soon, he'll learn to regret his actions.

1991 – Trev Rides Forth (TotM2): An act of senseless violence awakens a sinister force in this heavy metal fever dream.

1993 – The Power Within (TotM2): A grieving boy finds that he isn't as alone as he thought.

2008 – Rock Bottom (TotM1): Aussie backpackers come face to face with primal adversaries in the cold peaks of Nepal.

2012 – The Platinum Service (TotM1): When you have great wealth, you can buy your way out of most things. But sometimes, actions bring unexpected consequences.

2013 – Festival of the Damned (TotM1): Four teenagers are hired to perform at a country fair, but they soon realise that they were each chosen for a very specific reason.

2015 – The Enigmatic Skeleton (TotM2): When a professor tries to unravel the mysteries of a macabre human skeleton collection, he discovers that curiosity comes with its own perils.

2013 – The Sinful Child (TotM1): Held captive in her father's basement, Amelia struggles to escape. But reality isn't always what it appears to be and soon she will learn an earth shattering secret.

2018 – Terror from the Trash (TotM1): Climate change is a very real threat to the world, but scientists find new perils as something long thought to be dead, awakens.

2018 – The Morrígan (TotM2): Haunted by vivid dreams and witnessing strange events in the depths of the Irish countryside, an artist ignorantly stumbles towards a grim fate.

2020 – The Tattoo (TotM1): A hitchhiker and a lorry driver exchange tales on the road. Soon, they realise that neither of them is who they claim to be.

2020 – The Tokoloshe (TotM1): In South Africa there exists a demonic entity that can make wishes come true, but the consequences cannot always be predicted.

2021 – The Coconut Killer (TotM2): After coming out at school, a bullied gay teen attracts the wrong kind of attention.

2022 – The Heir Apparent (TotM1): Keen to support his parents' failing farm, Keith asks his wealthy cousins for a position in the family firm. As he becomes more and more entrenched in the business, he discovers that limitless ambition can be murderous.

2022 – The Wrong Crowd (TotM1): Tim just wanted to apologise to his girlfriend, but he soon finds himself in peril when he realises that he has accidentally joined a very exclusive and very deadly club.

2023 – 12 Minutes (TotM2): A text message arrives, triggering a terrifying countdown.

2024 – The Black Box (TotM1): Waking up from a coma after a severe accident, Jack finds that it is always better to read the small print when offering your body to medical science.

2028 – Welcome to Paradise (TotM2): When a troubled man arrives in the afterlife, he is assigned an idyllic mansion, but something isn't right and his memories are starting to return.

2348 – The Illusive Passenger (TotM1): In the distant future, a freighter captain picks up a most unusual cargo.

2518 – The Ghouls of Bangalore (TotM1): In outer space, greed and narcism still plague the human race. An engineer whose life is at its nadir learns a terrifying secret.

Also by Newton Webb

Collected Works

Tales of the Macabre, Vol. 1

Tales of the Macabre, Vol. 2

Contemporary

2013 – **Festival of The Damned**

2012 – **The Platinum Service**

Historical

1958 – **The Black Fog**

1864 – **Smoke in the Sewers**

1832 – **The Horror at Hargrave Hall**

1818 – **The Ballad of Barnacle Bill**

1194 – **Hunted**

NewtonWebb.com

Home to a wide variety of the authors free short stories and audio-books.

NewtonWebb.com

Printed in Great Britain
by Amazon

25194063R00159